Mile High

Up In The Air Novel #2

By R.K. Lilley

Mile High
Up In The Air Novel #2
Copyright © 2012 R.K. Lilley
Second Edition
All rights reserved.

ISBN-10: 0615752179
ISBN-13: 978-0615752174

Formatted by Midnight Engel Press

SERIES BY R.K. LILLEY

THE WILD SIDE SERIES

THE WILD SIDE

IRIS

DAIR

THE OTHER MAN - COMING SOON

TYRANT - COMING SOON

THE UP IN THE AIR SERIES

IN FLIGHT

MILE HIGH

GROUNDED

MR. BEAUTIFUL - COMING OCTOBER 15TH, 2014

LANA (AN UP IN THE AIR COMPANION NOVELLA)

AUTHORITY - COMING SOON

THE TRISTAN & DANIKA SERIES

BAD THINGS

ROCK BOTTOM

LOVELY TRIGGER

THE HERETIC DAUGHTERS SERIES

BREATHING FIRE

CROSSING FIRE - COMING SOON

TEXT LILLEY + YOUR EMAIL ADDRESS TO 1-678-249-3375 TO JOIN MY EMAIL NEWSLETTER.

CONTENTS

CHAPTER ONE

I took a deep breath, then winced. I was trying to enjoy basking in the Miami sun, but I was still a little sore. It had been over a month now since I'd sustained my injuries. I was fit enough to work now, but I still got occasional reminders of what had happened to me when I moved or breathed just wrong.

My phone chimed that I had a new text message, and I winced again. I needed to remember to keep it in the off position. It helped me to delay the inevitable. I reached down to the concrete below my pool lounge chair, gripped my phone, and held down the off button until it powered off.

Just seconds later, I heard the Kings of Leon song that served as Stephan's ringtone begin to play. He sighed heavily from his lounge chair beside me, then rose, heading into the hotel bar that was nearest the pool. If I hadn't been sure my text was from James, I was now. It was his pattern lately. He would call Stephan after failing to get ahold of me. And for some odd reason, Stephan felt obliged to answer his calls. It had been the cause of an unusual new tension that had sprung up between us.

A different figure loomed over me a moment later, casting a

shadow as it hovered near the seat that Stephan had just vacated.

"Mind if I join you, Bee?" Damien asked in his heavy Australian accent. I didn't open my eyes from behind my dark shades, but I recognized his voice easily enough.

I made a humming noise that meant I didn't care, and he lounged beside me.

Stephan and I had had to call in several big favors from another crew to get to Miami for our layover. But I had wanted so desperately to avoid New York this week that Stephan had made it happen.

Somehow Captain Damien and First Officer Murphy had managed to do the same, after Stephan had casually mentioned in a text that we would be missing our New York trip for the week. At first, I'd thought it was rather stalker-ish of them, but more and more, the two men were growing on me. Damien had made no overtures. He was, in fact, great company for a person who just wanted some peace and quiet. He had no problem being comfortably silent, occasionally making light-hearted comments that drew me out of my black moods. And he was accompanied by Murphy more often than not. Murphy could make anyone laugh. Even me in the depressed mood that was dogging me lately.

"That cover-up is gonna give you an interesting tan line," Damien said in an amused tone.

I wore a black swimsuit coverup that went to the top of my thighs. I wore it over my plain black bikini. The coverup was see-through, but it was just dark enough to mostly obscure the faint traces of bruises that still patterned my torso in a stark reminder of the violence I'd survived just weeks ago. They had faded considerably, but they were still dark enough to need covering. I would draw unwanted attention if I bared my skin for all to see. I'd already gotten enough unwanted attention lately. The paparazzi would take any excuse to make me a headline nowadays. I wasn't in any mood to encourage them.

"No one wants to see what's under this cover-up. Trust me," I told him, still not opening my eyes or even twitching.

He coughed back a little laugh that made me uncomfortable. I was perceptive enough to know that Damien was more than a little interested in me in a romantic way. Any reminders of the fact were unwelcome.

"I beg to differ," he said quietly, and I felt myself frown.

"Sorry, sorry," he said quickly, before I could speak. I let it go. As long as he knew I wasn't interested in anything beyond friendship, I was content to let sleeping dogs lie.

Damien was handsome and funny and great company. He was also a shameless womanizer. I figured it was just second nature to him to try to to show interest in any woman in his vicinity. And it was also in his nature to flatter any woman when given an opening. I was usually more careful about giving him that opening.

"Is everything okay between you and Stephan? I've never seen you guys like this before. You're so stiff with each other. Are you fighting?"

My gut clenched. Things did seem off between us, and I wasn't sure how to make it better. I figured he had to be at least a little resentful of me for making him miss his week's worth of Melvin time this week. Not that I had actually made him. I had told him more than once that I would understand if he still wanted to go to New York. The crew we had traded with had even agreed to just do a single trade with me. But Stephan had insisted we stick together. He was worried about me, I knew.

I liked Damien. I even thought of him as a friend. One of my few pilot friends. But I couldn't imagine discussing my difficulties with Stephan with anyone. It felt almost disloyal.

"He's just worried about me, I think. Since the attack, we've both been on edge," I explained. It was all true, but didn't address the reason for our awkwardness.

Damien made a neutral little hum in his throat. "What about that James guy? You two doing okay? I saw a little bit of the media circus that surrounds him. You get tired of all that, and drop him? You could have any man you want, you know."

I sucked in a breath. Damien was usually very good about not asking questions like that. It was why he had made good company lately.

"I don't want to talk about it," I said, my tone cool.

He got the hint. "Damn, sorry. I'm on a roll, putting my foot in my mouth, aren't I?"

I gave a half-smile, finally looking at him. I gave a little nod, and he laughed.

"Well, I guess I owe you now. You want to ask me any rude, prying questions about my personal life?" he asked. He had a great smile. It was all even white teeth, and self-deprecating humor. It would have been hard not to smile back. I didn't even try.

"Nope," I told him with no hesitation.

He laughed again, as though I was much more funny than I actually was. "I guess when you answer yes to that question, I'll know I have you where I want you."

I just wrinkled my nose and turned my face away.

"Wanna take a walk on the beach?" he asked, after several minutes of silence.

I realized in surprise that I did want to get up and move around a bit. I'd been so inactive lately, due to my injuries. "It's not a romantic stroll or anything, is it?" I asked him cautiously.

He sat up, grinning at me. He really was a good-looking man. He wore only low-slung black swim trunks. He was tan and muscular. His dark hair and warm brown eyes were hollywood material. I really didn't understand why he would put so much time into a passably attractive girl who wasn't even remotely interested in him. I tried to use that characterization as further proof that he was just being friendly, still strangely uncomfortable with his company.

I got up, moving slowly. I was still stiff, though I had recovered remarkably well, all things considered. I hadn't been released from the hospital until I'd had countless tests run, so I was in the clear of any serious injuries.

I started walking, and Damien fell into step beside me. He seemed to know better than to try to help me. I found the wooden crosswalk that led from our hotel to the beach, and crossed it resolutely.

I walked almost to the water line before I began to walk along the beach. My bare feet got wet, but it felt good after laying in the hot sun. I even got a few steps deeper into the tide before I began to follow the shoreline, passing the various ocean-front hotels. I counted the hotels we passed, absently keeping track.

"Some weirdo just got a picture of us," Damien told me as we walked.

Inwardly, I cursed. Outwardly, I shrugged.

"Want me to go beat him up and take his camera?" he asked.

I laughed. "The damage is done," I said. I could only imagine what they would print about me this week. I figured no matter what it was, it couldn't be worse than the tangent they had gone on a month ago.

They had called me every derogatory name in the book. I was becoming quickly immune to it. It was almost a pleasant surprise to me, how quickly I was becoming desensitized to being publicly insulted. Someday I might even stifle my unhealthy urge to check online for what they were saying about me. I wasn't sure I'd ever have enough self-control to keep from checking to see what they were saying about James...

"Are you really done with that James Cavendish guy, or are you just taking a break?" Damien asked, walking close to my side, as though afraid I would lose my balance. He probably wasn't totally wrong. I did feel a little wobbly, but it was mostly because I was so stiff.

I gave him a level stare. I decided to be brutally honest with him. "I'd like to think I'm sensible enough to be done with him. I'm realistic enough to know that, done or not, I'm ruined for other men. If you must know, he and I have certain...tastes in common. I don't really care to discuss it any more than that."

Damien touched my arm briefly, giving me a warm smile when I looked at him. "If you're a dominatrix, Bee, I can live with that. Feel free to tie me up and spank me, anytime you feel the need."

I laughed, because he was joking, and because it was the opposite of the truth.

"Um, no," was all I said to him.

"Are you in love with him?" he asked. "Is it that serious? You can tell me, Bianca. I won't judge. I just want to be your friend."

I grimaced. He was my friend. *Why is it so hard for me to open up?* I wondered. Even to a friend. I thought over the question, trying to suppress my natural urge to just close up at such a personal topic.

"Yes," I answered finally. "It's hopeless, I know. Maybe that's why my heart was perverse enough to give itself. But I do love him."

He squeezed my elbow. "Hey, I know the feeling. Don't beat yourself up so much. What will you do?"

I took a few deep breaths, really thinking about it. "That's what I don't know. I can't deny how I feel, but I can deny where it has to lead. He still wants me. Will I let him have me again? That's the million dollar question, I suppose."

Damien gave me a pained look. "It is."

I gave a small shrug, the one I couldn't seem to help. It was a gesture that seemed to drive everyone in my life insane.

"He'll grow tired of me, I'm sure," I said softly. "It's his M.O. The question is, am I so desperate for him that I'll just sign on for the ride?"

Damien didn't have an answer for that. Neither did I.

CHAPTER TWO

Damien and I walked slowly back to the hotel. We found more neutral topics to chat about on the return trip.

I noticed this time when my picture was taken by the man who crouched in the bushes outside of the hotel that bordered our own. He was a pudgy, balding man. I had the urge to tell him that he didn't need to bother damaging his knees by attempting to hide. He was very visible, even hiding.

I made myself ignore him instead. His publication would say something horrible about me either way, I was sure.

"Wanna hit up that Cuban restaurant on the corner?" Damien asked. We were almost back to our hotel.

I shrugged. "Let's see what Stephan wants to do," I said neutrally. The food sounded good, but I didn't want to end up going to dinner with just Damien.

"Okay. We'll make it a foursome. Murphy will no doubt have an opinion on where to eat," Damien said cheerfully. His attitude reassured me. I'd been half-worried he was trying to corner me into some kind of a date.

We found the other two men chatting with each other in our

crew hotel's large, crowded bar. Everyone agreed on the Cuban restaurant easily enough. It did have killer food.

We split up to change for dinner, meeting back in the lobby twenty minutes later. I just threw on some shorts and a tank top.

We walked to the restaurant, the men joking constantly, making me laugh. They really were good company.

I ordered black bean soup and rice at the restaurant. It was a simple, if fattening, meal. I didn't care. It was my version of comfort food. I gorged myself, as I rarely did. I even ordered a second order of the meal to go. It was a great breakfast, if you added orange juice. I did, grabbing a carton from the mini-mart a block away from the hotel.

Stephan carried everything for me without a word. Awkward as it was between us, he was still a gentleman to his core. His unusual mormon upbringing had ingrained in him a need to shelter me that I'd never been able to talk him out of. I accepted him too much to even try at this point. I just thanked him when he unburdened me of the bags.

Unexpectedly, he gripped my hand as we walked. I squeezed his hand back instantly. I couldn't stand distance between us.

"Are you mad at me?" I asked him. We walked just a few feet in front of Murphy and Damien, so I pitched my voice very low.

He sent me a wide-eyed, surprised look. "Of course not, Buttercup. I'm terrified that you're angry with me for keeping in contact with James."

I squeezed his hand again. "No. I understand very well how hard it is to ignore that man. He is persistent. I was just worried that you were mad at me for keeping you away from Melvin this week."

His mouth tightened. "Not at all. I've come to realize that Melvin isn't relationship material. He admitted to hooking up with another guy last week, even though we had said we were going to take it slow, but be exclusive. And I also think he tried to talk to the press about you and I. I feel bad that my judgement was so off about him. I was so attracted at first that I just saw what I wanted to see. You know what I mean?"

I cringed. "Sadly, I know *exactly* what you mean," I said, thinking of James.

He shook his head, giving my hand a little squeeze. "James isn't the same as Melvin, Bee. I'm sure of it. I just wish you could see it, too."

I just gave him a look. It was my 'drop it' look.

Murphy and Damien wanted to go bar hopping on South Beach.

I declined their invitation quickly. Stephan followed suit. Murphy turned to his phone, texting the rest of our crew. We had seen the three other flight attendants at the pool briefly earlier, but they seemed to be a room-bound lot for the evening. Murphy looked crestfallen. An antisocial crew was his worst nightmare.

"A movie? There's a theatre less than ten minutes away."

Stephan sent me a questioning look.

I just shrugged. What I wanted was to go to my room and crawl under my covers until morning, but I knew I would just drive myself crazy if I went that route. A movie seemed the lesser evil.

"Okay. Just let me a grab a sweatshirt. I always get cold in that theatre," I agreed finally.

My room was down the hall from Stephan's. Unfortunately, the hotel hadn't been able to accommodate us with adjoining rooms, as we preferred.

He handed me my bags of food and juice as we split up. I put the food in my mini-fridge, and grabbed a sweatshirt from my suitcase.

I set my phone on the end table by my bed, plugging it in to charge. Reluctantly, I turned it on. I was just intending to set my alarm for the morning, then leave the phone in my room, charging.

There were several missed texts and calls. There always were, lately. Most were from James, of course, though a few were from other friends, and a few were from a strange Vegas 702 number that kept popping up lately. I wondered briefly who that strange number could be, as it kept showing up more and more in my missed call log. I'd even taken the call once, though there'd just been a few seconds of background noise followed by an abrupt hangup.

My mind changed courses when, in a sudden total loss of self-control, I checked my latest missed text. I wasn't at all surprised to see that it was from James, but my heart still skipped a beat just seeing his name.

James: Just checking in to see how you're doing. I miss you.

I was texting back before I could stop myself.

Bianca: Doing fine. Please stop worrying about me. Just hanging out with the crew. Hope things are well with you.

He responded immediately.

James: Well enough. I'll be in London for most of next week, so please don't skip out on New York again just to avoid me. When can I see you again?

My heart ached with longing at just the thought of seeing

him, but my heart wasn't doing a good job of steering me in the right direction lately.

Bianca: I need more time. I'm sorry. I just seem to lose all self-control when I get near you. I need to get myself grounded again.

James: We can meet however you want. You make the terms. I would agree to anything, just to see you for five minutes. I mean that literally. I could meet up with your crew or we could meet up for coffee. Just tell me what you want and I'll do it. I'm desperate to see you.

I swallowed, feeling at sea. How I wanted to see him, even if only for five minutes. I should be able to control myself, if it were only five minutes...

Bianca: Let me think about it. You know my schedule. Let me know when we're in the same city and I'll try to find a brief, neutral way that we can meet up.

James: Don't tempt me so, Love. I'll be on a plane in thirty minutes if you really mean that.

My gut clenched.

Bianca: Don't do that. I meant if your schedule takes you to the same city. Please

don't travel on my account.

James: I need to take a business trip to Vegas soon. I'd like to see you when I'm there. Tell me the time and place and I'll work my schedule around it.

Bianca: Stephan and I are meeting up with some friends a week from Monday. We haven't decided on a time or place, but I'll let you know when we do. You can join us if you want.

James: I very much want. Give me the details when you have them. I'll count the days, my love.

I turned my phone off after that.

We all met back up in the lobby. I was the last to arrive. I felt bad that I had made them all wait, but no one seemed to mind.

They were having a good-natured argument about whether we should walk or share a taxi.

I wrinkled my nose at Murphy, who seemed to think it was worth it to take a taxi the short distance.

"It's less than a mile," I told him. "It's a waste of money. Especially since it's so nice out."

Damien poked Murphy's oversized belly. "It seems like you could use a walk, mate."

Murphy poked Damien's belly. "Don't foist your body image issues on me, *mate*. I'm sexy. When I want a six pack, I go to the liquor store. It's a hell of a lot more fun than spending three hours a day at the gym, like Mr. Universe here."

We all laughed.

Murphy saw that he was outvoted, so we walked.

The walk was pleasant, but once there, we had a hard time deciding on what to see. For some odd reason, the pilots were insisting on a romantic comedy. Stephan and I wanted to see a newly released Sci-Fi horror flick. I didn't like romantic comedies as a rule, but I particularly refused to see the one they were pointing out. It was starring a young red-headed actress whom I'd seen photographed with James.

If I watched the movie, I knew I'd just obsess about him and get depressed all over again. When I suggested that we just watch two different movies, the pilots finally caved.

"But if I get nightmares after this, Damien is getting a roommate tonight. I am always the big spoon. No exceptions," Murphy warned.

Stephan and I laughed, but Damien just gave him a disgruntled look, as though he was genuinely worried Murphy would try it. That look just made me laugh harder.

I thought the movie was great, but Murphy didn't agree. "That scene where that chick cut the alien out of her...I can't stop seeing that in my head. I'm going to be scarred for life now. You guys owe me for that. I'm making you all watch a lighthearted comedy next time," Murphy threatened as we walked back to the hotel.

Dark had fallen while we watched the movie, but the streets were well-lit and many people still walked along the popular street.

I noticed that Stephan had tensed up, and I followed his stare to a man taking pictures of us. I held his arm firmly, continuing to walk. Stephan looked about ready to punch the guy.

"We're going to have to just learn to ignore that sort of

thing," I told him quietly. "We can't stop them from taking pictures, and we can't control what they say, so ignoring them is our only recourse."

He gave me an assessing glance. "Maybe you are suited to James's lifestyle. It's pretty impressive that you're already accustomed to the paparazzi, considering that you've only been dealing with them for a few weeks."

I gave my little shrug. "It's not the end of the world. I could do without all of the horrible things they'll print along with the pictures, but I really just need to learn to stop reading it. It's all garbage. Before I dated James, I never would have even glanced at any of it. I need to get back to that mindset."

Stephan nodded firmly. "Me, too. I have Google alerts on you and James now. I need to quit torturing myself. It's not like we can stop any of it."

"If you see me looking up garbage gossip sites online, you need to stop me. This has gotten out of hand."

"Ditto, Buttercup."

CHAPTER THREE

The days passed slowly, as I looked forward to seeing James. Despite my reservations, I almost called him to arrange a meeting sooner several times.

In the end, I had hardly any contact with James, only texting him briefly the Sunday before I was due to see him. I just told him where everyone had decided to meet. It was a work affair that I wasn't particularly enthused about attending. But Stephan wouldn't go anywhere without me lately, and I was tired of keeping him home. I knew he loved to go out, so I had agreed to attend the work party almost two weeks before.

Bianca: We're meeting at 6pm at The Dime Lounge. It's just off of the strip, on the east side of Tropicana. It's going to be a lot of flight attendants and pilots.

James: I'll be there.

I started getting ready at 3:30, which was early for me. Giving myself more than an hour to get ready was unusual, so taking over two hours meant that I was nervous. Nervous and excited.

It took me an uncharacteristically long time to choose an outfit. I finally settled on a black mini-skirt that showed a lot of leg. I paired it with a sleeveless black button-up silk top that showed a tasteful but generous hint of cleavage. The all-black outfit put me in the mood for some loud shoes, so I dug out a pair of wedge sandals that were a bright mix of colors that didn't go with anything *but* black. They were a mix of orange, yellow, pink and blue that made me smile. They laced up my ankles in wide satin ribbons, and I tied them in neat little bows there. I never got a chance to wear the impulsive purchase, and I was pleased with the overall look of the outfit.

I found some big silver hoops for my ears. I eyed a silver box that had arrived in my mail the day I'd gotten home from the hospital. I'd glanced inside of it, seen the contents, and shut it without another glance. It contained the collar and watch that James had given me, before all hell had broken loose. I didn't know what to do with the jewelry. I didn't feel like I could keep it, since we weren't together. But I was also sure that James wouldn't accept it back. He obviously wouldn't, since the last time I'd returned it it had just ended up in my mailbox.

I did my hair and makeup, stewing about the jewelry.

Part of me wanted to just wear it. The collar would go well with my neckline, setting off my cleavage nicely. James would be happy to see me wear it, I knew. But it might also give him the wrong idea. He might take it to mean that I was willing to pick up again where we'd last left off. I wasn't sure I was willing to do that.

A change came over me when I was near James. A change that I wasn't sure I liked. He'd gotten me to fall in love with him after just over a week of knowing him. And if that wasn't bat-shit crazy, I didn't know what was.

I left my hair pin straight and hanging down my back in a pale, beige-blond line. I lined my eyes in a soft brown. I had a heavy hand with the black mascara and used a generous amount of gold eyeshadow. I went with a soft pink lip, liberally applying gloss. It was more makeup than I usually went with, but I thought it would suit a place like The Dime just fine.

The overall effect made me feel sexy and sophisticated, and that was exactly what I wanted. I needed to feel confident when I saw James again.

I heard my phone chime, and knew it would be Stephan, saying it was time to go. A look at the clock told me that.

Impulsively, I opened the silver box. I weighed the lovely choker in my hands. It was a silver color, though I had no idea what metal it was. I could never tell the difference. But it looked expensive, with diamonds peppering the whole necklace, and a loop on the front made entirely of alarmingly large ones. I hadn't realized how large they were before.

I took a deep breath, and reached back to put it on. The weight of it felt nice against the base of my neck, and I studied it, running my finger along it. I needed to go, but I couldn't seem to look away from the collar around my neck.

I glanced back at the box, and noticed for the first time that the box held more than just the necklace and watch. I opened another small box that I had overlooked with my previous cursory inspection. It contained exquisite, large hooped earrings made up of large diamonds that matched the details on my collar to the T.

I bit my lip, and put them on. *In for a penny, in for a*

pound, I thought recklessly.

I hurried out the door, and, sure enough, Stephan's car was waiting in my driveway. I got into his car, digging into my small clutch-purse as I did so. I checked to make sure I had all the essentials.

Stephan let out a low whistle at the sight of me. "You look *hot*, Buttercup. If you hadn't told me James was stopping by to see you, I could have guessed by that mini skirt."

I gave him a sharp look, but couldn't maintain it for long. He had a point. I hardly ever tried to dress sexy.

"Everyone is going to be there," Stephan told me happily as we drove the twenty minutes to the club. He started naming off the attendees. Some I would normally have been happy to see, but at the moment, not so much.

Everyone knew I had been attacked in my home. And that I had been hospitalized for over a week. The rumor was that I'd had a home invader attack me, but people would be asking me well-meaning questions about it nonetheless. I hated the kinds of questions that I knew would be asked. I hated that people had even a vague idea of what had happened to me.

I'd survived, and the rest were just details, I told myself firmly. It was a mantra that always snapped me out of self-pity mode. As usual, it worked. I was alive, and it was enough.

We had a good-natured argument as we drove about whether Stephan should pop the collar of his polo. He'd worn the collar up, and I'd noticed almost immediately. I just couldn't seem to get onboard with the style. There was just something inherently douche-baggy about the look. I told him so.

He eventually caved, straightening his collar with a rueful smile.

"Just because you like a look, that doesn't make it right," I teased him.

We got to the lounge a solid ten minutes before six. The doorman was checking our I.D's and even our airline badges. We both had them on us, since we had been told we'd need them to get an employee discount, but it was unusual to have to show them at the door.

I heard a familiar voice behind me. "These are Mr. Cavendish's guests. I'll walk them in."

I turned, giving a surprised smile to Clark. I inwardly cringed, thinking of the last time he'd seen me. I'd been a complete mess, running into traffic like a maniac. But it wasn't his fault he'd seen me in that state, so I tried to greet him as though it hadn't happened. "How are you, Clark?" I asked.

He smiled at me warmly. He seemed genuinely pleased to see me. "Just great, Ms. Karlsson. I'm very happy to see you looking so well."

I just nodded, automatically shying away from the subject of what had made me so *un*well recently.

Clark led us through the dimly lit lounge, heading straight to the small VIP section.

I sighed.

Of course James would be in VIP, but it kind of defeated the whole purpose of us being here, socializing with co-workers.

Sure enough, we were no sooner seated than Stephan was bouncing back up, spotting a friend of ours across the room. It was our friend, Jessa. I hadn't seen her in over a month, and I really did want to say hi.

I saw quickly that James was nowhere to be seen.

I sent Clark an apologetic glance. "Thanks for showing us to the table, Clark, but I see someone I want to chat with. Where is James?"

Clark looked uncomfortable. He was even fidgeting with his tie. The nervous gesture seemed very uncharacteristic for him. "In the car, finishing up some phone calls. I'm pretty sure he didn't think you'd be so prompt, or I know he would have wrapped his business up by now."

I just nodded and headed over to where Stephan and Jessa were hugging in greeting. She saw me and gasped. She gave me a hug that was hard enough that I had to hide a little gasp. My ribs were still a little tender, if they were pressed just wrong. She'd hit just the wrong spot with her exuberant squeeze. I hid my reaction and returned her hug.

"It's so good to see you looking better," Jessa gushed. "I'm sorry I couldn't come by the hospital or visit you before. Thing's have been crazy lately, and I didn't hear about anything until you were leaving the hospital. And I was out of town at the time." She glared at Stephan. "Stephan here kept it under wraps. Even from *me*."

"Please, don't give it a thought. In fact, let's never talk about it again. How've you been? Where have you been flying this month?" I asked her.

Jessa was from our flight attendant class. She was a tall brunette, nearly my height, with lovely brown eyes and the warmest smile. She was one of my favorite people. When possible, we tried to meet up with her at least twice a month to catch up. She had a great sense of humor, and loved to go out. Even Stephan was a homebody compared to her.

She was flipping her thick, curly hair behind her shoulders as she told us a story about some passenger on her last flight who'd tried to smoke in the bathroom and then lie about it. She was getting agitated just relating the story about the shameless lies the old man had tried to get away with.

I had to hide a smile. She was always getting agitated with the crazies. And her sassy way of dealing with them was just good comedy.

A cocktail waitress in a mini skirt and corset promptly approached us and got our drink orders. Stephan was drinking house cabernet. I stuck with water. I was off of alcohol, especially if James was attending. He abhorred the stuff.

I spotted Brenda by the bar, and waved. She joined us, smiling.

"We missed you guys this week," she said in greeting.

"Cindy and Lars are great, though, right?" I asked, smiling. The couple we had traded with were notoriously fun to work with.

"Oh, yeah, those two are a blast. We still missed you, though." She pursed her lips. "Jake and I, I mean."

We shared a wry smile. I didn't have to ask why she had left out Melissa's name. The other girl was acting more and more unhinged every time I dealt with her. I had known she wouldn't miss us.

She noticed my jewelry. "That is the loveliest necklace and earrings. So unique."

I fingered my choker, thanking her.

"Did your husband come?" I asked, glancing around. He often came with her to work functions, and sometimes even joined her on layovers.

"No, he didn't get off of work until six, and he says he's beat. I probably won't stay long. It's just so hard to miss out on an opportunity to see so many of the flight attendants that I rarely get to see. We should organize these parties more often."

Jessa agreed with her heartily, and they chatted about trying to do just that for a solid ten minutes.

Jake joined us amidst their plans, hugging everyone while

managing to seem interested in the current conversation. I hugged him back lightly. I had had a hard time with the flight attendant hugging situation right at first, but the custom had grown on me. When you had close friends that you only got to see once a month in passing, a hug seemed appropriate. Though everyone, even not so close friends, seemed to insist on the habit. I just went with it now. No one else understood my hangup, I knew. So I had just learned to keep it to myself.

A tall, slender, dark-haired man approached Stephan from behind, clapping him on the shoulder in greeting. The man leaned in close to Stephan's ear, whispering something. Stephan seemed to blush down to his toes.

I watched the whole thing as if in slow-motion, my jaw dropping in shock.

CHAPTER FOUR

It took me a long moment to recognize the man, since what I was seeing made no sense to me.

Javier Flores and Stephan were not exactly on friendly terms. Last I had checked, they were closer to bitter exes. The two men hadn't spoken for over a year. Or so I had thought.

Javier was Stephan's version of the one that got away.

The two men were as dissimilar physically as they were personality-wise. Though both men were tall and handsome, Stephan was much taller. Javier was maybe an inch shy of six feet. And where Stephan resembled a strapping Abercrombie and Fitch model with his blond good looks, Javier was almost delicate looking. His face was just plain pretty, with perfect, even features, and the thickest eyelashes I'd ever seen. He had jet black hair that hung to his shoulders, falling into his eyes artfully as he tilted his head forward, giving Stephan a wicked sideways smile. He was tall and slender, almost thin. His dark brown eyes were mysterious and lovely, but I had always found them a little cold and distant.

The two men had dated for just a month, over a year ago. It

had been an intense month, but it had ended quickly, and badly. Javier had a real problem being Stephan's secret lover, and he hadn't tolerated the situation for long. He'd given Stephan an ultimatum; Stop hiding their relationship, or he was out.

Javier had been shocked and hurt when Stephan had chosen the latter. He'd been giving Stephan the silent treatment ever since, avoiding him at parties like this. He'd even left the room at the sight of Stephan for several months after the breakup. Stephan had been crushed by the whole thing.

I had understood that Javier was hurt badly, but I still thought he'd been an asshole about the breakup. Still, I'd been upset about the breakup as well. Stephan had never looked at any guy the way he looked at Javier, and I'd really hoped, at the beginning, that the relationship would work out for them.

Javier saw me staring at him, and his smiled died a quick death. He'd always been polite and courteous with me, but I'd sensed that I made him wary. Not a lot of people understood the relationship between Stephan and I.

Javier surprised me by striding to me and enveloping me in a soft hug. "I'm so happy to see you well, Bianca."

I hugged him back automatically. He didn't let go for some strange reason.

"You don't hate me, do you?" he whispered in my ear.

I blinked, meeting Stephan's sheepish eyes over Javier's shoulder.

"Why would I hate you?" I asked him quietly. He'd thrown me for a loop.

"For being such a bastard to Stephan for so long. My heart was totally broken, but that's no excuse for the way I treated him. And I wasn't exactly nice to you. I stopped speaking to you as well, even though none of it was your fault. Stephan even tells me that you defended me, up until I threw a fit at that Valentine's party and embarrassed myself."

25

Javier had been on our crew for the month when he and Stephan had started seeing each other. I had never even given a thought to the fact that Javier hadn't spoken to me either, since the breakup. All things considered, I had just expected it.

"I know it sounds crazy, but I was jealous of you. I had myself half-convinced that something was going on between the two of you, and that was why Stephan couldn't seem to commit to being gay."

I stiffened. He hugged me tighter, though his hold was still soft. I doubted that the slender man had it in him to be rough.

"I know. Crazy, right?" Javier continued. "But me and Stephan have been talking again. Please, tell me you're okay with it."

I nodded, though I wasn't really sure *what* to think. Javier's about-face was just so sudden and unexpected, and Stephan hadn't said a word. I had just barely caught up with the fact that he wasn't seeing Melvin anymore.

"Yes, of course. I'm not Stephan's keeper, contrary to popular belief."

He kissed my forehead, pulling back to look at me. "I know, but you're his family. I just want us to be cool."

His eyes were earnest and pleading now, far from the cool way they usually looked. It gave me hope. Perhaps he just acted cool, to hide his feelings. I could well understand that.

I smiled at him. It was stiff, but not for lack of effort. "Yes. Okay. I want whatever makes Stephan happy. Always."

Javier nodded emphatically, finally stepping away from me. "Good. Great. Stephan was worried you wouldn't like us seeing each other again."

I sent Stephan a baffled look. He was still watching us, looking distressed.

"He should know better," I said.

Javier moved back to Stephan. I was floored by what

happened next. Stephan threw an arm over Javier's shoulders, messing up his hair playfully. He released the smaller man almost instantly, but it was still the most affectionate thing I'd ever seen him do in public with another man.

For some reason, I felt my eyes getting moist.

Stephan caught my eye, walking over to me. He pushed me into his chest, leaning down to speak into my ear. "Are you really okay with this?'

"What kind of a question is that?" I asked, my voice muffled against his pale orange polo. "And why is this the first I'm hearing about it?"

He was running a hand up and down my back soothingly. "It was just weird timing. I kept meaning to, but things have been so crazy. I could never find the right time. He actually called me because he heard you'd been hurt, and he wanted to make sure we were both okay. That's sweet, right?"

I pushed back, nodding at him. "What about your...issues?"

He swallowed, hard. "Javier and I talked about it. And I realized he has a very good point. I don't have to make an announcement to the world. I don't need a coming-out ball, yanno? But I don't need to lie about it anymore, either. I can just live my life. I don't owe any explanations to anybody. I always said I just wanted my private life private, but I'm beginning to see that there was more to it. And I have nothing to be ashamed of, right?"

He had tried to make it a statement, but I still heard the question in there. I gripped his arms, hard. "Not a thing. I'm so proud of you, Stephan."

He squeezed my arm. We avoided eye contact for a long minute, both blinking back embarrassing tears.

Finally, composed, he just nodded, heading back to stand near Javier. He gripped the other man's shoulder briefly before folding his arms across his chest, listening to whatever Jessa was ranting about.

I felt a little in shock about Stephan's sudden, drastic change of heart. But it was a good shock.

I watched the two men for several minutes, dazed by the change in Stephan. It wasn't full on PDA, but he kept playfully poking Javier in the chest, or tugging on a lock of his hair. Javier kept his hands carefully to himself, but he was giving Stephan the warmest, sweetest looks. I thought it was beautiful.

Murphy and Damien were the next to join our group, and made the rounds, hugging everyone. I realized that our little group had grown rather large and loud.

I searched the spacious lounge, thinking that James might have a hard time spotting me in such a large group, but I saw no sign of him.

I did spot Melissa across the room. She was sitting by the bar with Captain Peter. She was wearing a skin-tight red dress, staring at our group sullenly. I wondered, a little cattily, why she insisted on wearing colors that clashed with her hair. I mentally chastised myself. She was an unpleasant person, but that was no excuse for sinking to her level.

I gave her a little wave when our eyes met, resolving to at least be polite since she was a member of our crew for at least another month. She just nodded back, then looked away. At least she hadn't flipped me off.

I focused back on our growing group as we were joined by two more.

It was Judith and Marnie. They'd been on our crew a few months back. They were inseparable party girls. Judith had long black hair, and Marnie was a platinum blond. They were both very short with great figures and cute faces. They sort of reminded me of naughty pixies. Half-drunk naughty pixies at the moment.

I remembered that they often introduced themselves to men at bars as Ivanna Humpalot and Alotta Vagina. They rarely went back to their rooms alone, sometimes even sharing men with each other. They were a funny pair, but not for the faint of heart. Stephan and I had been at Judith's twenty-first birthday party about two months ago. It had been crazy. She'd made out with at least three men that I'd seen, and dragged two of them to her hotel room.

Marnie was a year older than Judith, just twenty-two. I was older than both girls, but the two of them had me beat by a lot of years in experience. They both thought any woman who had lasted to fifteen with their virginity intact was a prude. I didn't imagine they even had a word for someone who had lasted until age twenty-three, like I had.

Judith squealed in delight when she saw me. She rushed over and hugged me.

"I heard about the attack. How are you doing?" she nearly shouted.

I hugged her back stiffly, wishing she hadn't spoken so loudly. "Good. How are you?"

She cast a sidelong glance in Damien's direction.

"How much you wanna bet I'll wake up in Damien's bed tomorrow?" she whispered. "Then I'll be good. Marnie hooked up with him a few months ago. She says he's *hung*. The last guy I hooked up with was a real disappointment. It had to have given me some like good cock Karma, right?"

Her words surprised a laugh out of me. I hadn't known about the hook-up between Marnie and Damien, but I wasn't surprised.

"TMI, Judith," I told her with a smile. "I have to work with him every week."

Marnie had sidled up next to us, squeezing between us to hug me softly. "If Judith goes after him tonight, I'm joining them," she said with a wink. "I swear to god, if any man can handle two women at once, it's him. He's a marathon man."

Judith wrinkled her nose at Marnie. "I never get the really good ones to myself. She always wants a piece."

I didn't even try to hide my laugh. She was complaining, but her tone was more amused than upset.

Damien caught my eye from a few feet away. He didn't walk over, just gave me wide, questioning eyes. I was sure he was worried what they were telling me about him. I just smirked at him. He covered his face with his hands, and I swore I could hear his pained groan. I didn't feel real bad for him, since I was willing to bet he'd end up with the feisty girls by the end of the night.

"I heard a rumor that you lost your V-card. *Finally*. And to some super hot rich guy. Is it true?"

I grimaced. The rumor mill was alive and well, and apparently held some truth. "Yes. Please don't say it so loud."

I was still mortified that the two girls even knew I'd been a virgin. They had guessed it, strangely enough, considering I knew few people who knew less about being virgins themselves. We'd been in Judith's hotel room, watching some romantic comedy on a layover, when the two girls had started in on their favorite sex stories. They'd asked me to share, and I'd just blushed. They had guessed, with no little disgust, that I was a virgin. I had to give them a firm talking to when they wouldn't stop trying to find men to relieve me of the 'problem'. Marnie had even volunteered to lend me her on-again off-again boyfriend at the time. I had not taken the offer well. I'd gotten over it, though, knowing she was a little oblivious to other people's feelings when it came to things like that.

"Well, congratulations. Was he any good? Sometimes the really good-looking ones are horrible in bed. It's that whole, I'm so hot I don't even have to try, mentality. Yanno?" Judith elbowed Marnie playfully in the ribs while she spoke.

I just shook my head, wide-eyed. I most certainly didn't know anything about that. I couldn't imagine there was a man on the planet who was better in bed. I didn't particularly want to share that information, though.

"So he was good? Your first time was good?" Marnie pried.

I nodded, very uncomfortable. The sharing personal information thing was so not for me.

"On a scale of one to ten, what was he?"

I sighed. They were not gonna let up. "How would, 'I want him to fuck me to death, and he just might', rate on that scale?"

The women hooted with laughter, but their laughter died as they looked up and to my left.

I felt a familiar firm hand grip my nape. Soft lips that I was well acquainted with kissed my cheek. "That's a heartwarming assessment, Love," James murmured against my skin.

CHAPTER FIVE

I felt heat suffuse my cheeks in a rush, and a perverse shiver of pure pleasure rock my body.

Typical James timing. Showing up at the most disarming moment possible.

Judith and Marnie were just staring at him, stunned speechless for a long moment.

I turned to look up at him. His hand fell from my nape and we just stared at each other. I drank in the sight of him.

He looked...*wonderful.* He was dressed in a bright blue polo with dark washed, fitted jeans, and navy running shoes. It was the 'James's supermodel take on casual', I thought. Even his casual looked too sexy for public. I'd never seen him in jeans before. He made them look sinful. I saw just the hint of the top of his tan chest at his collar, and had to stifle my urge to check my mouth for drool. His caramel-colored hair just brushed that collar, and I clenched my hands to keep them at my sides. I wanted to touch him. But touching always led to too much, too fast, with us.

I met his vivid blue eyes. They were intense and unsmiling.

His eyes dropped down to my earrings and then to the collar at my throat. His jaw clenched, then unclenched. He ran his tongue over his teeth. My whole body seemed to clench.

"Thank you for wearing those. It was...considerate of you," he said in his most polite, if hoarse, voice.

He swallowed, shoving his hands into his pockets, then folding them across his chest. It made his upper arms bulge through his fitted shirt distractingly. His chest and arms looked bigger than I remembered, the muscles bulging as though he'd been lifting weights excessively. The material of his shirt looked so soft it made me itch to run my fingers over it. But that light touch would turn to a stroke. And then I would stroke harder to feel the resilient flesh beneath...

James's eyes were running down my body now, not for the first time. His eyes were on my very bare legs, then my cleavage.

"Your legs are outrageous. You make that mini skirt look illegal." He looked back at my face, finally. "You look beautiful." He took a deep, harsh breath, staring at me. It was gratifying. "But isn't that outfit a bit sexy for a work function?"

I wrinkled my nose at him, then pointedly looked around the room. This was Vegas, and we were in a bar full of flight attendants. My attire was downright modest compared to some of the outfits I saw.

"Did you want me to fuck you in front of all of your co-workers? Because that's all I can think about, when I see you in that outfit." His voice was pitched low, but I gasped at his words.

"This was supposed to be a short, casual meeting," I told him, a hint of accusation in my voice.

He took another deep breath, looking around the room, and away from me. I watched as he counted to ten silently.

"I missed you," he said finally.

I had missed him too, but I couldn't make myself tell him that. He still unsettled me too much for that kind of honesty.

Instead, I said the first thing that popped into my head. "You were late."

His jaw clenched again. "Yes. I was in my car, in the middle of the most annoying business call of my life. I think I may need to fire my manager in New York. I didn't see you arrive, and lost track of time. I apologize. I didn't want to miss a second of our time together, which made the phone call particularly annoying."

"It's okay. We got here early, for once, so I was just surprised to see that you weren't early, for once."

"Introduce us," Judith said loudly.

I wasn't surprised. The two party girls had shown a surprising amount of self-control in letting us talk quietly for as long as we had.

I turned, giving the women a rueful smile. Jessa moved closer, and we suddenly had the attention of the entire group.

I went around the group, naming all of the people that James hadn't yet met. I touched James's arm lightly as I finished. "Everyone, this is my friend, James," I said, feeling awkward. I had no idea what to call him.

"Boyfriend," James corrected, and I raised a brow at him. I didn't know what he was, but it didn't seem like he could call himself *that*. "Very serious boyfriend," he elaborated with a smirk.

I thought I knew what he was doing. He wanted to talk to me in private, and he knew that giving himself that title would antagonize me enough to draw me into an argument. I wasn't going to bite, though, I told myself resolutely. And he was overly possessive. He would say anything to warn other men off.

I sent Damien a glance. He was watching us, his mouth tight. I glanced away quickly, wanting to avoid drawing attention to the fact that he was staring at us rather intently.

Judith and Marnie began chatting James up mercilessly. I was more than a little surprised that they weren't hitting on him. Not even a little bit. It seemed more like they were interviewing him. I thought it was kind of sweet. They were the most flirtatious women I knew, but they were going out of their way to be completely platonic with someone whom they thought was my boyfriend. Someone who happened to be the most beautiful man on the planet. It made me see that they were good friends to me. Maybe better than I'd given them credit for.

I had a sad habit of being more cynical than was warranted. Kindness or consideration almost always caught me by surprise if it came from anyone but Stephan. I supposed he was the only person I'd ever allowed myself to have expectations of. I had plenty of friends. Mostly casual friends. But friendship and trust just hadn't been a connection I'd made. I listened to the girls asking James question after question, even their language cleaned up.

I suddenly felt old beyond my twenty-three years. I'd always thought they were the mature, experienced ones, but I certainly had them beat in the cynicism department.

I touched James's arm with just the tips of my fingers. "I'll be right back. I need to use the restroom."

James tried to walk me to the bathroom, but I waved him off.

"Go say hi to Stephan," I told him.

He gave me a stern look, but headed in that direction.

Judith and Marnie joined me. The top of their heads were right at a level with my chest. I always felt like a giant when I was hanging out with them.

"O M G, Bianca, that is the most beautiful man I've ever seen in my life," Judith gushed as we made our way across the bar. I flushed, but I certainly couldn't dispute the comment.

"That man is downright pretty," Marnie said.

I wrinkled my nose. The word pretty just sounded so feminine to me. And that was so not James.

"He's good in bed, too?" Marnie asked, clearly skeptical.

"That just isn't fair. If I looked like him, I'd never leave my house. I'd just stay home and fuck *myself*. If you tell me he has a big dick, I might become either a cutter or a lesbian."

We got to the line for the restroom, filing into the outrageous crowd that had already formed a good twenty feet away from the actual bathroom.

I smiled ruefully. "Then I won't tell you," I said.

Both women started making loud sounds of despair. I laughed at their theatrics.

"I guess good things really do come to those who wait." Judith said, sounding sad. "I can't go on one date without sleeping with a guy. And I can't go two days without finding a date, so I guess I'll never be getting anyone good."

"I can't wait to come either, so I guess I won't be getting anything that good. That kind of good only comes to those who wait twenty-three years, apparently," Marnie said forlornly. She brightened, snapping out of it almost immediately. "But we are gonna get a piece of Captain Damien tonight. He's a nice slice of something good."

I didn't point out that he hadn't even looked happy to see them. I doubted it would even slow them down. They were a persuasive pair.

"What's with all this tabloid garbage I keep seeing?" Marnie asked, leveling a rather serious stare at me.

I grimaced. "Mostly lies and just horrible people saying horrible things because it gets attention. I'm trying to ignore it."

Judith gave me a baffled look. "I think it's awesome. It feels like we know a celebrity now. I think it's all so fun and exciting. And he's so beautiful. There could be worse things."

She had a good point about the worse things, I thought.

I shrugged. "I can't change it, so I'm adjusting."

"So he doesn't have a longtime girlfriend?" Marnie asked. "I read somewhere that he was dating some gorgeous heiress, for like, the last eight years."

Talk about a mood killing change of topic.

I sighed. "He tells me she's just a friend. I guess the question is, do I believe him? I'm working it out. Trusting him is not my first instinct, but that doesn't really have anything to do with him."

Judith gestured at my jewelry. "And all this gorgeous bling. I vote trust him."

I laughed. They were starting to remind me of a half-drunk version of good cop, bad cop.

Marnie patted my shoulder. "Be careful, Bianca. That man looks like he could break hearts for fun, yanno?"

Judith pretended to fan herself. "But what fun, right?"

I couldn't argue with any of it. It was nothing that I hadn't thought myself.

There was a group of women huddled close, a few people ahead of us. They were whispering and rudely pointing me out. I didn't know any of them, but they were most likely other flight attendants that I'd never worked with. I guessed that they'd read something dreadful about me. I ignored them. It was something I was going to have to get used to.

It was all part of the media circus that surrounded James's life. And I had apparently decided not to give up on the man, despite my better judgement. He still wanted me, and he was a hard man to ignore when he was in hot pursuit.

The group burst into laughter. Even their laughter sounded catty, so I knew they were saying something awful. I forced my mind to focus on something else, a longtime habit I'd used for avoiding unpleasant things that couldn't be changed.

We eventually made it through the line and got in and out of the bathroom without incident. The group of mean girls had had Judith and Marnie about ready to brawl. They'd gotten progressively louder, emphasizing words like 'whore' and 'gold-digger', as they shot me strangely malevolent glances.

Whatever they'd read about me, I couldn't understand how it would affect them, or why they would care enough to be openly hostile to a stranger. It was beyond me, so I didn't linger on the musings long.

CHAPTER SIX

My back stiffened as we approached our group again. James was standing near Stephan and Javier, and they were laughing at something. But he wasn't alone. Melissa was practically plastered to his side, laughing along with them.

"You notice that bitch didn't say boo until we left. Then she swooped in like a vulture," Marnie was saying under her breath.

"I don't like her. She talks a lot of shit about people for doing less messed-up shit than *she* does on a regular basis," Judith added.

I tried to follow all of the shits in that sentence. I gave up as we got close enough for me to see the way Melissa's hands were sneaking in little touches all over James.

She touched his arm, patted his back, reached way way up and squeezed his shoulder. And then ran her hand along his chest and stomach on its way back down. James took a little step back, avoiding her touch, but I still saw red. Red as in crimson. Crimson as in blood. Blood as in I was going to make the bitch bleed.

I moved between the two of them in an odd haze of temper,

plastering myself to his side and pushing her roughly out of the way with my body. I ran my hand along the line of his chest and abdomen that she'd touched, as though my touch could erase hers.

I heard the ice cubes in her drink clink against her glass as she was jostled by my sudden movement.

She gasped in outrage.

I ignored her, looking up at James. "Why were you letting her touch you?" I asked him quietly.

He looked surprised, and half-amused. "I thought she was a friend of yours. I was trying not to be openly rude, but she was making it difficult. You have a drink while you were gone? You were gone for thirty minutes. Now you're acting a little...differently."

"You fucking bitch. You made me spill my drink on my dress," Melissa was yelling behind me. It was easy to ignore her, for some reason.

I ran my hands up and down James's torso again, using my fingertips to trace each muscle. He was unbelievably hard.

"Not one part of my body is this hard," I mused aloud.

"Careful, Love. You can't offer a starving man a feast and expect him not to take you up on it."

I stroked his chest again, pausing at one of his nipples. "I want to see your skin," I told him.

Now I'd done it. I'd gone and touched him, and it was worse than being drunk. I couldn't seem to focus on anything but touching more of him.

"Fucking Bitch!" Melissa said louder. "Do you have any idea how much this dress is worth? It's BCBG. Do you even know what that is, you skank?"

I saw James's eyes widen just a second before he spun me around, putting his back to the crazy redhead. I heard the sound of a drink being thrown, glass and all, against his rock-hard back.

It had been aimed at the back of my head, I realized,

stunned.

She was such a crazy bitch.

"Fuck," James said, glaring over his shoulder at a still fuming Melissa. "You need to get the fuck out of here, or security will be escorting you out. I think you've embarrassed yourself enough tonight, don't you?" His tone was positively scathing.

Melissa cursed fluently as she stormed away.

Our group erupted into chatter as she left. The general consensus was, 'Bitch is crazy'.

"Bitch be cray cray," Murphy summed it up, as only Murphy could.

Everyone laughed, breaking the last bit of tension.

I looked up at James, pursing my lips. "That was gentlemanly of you, taking the shot for me," I told him. "Thank you."

He shook out his shirt, ice cubes still flying off of his back. I checked his back. His shirt was soaked. Even his jeans were soaked. I was relieved to find, though, that the glass had broken on the ground, leaving him unscathed.

A waitress showed up with a bucket and mop and began to clean up the liquid and broken glass. We moved out of her way.

"It looks like you're going to have to take off all of your clothes," I told him with a smile.

He smiled back, but his smile was all heat. "I have a change of clothes in the car. Come with me?"

I leaned in closer to him, inhaling deeply. He smelled so good that I felt my eyelids drift closed with the pleasure of his scent. It was so good that I wanted to put a name to it, and bottle it up.

"Convince me," I told him softly, as I forced my eyes back open to look at him.

He glanced around, running his tongue over those sexy as hell teeth. "Okay. Did you have something particular in mind, or do I get to pick how? I'm trying to play nice here, since I don't want to scare you off again. You're not making it easy, though."

"Your shirt's all wet. I want you to take it off. I want to see your skin."

He gave me an appraising look. "That's it? All I have to do to get you to my car is to take my shirt off?" He was whipping it off before he'd even finished his question.

Hoots and whistles were starting up around the lounge as people took in the spectacular sight of his naked torso.

I gasped at the sight of all of his bare skin. He had *definitely* bulked up in the month we'd been apart, his already impressive chest swollen attractively. It was distracting, to say the least.

"You've been lifting more weights," I observed.

His smile was a little pained. "I needed a little more physical activity to adjust to the whole celibacy thing. I usually work out for two hours in the morning. I added two more in the evening, as well, as a sort of...sleep aid."

I felt a strange stirring of guilt, and a not so strange thrill of joy at his mention of celibacy. I opened my mouth to say...something, but I couldn't seem to hold a thought, with all of his bare skin in front of me. My captivated gaze moved lower.

His jeans dipped low. I traced the skin just above his jeans. It was dangerous territory, dipping into a sharply defined V. An impressive and growing arousal was making his jeans more obscene by the second.

He gripped my hand. "Unless part of my convincing you was that you want to get fucked against the nearest wall, I'd start walking, Buttercup."

He grabbed my hand and started moving toward the door.

"I need a new shirt," James called in Stephan's direction as we passed. Stephan gave him a wide-eyed look, but just nodded. "We'll be back."

"I want to have his babies," someone muttered as we passed.

I sent a glare in their general direction. I couldn't get real mad about it, though. I had made him bare the finest chest in the world to a room full of hungry flight attendants... And if anyone got a glance at his jeans, it certainly wouldn't lessen their interest.

Clark met us at the entrance of the club, holding the door open, face impassive.

"Nice catch, Sir," he said quietly.

I smiled at him, knowing he was referring to James moving to protect me from the thrown drink.

"Any paparazzi in the parking lot?" James asked brusquely.

"Max just did a sweep. Looks clean so far, Mr. Cavendish."

James just nodded, almost dragging me through the small back parking lot.

Clark managed to get in front of us again to open the car door. "Your suitcase is already in there, and open."

James nodded. "Very good," he said, ushering me into the car first.

I sat down, then scooted across the seat to make room for James. He crowded in behind me without a pause, the door shutting behind him. I heard him take a few ragged breaths, and then he was on me.

He had me on my back between one breath and the next. He opened my legs wide, crawling between them. He unbuttoned his jeans, pulling his stiff erection out with a harsh groan.

"I wanted to take my time with you, when I finally got my hands on you again, but I can't wait. Unbutton your blouse. I want to tear it too badly to touch it." As he spoke, he was inching my skirt up over my hips. It was a little stretchy, luckily. I thought that he wouldn't have hesitated to tear it if it wasn't.

My panties weren't so lucky. He gripped the lace in his hands and ripped both sides. I wriggled my lower half while working on the small buttons of my blouse. When I had released the last one, he was pushing my shirt open impatiently. His hands were already on the front clasp of my bra when what he saw made him freeze. My torso was still dotted with the last vestiges of what had been some truly heinous bruising. I saw his hands shake a little as he unclasped my bra. He brushed along the fading marks with just his fingertips.

"Over a month later, and it still looks like this?" His voice was deep with agitation.

I turned my face away. "I don't want to talk about it. I've talked about it enough."

He gripped my chin, turning my face back to him. His eyes were wild. "I couldn't stand it if something were to happen to you. Do you understand that? I've never felt so powerless or terrified in my life as I did when I watched that ambulance driving away with you, having no clue what had happened, or even if you were alright. And then to find out that *some monster had put his hands on you?* I want to kill him. I *need* to protect you."

I just set my mouth in a hard line. "That's not what I want from you. And I don't want to talk about it."

He was kissing me suddenly. It was an angry, passionate kiss. I kissed him back with just as much passion. Just as much anger. He was thrusting into me so fast that I was filled before I knew his intent. I was wet and ready but I was so tight and he was so big that it still caused a delicious friction that bordered on pain.

I gasped, my head falling back, my eyes closing.

He gripped my chin, hard. "Look at me," he ordered.

I did, watching the fervor in his eyes with a wistful pain that I felt deep in my chest. I would have given anything to have him *feel* the way he looked at me when he was deep inside of me. He looked at me like I was more dear than his next breath at times, and it was almost more than I could bear.

His hair trailed over his face and into mine as he leaned his face close. He held my wrists above my head, using his hands as shackles. He moved my wrists into one hand, the other moving to my jeweled collar, tugging at the ring roughly. His thrusts never let up or slowed. "You're mine, Bianca. Say it."

My words came out as a rough gasp. "I'm yours, James."

"Come," he ordered, thrusting so fast and hard that I sobbed as I came.

He groaned my name again and again as he poured into me.

Afterwards, he braced himself carefully on his elbows, protecting my still tender chest and ribs.

He grabbed a clean t-shirt from his open suitcase to wipe me, and then himself. I lay and watched him almost lazily as he changed into a new pair of boxer briefs, jeans, and a soft light gray V-neck shirt.

He crouched beside me once he'd changed, straightening my clothes almost tenderly.

"Did I hurt you?" he asked as he buttoned my shirt.

"Mmm, no," I said. Anything that could be considered pain certainly hadn't bothered me at the time.

"Not even your ribs?" He smoothed my shirt as he finished with the buttons.

I took a deep breath, but no, there was still no pain. "No, not at all. They finally aren't bothering me so much. Breathing was a little rough there for awhile."

His mouth tightened as he smoothed my skirt back down. "We don't have to do any of the rough stuff, if you don't want. I don't just mean while you're healing. I could give that stuff up completely, if it isn't what you want anymore."

"I still want it. Nothing's changed in that regard. What he did... and what you do, I don't see them as the same thing. I can't explain it, but the one helps me cope with the other. Can we not talk about this anymore?"

He smoothed my hair back from my face, kissing my forehead. "We need to talk more, not less. About a lot of things. If you would just let me talk to you, we could get things settled between us. I can't stand this constant uncertainty where you're concerned."

I sat up, feeling a need for some distance.

"Let's make a deal. How about we not talk. I'll go home with you tonight. I'll stay at your place. We can do anything you want. You can fuck my brains out all night." My voice was getting embarrassingly thick, even a hint of accent was coming out. "But I don't want to talk about the attack, not any part of it. And I don't want to talk about our relationship, or lack of one."

His jaw clenched, but I saw almost immediately that he wouldn't turn me down.

"Do we have to go back to the party first?" he finally asked, his mood clearly darker.

"Yes," I said firmly.

CHAPTER SEVEN

We walked back into the building without another word. James gripped my elbow in a proprietary manner.

We re-joined my group of friends. A few people gave us good natured smirks for our absence, but no one said anything about it.

James was quiet and withdrawn. I had a hard time enjoying myself when I knew I had put him into his sudden dark mood. He was barely even touching me. It wasn't until Damien engaged me in conversation that he became suddenly affectionate. Damien was asking me if I had any plans for the next New York layover when I felt James press against my back, wrapping his arms around me very carefully, just under my breasts.

Contrary man, I thought darkly, as he buried his face in my neck.

"Um, no, I don't think so." I tried to answer Damien, distracted by the mercurial man at my back. He'd pressed his groin against me, and I had no doubts as to what he was thinking about.

James raised his head at my answer. "I have an event I'd

like you to attend with me, if you're up for it. It's a formal affair, for charity."

I stiffened, bewildered by the offer. It was an about-face for him, asking me to something so public. We had established from the start that we weren't going to date. It wasn't what either of us had wanted from each other. I had quickly found myself hurt by the arrangement, but I hadn't known he'd changed his stance on any of it. When had it changed and why? Or was this just a stunt to show his ownership to Damien?

"Um, I don't have anything to wear to something like that," I said, naming off the first excuse that came into my head.

His hands started moving along my stomach, stroking. He grabbed my hips, holding me still as he straightened behind me. The motion brought his erection more flush against my butt, and I had to stifle a gasp. I didn't want anyone to see just what he was doing. I tried my best to look normal, but had no idea if I succeeded.

"I've had my dresser select a wardrobe for you, to keep at my place," he said in a perfectly casual tone. "And she'll be there Friday morning to help you either select something from the wardrobe, or find something else. She'll have a sampling from several designers for you to try on."

I blinked, not sure what to think of that. "You shouldn't—"

"It's only fair, if I want you to attend a bunch of stuffy affaIrs with me, that I provide the clothes you'll need to wear to them. And besides, we've already discussed the gift thing exhaustively. If I recall, that was one of the concessions that you actually agreed to." He was moving against me as he spoke. It was hard to hold on to a thought when he did that.

"When did you do all that? The wardrobe thing?" I asked, baffled.

"Weeks ago, when I realized that I was just going to have to get used to the idea that I couldn't shelter you from the paparazzi, so I might as well show you off."

I just blinked.

Damien was looking between us, studying James. I had almost forgotten, for a few minutes, that he was even there. James had that effect on me.

"You'll come with me, won't you?" James murmured in my ear.

He wrapped his arms around my shoulders, his arms moving slowly, rubbing against my nipples. There was no way that he wasn't aware he was touching them. They were hard little pebbles that he had to feel through the material of my thin shirt and lacy bra.

"I, um, I don't know. The invitation is unexpected, as I'm sure you know. I've never been to anything like that."

"There's nothing to it. We just get dressed up and walk around, mingling. I won't leave your side, if you're nervous. I just want your company."

Damien walked away, likely feeling ignored. He made his way to Murphy, who was telling a story loud enough for the entire room to hear.

I pitched my voice low, speaking over my shoulder. "I thought we weren't doing any of that. You said from the beginning that we weren't dating."

"I'd talk to you about it, but I'm not allowed to talk tonight, remember?" His deep voice was a rumble against my ear.

I saw his game. He wanted to get me curious enough to take back my own words. I wouldn't do it, though, even if my curiosity *was* eating at me.

I poked an elbow behind me. "Fine then, let's not talk about any events either, while we're at it. That raises too many questions about our relationship."

He made a displeased little hum behind me that I could feel rumble through me. He didn't speak for several minutes. I had to bite my tongue to keep from asking him questions.

Finally he broke his silence. "Do you like horses?" he asked.

"Horses?" I asked, baffled.

"Yes, horses. Do you like them?"

I thought about it. More about why he was asking than what he was asking. Finally, I just focused on the question. "Yes, I like horses. Doesn't everyone? Why?"

"Have you ridden?"

I flushed. "Once. It was just a two-hour guided tour, up in the mountains, so I'm not even sure it counts, but I loved it."

"Do you think you feel well enough to try riding now? Or do you need to heal up more?"

I cast him a suspicious glance. "Do you have horses in town?" I hadn't noticed any stables at his property, but I also hadn't exactly gotten a proper tour.

"I do. I need to show you the entire property sometime, including the stables. They're set away from the house. But that isn't what I had in mind. You said I could do whatever I wanted with you. You didn't give me any restrictions, including staying in town. I would take you to the beach, to relax, but I find that lately I absolutely despise the beach."

I raised my brows at him. "You don't like the beach?" I asked him, baffled.

He set his jaw and looked across the room with a steely glare. I followed his eyes. He was staring at Damien as though he wanted to do the man bodily harm.

"Currently, just the thought of the beach makes me want to do violence," he said, his tone quiet but ominous. "So I have another idea, if you're up to try some riding."

I studied him, trying to follow his odd thought patterns. "Where did you want to take me?"

He turned that steely glare on me. "You said I could do anything with you tonight. And you did not say I had to tell you what or where. All I want to know is, do you think you can ride a horse?"

I glared back. "I'm not sure. I feel okay. If I didn't do anything too crazy, and it was a calm horse, I suppose I could."

He nodded decisively. "Okay, we'll take it easy. Let me make some phone calls."

I watched him walk outside, a little stunned by the sudden turn of events.

He always seemed to do that, turn everything around until I was dizzy and panting and giving into his whims without a protest. It was infuriating, and exhilarating. I had thought my life was content and full before I met him. I had thought that excitement was the last thing that I wanted for myself. And the thought of falling in love had been anathema to me. *How could meeting one person make everything change so suddenly?* I wondered, not for the first time. I didn't know where he was planning to take me, but it didn't matter. I would go. My self-control became an elusive quality when I got into his orbit.

I approached Stephan, listening to the long-winded story Murphy was into before I was noticed. He was walking everyone through the horror of waking up with two women and a new tattoo with one of their names on it. Only he hadn't remembered either of their names, just that one of them was Lola, since it was written in big black letters on his chest.

I blinked at the ridiculous story. Surprisingly, I hadn't heard it before, though I had seen the tattoo when he was lounging by the pool. I listened, as interested as everyone else to find out which woman the tattoo was for, and why.

"Turns out, it was *another* woman I'd met earlier that night. She'd left in a jealous rage after the tattoo, when I started talking to the two I woke up with. I was just being friendly, I'm sure!"

His defensive stance about two women he'd woken up in bed with made everyone laugh. He was still genuinely offended by the woman who'd inspired his tattoo and never spoken to him again.

Four other pilots had joined the group. I recognized them only vaguely. They were part of the younger generation of pilots, and I knew they were friends with Damien and Murphy, but I couldn't recall any of their names.

"He calls her the one that got away every time he gets really trashed," Damien said in an amused voice, making me start. He was just behind me.

I turned to give him a slight smile.

His voice was pitched loud enough for the large group to hear, but he seemed to be speaking to me. "He doesn't even remember her, but he says he trusts even his drunk judgement enough that, if she inspired a tattoo in one night, she must have been 'the one.' Every time he goes on a rant about how he hates being single, he blames Lola's damned temper."

I looked at Murphy, laughing. He had a sheepish, good natured-grin on his face. It sounded like something he'd say, and he didn't deny it.

"Where was this?" I asked him.

"Melbourne, Australia. I bet she had a sexy accent," Murphy said in a dejected tone.

"We all know how much you love sexy Australian accents," one of the pilots added, sending everyone into new peals of laughter.

"Hey, now." Damien said, raising his hands. "Don't drag me into this. I've been with Murphy for years, and he has yet to get a tattoo for me on any part of his body, sexy accent or no."

"Now we know for sure he's never slept with you," Marnie interjected. "If he had, there would be a Damien tattoo somewhere on his body, I can attest. One night, and I had to check the urge not to brand you on my ass."

Loud hoots and hollers followed her brazen announcement, Murphy laughing the loudest. His laugh was particularly infectious.

I had to give Damien a second look. I'd have sworn he was blushing.

"Don't think I haven't tried," Murphy gasped out, still laughing. "He's just about the prettiest man I know. Prettier than at least half the women I've been with. But I can't even get a cuddle when he's drunk."

Our laughter was loud enough that even in the boisterous bar, most of the people were staring our way.

That was about the time James strode back inside.

I was standing closest to Damien, though we were still a good two feet apart. And I couldn't stop laughing, even seeing the storm that immediately overtook his lovely features at the sight of us standing near each other again.

I knew that he had a problem with Damien. He seemed to think there was something between us. I just didn't understand why. I'd known Damien for years before I'd met James. If we had shared a real interest in each other, obviously something would have happened by now. I understood Damien's appeal, but he just didn't do it for me. I had more...exotic tastes. I thought that all should have been very obvious to James, so it was hard to humor his strange dislike for one of my good friends.

James strode to me, looking much too fine even in a pique.

I marveled, as I did much too often, at how beautiful he was. His longish, sandy brown hair fell artfully out of his face as he walked. The chiseled muscles of his arms and upper body were clearly defined by his thin shirt. His clenched jawline was perfection. His mouth was almost bow shaped but held too firm of an edge to be pouty, though it sure was pretty. His arched eyebrows and thick lashes were a shade darker than his hair, drawing attention to his vivid turquoise eyes. His nose was straight and flared appealingly at the tip, sitting just right in his unrivaled face. He was simply beautiful. He was in no way feminine, but the word handsome just couldn't do those refined looks justice. He was long and lean, but in tight fitting clothing, it was clear that he was well muscled, rather than thin. *He's perfection,* I thought absently. *What is he doing with me?* Was always my follow up question.

He moved in close beside me, but didn't touch me.

"Looks like I missed all the fun," he said quietly to me, his voice strangely empty.

My smile began to fade.

"The arrangements have been made," he said shortly. "You're all mine, whenever we finish up here."

"What about you two? You look like you're hot enough about each other to break out the ink. When are you going to tattoo your names on each other?" Marnie called out to James and I, smiling and wiggling her eyebrows suggestively.

I sent him a sidelong smile.

He gave me the tiniest smile in return. "It would be a waste to mar her perfect skin just for a little ink," James said. "But I would happily get a Bianca tattoo, if that's what she wants."

I arched a brow at him as the crowd erupted, shouting encouragement for the folly. I'd seen James's body. He didn't have one tattoo, so he was just messing with them, of course.

"You wouldn't return the favor, Bianca?" Judith called out, sounding aghast.

I shrugged, giving James a narrow-eyed glare. "I guess if he got a tattoo for me, I'd let him pierce my nipples," I said more to him than the crowd. But the crowd absolutely roared at the joke.

He ran his tongue over his teeth in that mouthwatering way of his. He held out a hand to me, as though to shake. "You have a deal, Love. Please, shake on it. Nothing would please me more."

Someone sounded like they choked on their drink just behind me. I heard Stephan shouting something along the lines of, "What the fuck, Buttercup?"

I looked at his hand, wondering why he had to take the joke so far. But I shook his hand without giving it much thought, just going along with his over the top antics. One of Murphy's favorite lines about telling jokes came to mind, for some reason. Always go with the bit, he liked to say. *Can't deny the bit.*

"You first, though. I want to see that ink before I pierce anything," I said, making sure I had insurance, just in case he really had gone crazy.

He smiled, and it was positively wicked. "Of course."

"And I want to see those piercings, Bee!" someone called out. I couldn't even tell who it was.

"We want to see, as proof that you both held up your end of the bargain!" I recognized Judith's voice that time.

"You should put her name on your cock, in that case!" Marnie called out. She got enough of a shocked response to call out, "Too far? Was that one too far?"

James threw an arm around my shoulder, anchoring me close against his side. "No one gets to see her piercings, but I'll show the tattoo. Bianca can even pick which part of my body she wants to mark."

The joke had gone on long enough. I pulled back to give him a stern look, opening my mouth to speak.

He pressed his hot mouth against mine before I could get a word out. He kissed me, a hot, not fit for public, kind of kiss. His tongue swept deep into my mouth, just begging me to suck it. I pushed against his chest at first, having every intention of avoiding his need for PDA. His hand fisted in my hair, the other hand going to my lower back to press me firmly against him.

I struggled for only a moment before I was lost, softening against him, sucking at his tongue like my life depended on it. My hands fisted helplessly in his shirt, my wrists aching for the feel of the restraining pressure that I craved.

I forgot about my friends, forgot about the joke he'd taken

too far. He could have taken me there, against the wall, if he'd wanted to. That was his power over me.

He was the one to pull back, smiling. He looked over my head, and I knew he was grinning at Damien, a cold, triumphant grin.

"If you don't pick a spot, I might just have to take the only other suggestion I heard, something about your name on my cock." He spoke loudly enough to get some hoots and hollers from the crowd.

I couldn't even form the words to respond. He took one of my fisted hands, spreading it flat over his heart.

"Or how about right there, Love?" he whispered to me.

I licked my lips, opening my mouth to speak. I knew I should say...something, but my mind had just gone off into space. Off into, thinking about the things he could do to me, territory. He laughed, clearly enjoying the state he'd put me in.

He was smug and gloating as he stroked a hand over my hair. I couldn't bring myself to care. I was soon to be at his mercy for the night. The thought was all-consuming. I was excited, and aroused, and scared.

Was it too soon, since my injuries? Would I bring back some of the shadow pains that had so recently faded? Would he take it easy on me, or push me hard? I wanted to know the answers more than I feared the pain.

One thing I knew for certain. He was going to fuck me mindless, and I could barely stand the wait.

CHAPTER EIGHT

"**A**re you ready to leave yet?" James murmured to me a few minutes later.

We'd grown silent as the group moved on to another topic. James was stroking me lightly, touching me everywhere, falling just short of indecency.

He would touch my collarbone, but stop just short of my breasts. One hand lingered at my hipbone, dangerously close to dipping low enough to be obscene. I was getting more and more lost in his touch, losing all sense of what was appropriate, and losing sight of all of the reasons that I'd ever had any reservations about him at all.

This was the reason I had tried to keep my distance from him, but also the reason that I couldn't. I simply couldn't resist him. I had held out for a time, but if I was honest, it had only been a countdown to my capitulation.

I didn't answer him, and he took it as a challenge. He kissed me again, holding nothing back this time. He was gripping my hair almost to the point of pain, his other hand grabbing my butt as he ground against me. He was aroused and I moaned into his mouth, the sound barely registering in my lust fueled haze.

He pulled back, his breath ragged now. "You ready to leave now? I don't find the idea of fucking you against that wall behind you even slightly unpleasant. Exhibitionism has never been a problem for me. Is that something you'd like to try?"

He ground against me with every word he spoke, and his voice was mocking, almost angry. His words were barely registering, as my focus was on what he was doing.

"Hmm?" Was all I managed to get out.

"Are you ready to leave now? Or would you prefer that I fuck you in front of all of your co-workers?" James bit out in a hard enough tone to finally bring my mind back to the surface.

"No," I said, breathless and agitated.

How could I so quickly forget where I am, and that we're in a room crowded with people that I know?

"No, you're not ready to leave? Or no, you wouldn't prefer that I fuck you in a room crowded with your friends? Where they can all watch me bury my cock inside of you against that wall, not ten feet behind you. Is that something you want them to see?"

I just stared at him for a while, my mind moving like molasses.

He seemed to be getting angrier by the moment. "Answer me. Do you want me to do that?" he asked, each word biting and harsh.

"No," I said, shaking my head. "No," I repeated, trying to make it sound convincing. "We need to go."

He ground his teeth together. "I'm aware of that. Go say goodbye to Stephan," he ordered.

I stepped away from him, catching my breath for long moments.

I counted in my head as I made my way to Stephan, trying to get my mind onto the matter at hand, and off James.

Stephan gave me a slightly worried look as I approached.

"You okay, Bee?" He leaned near my ear as he spoke.

I just nodded, looking only at him. "James and I are leaving. I'm going home with him. I'll call you tomorrow," I told him.

He began to look around as I spoke, searching for James. He met the other man's stare as James approached. James leaned in, saying something in his ear, pitched too low for even me to hear.

Stephan nodded slowly, giving the other man a severe frown, but saying nothing.

James led me from the room by the hand, his own grip uncompromising. We didn't speak to anyone else. I was lucid enough to know I should be a little embarrassed at how far I'd almost let James go in a room full of people.

James was close to dragging me by the time we got to his car. He ushered me, rather forcefully, into the low limo the second Clark opened the door. He was a hard presence at my back as I moved across the seats. He sat close to me, but made no move to touch me again. I didn't mind, taking the reprieve to try to compose myself.

Several minutes passed in silence, James staring out the window as though he was avoiding even the sight of me. I could tell he was angry, but I couldn't even begin to guess why.

"So you've done that before?" I finally asked him quietly. My mind had been stubbornly lingering on the idea in the long silence. "You've had sex in front of other people before?"

He looked at me, his brow arched, his expression cold. "Yes. Are we sharing information now? I thought that was strictly off-limits tonight. Your idea, if I recall."

My eyes narrowed on him. "Don't bring things up that you aren't willing to talk about, then."

His brows flew straight up at that. "Is that a rule now? So you're saying that if you bring up a subject, you have to answer my questions about it, as well? If you'll agree to reciprocate, I'll accept those terms."

I bit my lip, wondering how this was going to backfire on me. I knew it would, eventually. How badly did I want to know about his exhibitionist tendencies?

Badly. "Fine. Tell me."

He pursed that pretty mouth. "Tell you what, exactly? About having sex in front of other people?"

I nodded.

"Is it something you're interested in doing, or are you merely curious?"

My eyes widened in dawning horror. Had he thought I would want to do that in front of my co-workers, if I was thinking at all clearly? The thought was abhorrent.

"Merely curious," I said with a blush. "About you more than the practice. I want to know what you did in front of other people, and with whom."

He spread his hands. "I've done it several times. There are...events for people like us. BDSM demonstrations. I've dominated, and spanked, and fucked several women at things like that. In front of a few people or even crowds. I never had a problem with it, though it was more a novelty than one of my actual preferences. And I fucked a few women at some frat houses in college in front of crowds, a few times on a dare, if I recall. I wasn't exaggerating when I said I used to be a real slut. I've been more circumspect in recent years, but only in comparison to my past exploits, really. Anything else you want to know about it?" His voice was tight with agitation by the end of his explanation, and his question was downright angry.

I felt sick to my stomach suddenly, the last vestiges of arousal leaving me completely. "And you'd have no problem doing that to me, in front of a crowd?"

His jaw clenched hard, and he turned his head away. He was silent for so long that I didn't think he was going to answer, though the answer was important to me.

"I have a *huge* problem with it," he said finally. "That doesn't mean I wouldn't do it. Even knowing how much I would have regretted it after, I still had a hard time stopping myself. I felt like you wanted me to, and that made it so hard to stop. I'm starting to see that that's not what you wanted. Still, I would have been furious with us both if it had gone that far."

"Why furious? You said yourself you've done it several times."

He gave me an almost malevolent glare. "Because you're *mine*. I don't want other people to see you like that. I don't want to share you like that. When I've done it before, it's been with women who were...dispensable. They were all dispensable, Bianca. I'm not proud of that fact, but it is the truth. Even the few subs who I've had under contract longterm were dispensable, in a way. I never shared them, but I certainly didn't care if anyone saw me fucking them."

I licked my lips. "You had subs under contract? Longterm?" I asked, feeling the sickness growing.

He sighed. "I did bring it up, didn't I? Yes, I've had a few subs under contract. They were amenable, though only two were compatible for what could be considered longterm. It can be a necessary arrangement, when you have a lot of money and your sexual proclivities are...unusual. I wanted no misunderstandings, and certainly none of them were strangers to the scene."

"Is that something you would try to do to me? The contract thing?" I asked him, my voice smaller than I preferred.

He gave me a baffled, wild look.

I had a horrible thought. I hadn't wanted the arrangement, would certainly have turned it down, but what occurred to me next was even more appalling.

"Oh," I said, the sick knot in my stomach growing by the moment. "That's a more longterm arrangement than what you had in mind for me, I take it." I made my voice and face empty of emotion as I spoke, wanting to take the blow with some grace. "You would obviously want someone more experienced with the things you like, to fill a role like that. Well, that's for the best. I couldn't make a commitment like that, anyway."

His head dropped forward, his hair covering his face. I saw his fists clenching and unclenching.

He was silent for a time. His voice was low but harsh with intensity when he spoke. "That is not the contract that I had in mind for you. But which is it, Bianca? Are we talking about our relationship, or am I not allowed? Because you keep saying the most infuriating things, and I'm finding it increasingly difficult to bite my tongue. So are we talking about our relationship tonight, or not? I've wanted to explain myself to you for a long time, but you always run away before I can even begin."

I swallowed. I suddenly wanted to know, quite desperately, what he would say if I encouraged this conversation. But I lost my nerve, feeling terrified enough of what he might say to postpone it for another day.

"Not tonight," I said finally.

A chilly silence filled the car after that. He didn't move, didn't speak, didn't touch. I withdrew into my own thoughts, for a time. We stayed that way until we pulled into the parking lot of Las Vegas's private airport. It was close to the main airport, but I'd never actually been to it.

"What are we doing?" I asked James.

He didn't look up. "You said I could do anything with you that I wanted. I am."

I gave him an exasperated look that he didn't see. "I don't have anything with me. I haven't even packed a bag. And it's late."

"I've taken care of it."

"It will be morning by the time we get anywhere. I can't

wear this outfit anywhere but a night club."

"I know. I said I've taken care of it."

We had stopped by then, and Clark was opening the door scant seconds later. James got out in a flash, pulling me out as soon as I got within his reach. He gripped my elbow firmly, guiding me into the small terminal.

"We should be able to depart immediately," he said brusquely.

"Are you going to tell me where we're going?"

"No. Not to a beach. I'll tell you that much."

I nearly laughed. "What is your issue with beaches? Everyone loves the beach." I looked at him, smiling to draw him out of his mood.

His face darkened. "I'm aware," he said, his tone scathing. The beach was a topic off-limits, I noted. I tucked away that little piece of information.

"I need a change of clothes," I complained.

"I'm aware," he repeated.

"You're the moodiest person I've ever met," I told him, my own tone dark now.

He squeezed my arm, hard. "You make me crazy. If you would give me some clue what you were thinking or feeling, if you even *feel anything* for me, I think I could handle our situation with a little less volatility."

His words struck me silent, and we walked like that through the smaller airport. We went through all of the motions, my mind reeling.

He wanted to know if *I* felt anything for *him?* It was a strange notion to me, one I couldn't credit. *He's worried about getting me to care for him?* I mused.

I dismissed the thought after mulling it over. I'd had this type of interaction with men before. It wasn't that he cared. It was that I came across just aloof enough that it made me a challenge.   James couldn't have felt challenged to gain the affection of many women. One night with him, and most probably professed undying love. Because, frankly, there was so much *to love*. But I wouldn't humor him, not at the cost of what little pride I intended to retain at the end of our affair.

CHAPTER NINE

We were boarding his jet in record time. I'd never been on a private jet before, and his was impressive. I studied the beautifully designed interior, keeping my features schooled into passivity as the flight attendant greeted us warmly.

He led me directly to a seat, buckling me in without a word, his mouth tight. We hadn't spoken since his odd statement, and I didn't know what to say.

He sat beside me in an oversized leather chair, buckling himself in. The seats made my airline's first class seats look tiny in comparison.

"The decor is lovely. Your decorators, as always, have exquisite taste," I told him. The plane's interior was done up in a muted red color with deep brown accents. I wouldn't have even known it was a plane, if I'd only seen the interior.

"Well, thank you. I decorate most of it myself," he told me, flushing a little.

I was surprised. "That's...impressive."

He shrugged, looking uncomfortable. "I own hotels. It always made sense to me, that I should have a hand in all of it, so

I've been making many of the decorating decisions since I was a teenager. It goes without saying that I choose my own decor on my private properties. I like things a particular way."

I flushed a little at that. He was a control freak, was what he should have said. Strangely, that thought only ever turned me on. "Do you enjoy interior design? Or is it merely a necessary evil for you?"

He looked thoughtful. "I enjoy it. If I'm honest, I even enjoy shopping. Do you think less of me now?"

I gave him a tiny, teasing smile. "Hardly. I far prefer *these* revelations to ones about you being an exhibitionist."

He had begun to smile, and just like that, it died. He grew broodingly silent again as the plane was prepped and we took off.

"Do you think you'll be able to accept my past? Or is it all just too sordid for you?" he finally asked quietly. His head was tilted back as he rested in his chair.

I blinked. "I suppose, as long as it is actually in the past, I could cope with it, if you're always honest with me."

He nodded, looking relieved, but oddly sad. "I will be. I have been. I've gone out of my way to tell you even the things I don't want to, because you asked it of me. You just need to give me some time to prove it to you. To gain your trust."

I thought about that as he went silent again.

The flight attendant was attentive, asking us if we needed anything mere seconds after we reached ten thousand feet.

She was beautiful, I noticed. Her hair was long and black, hanging straight down her back and parted down the middle, her features stunning. She had a slim but shapely figure. Her uniform was a plain black skirt with a fitted, almost too tight white dress shirt tucked in. She wore four inch red stilettos that she worked like a pro. I couldn't have walked in those shoes to save my life.

I remembered James's offer to hire me as his personal flight attendant. Was that how she had gotten the job? Did I want to know? The masochistic side of me certainly did.

"Have you slept with Helene?" I asked James, my tone very nearly idle.

He studied me. He hesitated, and I had my answer.

I looked out the window.

"Once, when she first hired on," he said slowly. "She offered rather blatantly, and I accepted. We've been nothing but professional in the years since. Are you upset?"

"Is she a submissive?" I asked.

I heard his breath puff out in a frustrated sigh.

"It's almost as if you're toying with me, hinting that you might be jealous. I shouldn't hold my breath, huh? No, she is not. We weren't compatible in that way. I didn't even consider it. As I said, it was years ago. I was more promiscuous then. She was beautiful and amenable, and it was enough, at the time."

Ick, ick, ick, I was thinking. Ouch, ouch, ouch, was what I was feeling. "It doesn't seem very professional, sleeping with your employees like that," I said stiffly.

He covered my hand with his own. "It wasn't. I don't do anything like that anymore, even before I met you."

"Will we be running into women you've slept with everywhere we go?" I asked.

He squeezed my hand. "Not everywhere, but occasionally, yes. If it bothers you too much, I could let her go, or reassign her. I hate to make you uncomfortable."

I looked to where the flight attendant worked in her tiny galley. She had been nothing but professional and efficient.

"Does she hit on you anymore?" I asked.

"No. I told her quite clearly after the first time that it would not be happening again. She took it with grace. She is a real professional. But I will accommodate you, however you like. I want you in my life, and I will make any concessions needed to see that happen. Do I need to let her go?"

"Of course not," I said, not looking at him. If we were having sex, he never would have allowed my looking away from him in such a way. He never would have allowed the distance it gave me. But, for whatever reason, he seemed to be giving *me* the control outside of the bedroom. "She seems to be good at her job."

"She's quite good. And always available to fly at a moment's notice."

"Where are you taking me?" I asked him, changing the subject. Talking about and looking at the other woman was depressing me, for obvious reasons.

"Wyoming," he answered.

I blinked at him.

"It's a fairly short flight, but there's a bed in the back, if you want to get a little sleep. There's also clothes and toiletries for you," James went on.

"What's in Wyoming?" I asked.

"I have a horse ranch there. It's very secluded and peaceful. I thought it might be a nice reprieve for us, for a day or two."

"You don't need to work?" I asked him.

"I'm grooming a North American manager to take over some of my duties. I have micro-managed my businesses for too long, I'm recently realizing. I have a man who I believe is capable, so he should certainly be able to handle things for a few days. I need to be able to have a life outside of work. For once, I actually want that. So this will be a test for him. When I want to take a few days, or even a few weeks off, I want to leave things in capable hands."

I hadn't expected my casual question to elicit such an in-depth answer. He always surprised me, and unwillingly, I felt some of my walls weakening.

"I have to be back to work Thursday night," I told him.

He smiled at me, his mood lightened. "Yes, I know."

I realized I was tired enough to sleep with a sudden yawn.

James saw, giving me a hooded look. "Ready to go to bed?" he asked.

"Are you tired?" I asked him, about to tell him he didn't have to join me if he wasn't.

His eyes seared me. "Love, I've been waiting for weeks to see you. Sleep is the last thing on my mind." As he spoke, he unbuckled me, pulling me to my feet and leading me to the back of the plane, without further ado.

Just before we reached the closed door at the back, he let go of my hand, reaching up to the ring on my choker, hooking a finger inside. He didn't even glance back at me, but I felt a change in him.

He opened the door, pulling me into a surprisingly large bedroom. He led me around the room, showing me where I could find the things I'd need. Half of the clothes in the closet were women's clothes. *Dare I ask?* "Will those fit me?"

"I would hope so," he answered in an icy tone. "I had my shopper buy them for you, and she had all of your measurements."

The bathroom was tiny, but held the essential toiletries that I might need.

He was unbuttoning my blouse, his chest against my back, before we'd finished the short tour. He pulled it off my arms, unsnapping my front clasping bra with one swift motion. He had my skirt unzipped and falling to my feet in a flash.

Unexpectedly, he bit down between my neck and shoulder, right on the tendon, hard enough to make me jerk. He sucked on the wound he'd made, and I moaned.

"Leave the shoes on. Lie down on your back, and spread your legs," he ordered.

I obeyed.

He pulled restraints from under the mattress, fastening my wrists, and then my ankles. I felt a sensual haze overtake me as I gazed at him. I was spellbound as I watched him undress.

He shrugged out of his shirt in one smooth motion. I held my breath as he undid the button and zipper of his pants, releasing his erection. He pushed them to the floor, stepping out of them and immediately stepping up to the bed.

He studied me for long minutes, his intense eyes drinking me in, as though memorizing the sight.

"I missed you," he said, his voice a harsh whisper, and I believed him.

He crawled onto the foot of the bed, burying his face between my legs before I saw his intent.

I gasped as he licked at me with long, perfect strokes. He sucked at my clitoris and I whimpered. He had me on the brink of orgasm in seconds, but pulled back suddenly, going back to slowly licking me.

"James, please," I begged him.

I got no response, just the slowest lick along my core.

"Mr. Cavendish, please," I tried again.

He moved up my body, licking and sucking at my naval. He spent drawn-out minutes at my breasts, sucking hard on my nipples for endless minutes, kneading at my full breasts, until that alone had me close to the edge. He stopped short there, as well.

I sobbed.

He left no part of my exposed body untouched, rubbing, pinching, sucking, biting. It was the most exquisite torture.

His heavy arousal dragged along my body as he moved, and I tugged hard at my restraints, trying to get closer to that part of him. I pulled so hard at them that my hands and feet began to go numb, but James never let up.

I tried begging again. "I beg you, Mr. Cavendish."

He ignored the words, never speaking, never letting up.

"Are you punishing me, Mr. Cavendish?" I finally cried.

"Of course I am," he murmured against my skin, and there was steal in his voice. "I can't whip you. This is the alternative.

Do you prefer the whipping?"

"Yes," I said without hesitation. There was no comparison in my mind. One liberated me, and the other made me feel desperate and exposed. Tears seeped down my cheeks as he relentlessly worked on my body.

"Why?" I asked breathlessly.

He thrust two fingers into me suddenly, and my back bowed on a gasp.

His own breathing was harsh as he spoke, stroking me purposefully. "Just to give you a taste. I was *desperate* for you. To comfort you, to tend to you. Hell, just to look at you. But you withdrew from me completely, until I was pathetically grateful for just a text from you, and even that you withheld most of the time. So I needed to give you at least a small taste of the wanting." He worked his fingers along just the perfect spot as he spoke.

I was tensing with my approaching orgasm when he pulled his fingers out.

I screamed in frustration.

He kissed me. It was a bruising kiss, and I tasted myself on his mouth. He plundered my mouth as he positioned himself above me. I began to whimper loudly as I felt his cock right at my entrance. He teased, rubbing in circles there. I tried to thrust up at him, but merely served to further strangle my ankles in the process.

"I-I'm sorry I did that," I told him finally. "You scare me. The way I feel about you scares me, so I ran."

He thrust inside of me as I spoke.

I screamed. He moaned.

He propped himself on his elbows, thrusting furiously, but holding my gaze with his own. He tugged on the loop of diamonds on my collar as he thrust, and I felt the pull there, the connection that it symbolized.

"Nothing in my life has ever felt as perfect as being inside of you," he gasped out, cupping my face, his punishing pace never letting up. "Come, Love," he ordered.

I did. "James," I cried, and I watched his eyes as his own release took him.

The way he looked at me then made me want to cry with longing. If I was foolish enough to believe that look, I'd be lost forever.

CHAPTER TEN

I was already on the edge of sleep when he undid my restraints. I heard first a pained noise escape his throat, then a harsh string of cursing. It brought me back from sleep enough to open my eyes. He was studying the marks the ropes had left on my skin. I couldn't even feel the marks that were apparently bothering him, so I just closed my eyes, and drifted off.

He was sliding panties up my legs when I awoke. He was already dressed in a fresh white T-shirt and jeans.

I felt surprisingly good as I sat up. He'd laid a T-shirt, jeans, and a bra for me on the bed.

"You can pick something else, if you prefer. There's plenty to choose from in the closet," he told me, and strode from the room, closing the door with a loud click behind him.

I went into the small bathroom to change. I freshened up in a hurry, pulling the jeans on, pleased to find that they actually fit. They were the right size. They were even long enough, which was rare. They were Diesel brand, which I'd never worn, but I quickly became a fan. They were bootcut and hugged my butt just perfectly, with a little bit of stretch in the material. The dark wash was flattering. I was impressed with his dresser's success at picking out jeans for me, a task that usually made me want to gnash my teeth in frustration.

I shrugged into the white t-shirt. It was soft and thin, with a small pocket right over my left breast. It was much more tight than something I would have chosen for myself, but beggars couldn't be choosers. I fingered the lovely collar at my throat, clearly visible with the T-shirt's neckline. I noticed for the first time that my earrings from the night before were missing. James must have removed them, and I had no idea where they were. I made a note to ask him about it.

I saw that he'd laid out navy running shoes for me by the door. As I slid them on, I noted that they looked oddly familiar. I was still staring at them as the door opened and a matching men's pair of them came into view.

"We have matching shoes?" I asked him, and I couldn't keep back a smirk.

He pulled me against him, rubbing my back and then my butt. "Shoes and shirts, and the jeans are pretty damn close."

I laughed. "Is this a fetish of some kind? You like to match?"

He smoothed my hair back, tilting my face up as he began to braid it. "It wasn't deliberate, exactly. I just saw that you had things similar to mine, and unconsciously picked them out. I kind of like it, though. No one could doubt that we're together when we're dressed like this." He finished braiding my hair, using a hair tie from his wrist to tie it off.

He fingered my thick metal collar, his eyes soft. He surprised my by pulling a small box from his pocket. It looked like a small ring box.

My breath caught, my mind going a little panicky at what it might contain. I was almost relieved when he revealed the large, square cut, light blue gem stud earrings. They were beautiful and unexpected, and I was stunned enough to let him put them on me without protest. Foolishly, I'd had a horrifying moment where I thought he might be trying to give me a ring of some kind. I was relieved but baffled that it was something else entirely.

"It's too much, James. You don't need to shower me with gifts. It's really not my thing."

He touched my ear lightly. "No, it's not your thing. It's my thing, so humor me. And they match your eyes. I knew they would."

"What happened to the other ones? The ones I wore last night? I hope I didn't lose them."

He just smiled at me. "You didn't. I packed them. When will you learn that I'm a man who thinks of everything?"

I sighed at his description of himself, oddly resentful at the aptness of it.

He kissed my forehead, grabbing my hand and leading me from the plane.

Helene nodded at us as we left, calling out a polite good-day. I nodded back, uncomfortable but civil.

We emerged into a landscape of rolling green hills, surrounding a tiny landing strip that I doubted anyone could call an airport. It was an instant, pleasant change from Vegas.

"How pretty," I said, as he led me to a sleek silver convertible sports car. Two black SUV's were parked behind it, and I saw Clark getting behind the wheel of one of them.

The convertible's leather seats were a bright blue that contrasted with the gunmetal color of the car. The emblem was a crown, and I had no idea what brand it was, but I knew nothing about cars, so I shouldn't have been surprised. It was a given that the brand was out of my price range.

He opened the passenger side for me, handing me in, and even buckling my seat belt. I gave him a wry look as he did so.

"I could never pass up an opportunity to restrain you," he

said softly, as he ran his hand along the belt.

He got into the driver's seat, reaching into the glove box and taking out two pairs of sunglasses. I took my pair, thanking him.

"You thought of everything," I said, reaffirming his own words from a few minutes ago.

His right hand, which had been gripping my knee, went to my wrist. The marks there were harsh and red, the skin raw in places.

"Not everything, apparently. This went too far." He started the car, signaling the SUV's. Clark's car went in front of us, the other falling into place behind.

Clark sped ahead in a hurry. He had to be speeding as he drove almost out of our sight on the two lane highway. I watched the lovely rolling hills pass us as James handled the sports car, as he did all things, with consummate skill.

The rolling hills quickly turned into pine covered foothills and plateaus. It was a lovely, pleasant drive. Even the weather was perfect. We had been transported from the desert and into a green haven.

James kept his hand on my thigh, rubbing and squeezing as he drove, only lifting it to shift when necessary.

I shifted slightly in my seat, already a little sore from our activities of the night before.

James noticed immediately. "You sore?" he asked me. He had to raise his voice a little to be heard above the sound of the car and the wind.

I gave a little shrug. "Nothing that I mind," I answered. "Certainly nothing that would make me want to keep from doing it again."

"How about a half a dozen times?" he asked me with a warm smile, his eyes hidden behind dark shades.

I couldn't keep from responding with my own soft smile.

Less than twenty-four hours with him, and he already had

me wrapped around his little finger again.

It was hard to stay away from him, even while he was driving. A rather obtrusive console separated us. I slid my hand over to his waist, pressing my hand over the bulge in his jeans.

His hand covered my own and he shot me a rather surprised look.

I checked the SUVs escorting us. They both seemed safely out of sight for the moment.

I fumbled with the button on his jeans, finally unbuckling to use both hands. I uncovered his growing erection, and he sucked in a breath as the air hit him. I arranged myself over the console, taking him into my mouth before he could protest. The console dug into my ribs a little painfully, but it wasn't enough pain to stop me.

His hand gripped my hair roughly. "Fuck." His curse was low and hoarse. "That's not safe, Bianca," he said, but he didn't stop me.

I lifted my head briefly to say, "So come fast, and we'll be out of danger quickly." I took him back into my mouth, stroking his base hard with both hands. His grip on my hair grew painful as I bobbed my mouth up and down on his cock relentlessly.

He was coming in my mouth in under two minutes. I hadn't even known he was capable of coming so fast. He cursed and moaned as I swallowed his hot cum.

"Fuck, fuck, fuck. Bianca, you're too much. I almost went off the road. My vision got way too fuzzy there."

I sat up, buckling in. I smiled at him, a wicked smile, my lids heavy but hidden.

He stared, mesmerized. "You're going to be the death of me, aren't you?"

We were on the highway for just over an hour before James began to slow down, seemingly in the middle of nowhere. Clark had turned off of the road in front of us, I saw. James followed him, turning onto a well-paved but small road. We passed through heavy gates almost immediately after turning off of the main road. It was set up so that you couldn't even use the road to turn your car around without the gate open.

We were on the small road a good twenty minutes, passing through rolling hills, then a forest of oaks, then between twin plateaus. The grassy hills were dotted with pine trees here. It was a mercurial, changing landscape. Land just like the man who owned it all.

"Almost there," James said, his hand on my knee.

I saw the sprawled-out buildings minutes before we reached the ranch. It seemed almost unreal, this secluded compound in the middle of nowhere.

James pulled directly up to the main building. All of the buildings matched, built in an elegant dark brown wood in a modern log cabin style, with huge reflective windows. It looked like an ultra modern take on a cabin in the woods. It mixed the modern with nature, taking elements of the area and adding a stylish flair. It seemed to be the Cavendish designing trademark.

"It's lovely," I told him.

He smiled, pleased. "The stables are in back, but let me show you the house first."

"I could see them from the road. What are all of the other buildings? The house seems so huge just by itself."

"For staff," he said, as he pulled me inside.

He showed me the house room by room. It was beautiful, of course.

"You decorated this," I stated. I didn't have to ask. I was starting to recognize his personal touch. The stark modern floors and walls mixed with rustic tables and furnishings that had an authentic Wyoming feel to them just had his stamp all over it.

He just nodded, leading me through the entryway and through a mammoth living room. He showed me each room of the main floor, pointing out details of the design.

"What? No antlers?" I asked him, as he led me around.

He gave me a mock glare.

I realized I needed a nap as he led me up the stairs. I tried to stifle a yawn.

He glanced back at me. "Nap-time," he told me.

I just nodded, though it hadn't been a question.

"We'll finish the tour later," he said.

He led me to what was obviously the master bedroom and into a ridiculously huge closet. Half of it held what were obviously women's clothing. I shot him a look.

"Whose clothing is that?" I asked. I'd been going for a casual tone, but it came out stiff.

He gave me a censorious look. "Yours. I told you I had my shopper pick out a wardrobe for you. You can add whatever you like, but I thought it would be convenient, for the moment, to have at least the essentials available for you, so you don't have to pack every time we want to go to one of my houses."

"You said you had done that in New York. And I didn't imagine it was anything like this. This is too much, James."

"It's nothing," he said curtly, pulling a tiny transparent slip off of a hanger and thrusting it at me. "Put this on and get in bed," he ordered, and started to strip.

"Do you always do this? Looking at this closet, you'd think you were living with a woman. Is this your usual...arrangement?"

"Of course not! I've never lived with a woman, never even considered it. You will be the first, when I've talked you into it," he told me, pulling off his shirt.

"It will be an easy transition once I convince you," he continued blandly, "since all of my properties have been stocked with your things. As I said, you can add whatever you like. And if there's any decorating changes you'd like to make, please feel free to do so. I know I can be controlling and possessive about my things, but I want you to feel that what's mine is yours."

I froze in the act of unbuttoning my pants. The things he was saying, and in that dispassionate tone, just weren't computing in my head.

"You can't be serious," I said softly.

"About what?"

"Living with me."

"I see by the look on your face that you aren't pleased with the notion, but I'm a very determined man. Start getting accustomed to the idea."

I went back to undressing, dismissing the notion. Maybe he was trying to say outrageous things just to get me to talk about the things I didn't want to. I didn't know. But, instead of feeling caged or trapped by the arrangement he was proposing, I felt...nothing. Denial was my reaction, and I welcomed it.

"You're insane," I told him lightly as I pulled on the tiny slip he'd handed me.

I crawled into the luxurious covers of yet another of his ridiculously oversized beds. I felt him hovering near my side, standing over the bed.

"Well, I suppose that's not the worst reaction I could have gotten. I was scared you would run screaming from the house, so this is actually a positive, compared to that," he told me, his voice still so dispassionate. I'd heard him use that tone on the phone before. I realized it was the one that he used for business transactions.

I heard him go into the bathroom, not shutting the door. The shower began to run. I was asleep before he joined me in bed.

CHAPTER ELEVEN

James was a hot weight enfolding me from behind when I awoke. The clock on the bedside table read 1:30 p.m. I'd slept at least four hours, and I desperately needed a shower. I slid out from under his heavy arm, going into the bathroom. I shut the door behind me as quietly as I could. The man seemed to get so little sleep. I'd feel bad if I woke him, when he seemed to be sleeping so deeply.

I was rinsing conditioner from my hair when he pressed his naked body against my back. I gasped.

"Good morning," he murmured, reaching around me to pump some soap into his hand. His arousal was already hard and pressed against my backside. He rubbed the soap over me with one hand, kneading at my breasts. I was already clean, but I didn't protest. *Who would?*

He was washing himself with his other hand, and I felt it as he reached his own arousal, stroking the length, again and again. He reached between my legs as he did so, his expert fingers giving attention to every fold.

"Put your hands against the wall," he rasped into my ear after he'd teased us both for several minutes.

I laid my hands flat against the wall, and he grasped my hips roughly. He buried his face in my neck as he drove into me. It was a smooth entry, but he hammered into me, again and again, holding nothing back. Every stroke pulled along that perfect spot, and I arched my back, sobbing. One hand held my hips anchored while the other slid up to a wet breast, gripping it roughly. He pinched the nipple, twisting hard enough to make me cry out. He bit my neck at the same moment.

I came instantly, sobbing out his name brokenly. The name James had never had so many syllables.

"Fucking perfect," he groaned into my ear. "Tell me you're mine. I need you, Bianca. I need you to know that you belong to me."

"Yes," I gasped, already building inexorably towards another powerful climax.

"Say it," he bit out.

"I'm yours, James. I belong to you."

"Now come," he ordered, spilling into me with a rough shout.

The shout did it, and I was lost again in the rolling waves of pleasure.

He washed me again, leaning my near limp body against him. "No one else can do this for you, Bianca. Don't ever even consider it. You were made for me."

He dried me and nearly carried me to the bed, laying me down. "I'll get your clothes. I want to dress you."

He didn't return for several minutes, and when he did the sight of him made me prop myself up on my elbows to study him more thoroughly.   He was wearing skin-hugging tan riding breeches, with dark brown chaps that came to his knees. He wore a thin bright white V-neck shirt. The getup hugged nearly every muscle of his body, leaving nothing to the imagination. It was absolutely, mouthwateringly sexy. My jaw dropped. He smiled, and it was wicked.

He set a bulky pile of clothing on the bed beside me, and began the drawn-out process of gearing me up to ride. He dressed my bottom half first, slipping on my tiny panties, caressing every body part that he passed. He had to work the tan riding pants up my legs more slowly, they were so tight.

"Are they too small?" I asked.

"No. This is what they're supposed to do, until you break them in. They will fit like a glove soon enough." He worked them to my waist as he spoke. He kissed my belly, running soft fingers over the fading bruises along my torso. He did that so often, it was becoming a sort of ritual.

He slipped thick soft black socks onto my feet, kissing my arches. Next, he worked on stiff dark brown ankle-length boots that matched his own. "These will take breaking in as well. The leather's been softened, so it shouldn't be too rough," he explained.

He worked dark brown leather half-chaps onto my legs next. He named all of the clothing as he dressed me. The chaps hooked just under my heels, fastening to my legs with heavy velcro. It allowed him to size them to my long, thin calves perfectly. "I got you some full chaps as well, but this is the best gear for learning."

He moved to my top half next, managing to slip me into a snug sports bra without making me sit up. It zipped in the front, and he sucked on each breast thoroughly before zipping it up with a look of regret. It was only then that he sat me up, slipping a skin tight white V-neck shirt over my head, pulling each of my arms through gently.

I laughed at him. "We match again, you weirdo."

He grinned back at me. "I find that I like that. I can't say that this will be the last time, either." He pulled me to my feet, straightening my shirt as he did so.

"You realize that I can dress myself, don't you?"

He just smiled, content. "If you don't mind my eccentricity, I prefer to do this."

I gave him my little shrug. I hadn't known pampering like this before, and I found myself unexpectedly relishing the experience. "It makes me feel special. I find that I love it. I find that I love everything you do to me."

He cupped my face, his eyes fiercely tender. I had to force myself to meet that searing gaze. "You are special. You're the most special person in the world to me. I don't known how to make you see and feel that."

I was speechless. He kept saying the most disarming things to me, things I had never prepared myself to hear.

My stomach growled loudly, interrupting the too intense moment.

He kissed my forehead, taking my hand. "Let's feed you, poor thing. I've been negligent."

He led me swiftly to the kitchen, where an attractive black-haired woman was busily preparing a meal that smelled divine. She beamed at James but greeted me more cooly, while remaining wholly professional. "I've prepared slow cooked three-bean chicken chili, Sir. I could also prepare sandwiches, or anything else that you'd prefer for lunch."

"We'll take sandwiches, and fresh vegetables from the garden. We will eat in the formal dining room for lunch, and have the chili for dinner, Sara," he said without asking me, leading me into the daunting dining room.

"Why not use the smaller dining room for just the two of us?" I asked.

"This room is more private," he said with a shrug.

He pulled me onto his lap for a long kiss. It was a sweet, affectionate kiss, but it left me hot all the same.

I felt his hands in my hair, and it was a drugging moment before I realized he was braiding it. I pulled back with reluctance.

He just moved his mouth to my neck, braiding all the while. He'd barely finished that task before he was spreading sunblock on my arms, keeping me on his lap the entire time. I hadn't even seen the little bottle on the table, he'd had my attention so completely glued to him.

He set me onto my own chair only when Sara was carrying a large tray into the room. It held several Turkey sandwiches on dark wheat buns, with some sort of white cheese that I couldn't have named, and loaded with vegetables. They were delicious, the vegetables tasting fresh from the garden. Each sandwich was smeared with a spicy hummus. She brought out a large dish of fresh, raw vegetables as well, with a serving of hummus for dipping.

I ate heartily. I'd gone too long between meals. "I'm going to lose some weight hanging out with you. I try to eat healthy normally, but not surprisingly, you take healthy eating to the next level. You don't even know the meaning of the term 'half-assed'."

He gave me his censorious look. "You don't need to lose weight."

I gave a little shrug and went back to eating. *Easy for Mr. No Body Fat to say*, I thought.

James finished eating before I did. "Do you mind if I make some calls?" he asked politely.

I shook my head that I didn't mind, knowing he was skipping out on a lot of work just to be there.

I finished eating, and waited for maybe five minutes while he made call after call, working on his laptop as he did so.

"Do you mind if I go look at the horses while you work?"

He nodded, waving me off absentmindedly.

"Take your time," I told him as I left. I had a general idea where the stables were, so I headed that way. I nearly got lost just trying to leave the palatial house, but finally found a door that led out of a room adjacent to the kitchen. I'd walked in a circle just to get there. It was easier to take a direct route to the stables after I got outside, since the buildings housing the horses were so huge that I couldn't possibly miss them.

I walked inside the wide opening into the shaded stalls, looking into each one. Many of the stalls were empty. I stopped at the first stall that wasn't. It held a beautiful chestnut who came when I clicked to it softly. It let me pet it, sniffing around for snacks. I hadn't thought to bring any, hadn't known where any were.

"She'll love you if you give her an apple," a deep, unfamiliar voice drawled behind me, a hint of a strange accent detectable. I thought it may be French, but wasn't sure. I turned, a little startled, though I shouldn't have been. Of course there would be people in the stables. The sight that greeted me, though, was startling.

The man was tall and smiling, his black hair shaved close to his head. He was devastatingly handsome, with a dominant but attractive nose and smiling eyes. His strong jaw had an appealing five o'clock shadow. I guessed he was in his early thirties. He was geared up in clothing similar to my own, and the tight apparel showed his heavy muscles to distraction. His teeth were even, his smile engaging. I met his light brown eyes, smiling politely.

He sized me up as I had him.

My breath caught as I saw the riding crop in his hand. It was for the horses, of course, but he looked like a man who could dominate a woman, and my newly awakened sexuality made my mind drift to the things he might do to a woman with that crop.

He held a hand for me to shake, stepping closer to me to pat the horse on the neck while he did so. I shook his hand, and he gripped mine firmly, lingering. I pulled away hastily.

"This one is Nanny. She's a good horse." He went to a bag near the door of her stall, pulling out an apple, and handing it to me. "If you're looking for a horse that will adore you, look no further than Nanny. She's as docile as they come. You don't look like a woman who appreciates docile, though. I'm Pete, by the way. I train horses for Mr. Cavendish. In fact, I do just about anything horse-related for the boss."

I smiled at him while I tried to feed Nanny the apple. I pulled back with a startled yip when she tried to take the apple from my hand, fingers and all.

Pete laughed, stepping in close behind me. "Not like that, ma chere." He positioned my hand around the apple so that my fingers weren't sticking out like tempting targets. "Never give a horse your finger, or sure enough, they'll take it." He held the apple to her with me, and she took it this time without touching me with her teeth.

I moved hastily away from Pete after Nanny had the apple.

"I'm Bianca," I said, strangely breathless.

He winked at me. "I know who you are. The boss's lady. Come with me. I have a special treat for you." He turned and walked away, just expecting me to follow him.

He knows I'm with James, so he should be safe. Shouldn't he? I wondered.

I hesitated, then followed.

CHAPTER TWELVE

He led me to a large, open corral that held a lovely pale horse that captured my attention immediately. "She's what we call a palomino, based on her coloring. The tan coat with the white hair. She's a palomino thoroughbred, which is rare. Her name is Princess, and the boss wants you to learn to ride on her. She doesn't have any bad habits, so she won't be teaching *you* any. But she's real particular, so it might be tricky."

I continued to stare at the beautiful creature. She was already saddled and tossing her head restlessly.

I noticed absently where all of the horses from the stalls had been. The were frolicking and eating in a large pasture just behind Princess's corral.

"You want to get on her, see how she feels?" Pete asked, smiling at me. He had his elbows propped up on the high post of the corral. "Mr. Cavendish said you had some injuries, so we can just work on your seat for today. You set the pace. We'll go however fast you want."

"You're going to teach me to ride?" I asked him, surprised. I had oddly assumed James would be teaching me. This made more sense, I supposed.

He shrugged, smiling. "Who else? I train the horses, so why not the people that ride them?"

"Okay, yeah, I'd like to ride her. She's exquisite."

He gave me a wicked grin.

It made me want to shiver, but not in distaste.

"Like her rider," he said, his tone rich with sin. "I can see why the boss wanted to see you on her. Come on, ma chere, let's get you mounted."

I blushed at his terminology, but followed him to the palomino.

I petted her nose first, and she sniffed me, flipping her lovely white hair.

"She seems to like you fine so far," Pete observed. She had lovely amber eyes. "Come here, ma chere," Pete said, standing at the horse's side.

I stepped closer to him, but not too close. He tsk'd at me. "I won't bite. Come here. I'll help you on her back."

I stepped even closer, until I felt like I was way too close. He turned me by the shoulders, his touch gentle but dominant. I sucked in a breath.

He grabbed my hips and lifted me suddenly.

"Left foot in the stirrup, right over the horse," he said, not even breathless from the impressive lift. I did what he said, and Princess shifted restlessly when I sat in the saddle. "Now, your seat is the most important part. If you have that down correctly, it'll make everything else work right. You actually look natural on that horse, Bianca." As he spoke, he gripped my thigh, pushing it against the horse firmly.

His grip moved down to my foot, pushing my toe in slightly, and my heel down. "Heels down, toes in. And remember to grip her real, real tight with your thighs. She has a sensitive mouth, which is good. That's what I meant about her not having bad habits. But it means you're gonna be real light with the reins. Real light. Most of your control will be gained from the movement of your legs."

I followed his instructions carefully, mindful of every part of my body, not wanting to mess up.

"Good," he said approvingly. "Your legs look amazing. Mr. Cavendish said you hadn't ridden before, so you must be a real natural to look so good, so fast. It doesn't hurt that you have killer legs." He gave me an appreciative smile at his last comment, and I blushed involuntarily.

The man was flustering me, for some odd reason. He moved to my other side, making a pleased sound in his throat. The sound made me blush harder.

"Look at you," he murmured. "I didn't even have to touch this leg, and you fixed it perfectly."

He brought out the riding crop he'd tucked into his chap, and brushed it lightly along my back. My eyes flew to his in shock, trying to read his intent.

"Arch your back, ma chere," he instructed. I complied automatically, the motion seating me more securely in the saddle. "Perfect. Your seat is looking great," he said, still not removing the crop from my back. "You think you feel up to walking her a bit?"

I was nodding as I caught a movement out of the corner of my eye. I looked up to see James striding towards us out of the stable, looking positively livid.

Pete spotted him at the same time I did. He gave his boss an inquiring look.

James didn't speak until he was intimidatingly close to the other man. James was maybe an inch taller than Pete, but he made that inch work to his advantage, glaring down at the other man.

"Give me that crop, Pete," James said through gritted teeth.

Pete obeyed, looking startled.

"I'll be training Bianca. And don't ever lay another finger on her. Or anything else, for that matter. Do you understand?" James asked, his voice filled with rage. His hands were clenched, one around the offending crop.

Pete nodded, his mouth curving down in a frown.

"Leave us, Pete," James ordered coldly.

Pete left instantly, without saying one word, though he adopted a leisurely pace.

James turned his livid eyes to me. He looked furious, but I saw the hurt there, too. I didn't understand it, didn't understand him.

He gripped my thigh with his free hand, his head dropping forward suddenly, and he laid his cheek on my thigh, putting his hand on my horse's neck. I stroked my hand over his hair, and he shuddered under my touch.

I should be mad at him, I thought, for embarrassing me, for embarrassing his trainer, but I just wasn't. He seemed almost injured by the exchange. While I didn't understand it, I wasn't immune to his pain.

"I can't stand seeing that," he told me finally, his voice harsh and raw. "When I see another man touch you, I want to kill him. Why were you letting him touch you, Bianca? Do you want him?"

I stroked his hair. "I thought he was supposed to teach me to ride. You overreacted, James. He was just showing me how to sit."

"I saw your face. You were *reacting* to him. Don't lie to me. I know that look. And he wanted you. I saw his face, as well."

I froze. I had been reacting to him, in a way, though I hadn't been about to do anything about it. It had been the simple reaction of a woman meeting a man whom she sensed could please her, a man who wanted to. I had simply felt an attraction, when I was seldom attracted. But it was nothing to compare to my reaction to just the sight of James, just the thought of him.

91

I licked my lips. "I-it was nothing. I was startled by the crop. I think you know why. I couldn't believe he had used it in that way."

"He was dominating you, and you were submitting to him. I know what I saw."

I continued to stroke his hair when he fell silent, searching for the right words. "If that was what was happening, it wasn't deliberate, and I didn't understand it. Even if he had made a pass at me, which he didn't, I would have turned him down."

He was shaking his head before I finished. "It's not enough, Bianca. It's not just about the sex. It's about the ownership. I want you to promise me that you won't let another man touch you. And if they do, you need to pull away immediately. Even if it's just here." He reached up, touching my elbow, his eyes angry and charged.

My brows drew together in a frown. "Stephan-"

"I'm not talking about Stephan. Stephan is the exception, of course."

I sighed at him, wanting to get down from the horse. "You're asking too much, James. Flight attendants hug every time they see each other. I'm already odd enough, without finding new things to separate me from everyone else. And most of the men I touch are gay, you know."

"Fine. I'm not talking about them. I'm talking about you thinking about how I would react to seeing who was touching you, and to react accordingly. If you think it would bother me, don't do it. How about that?"

I glared. "And what about you? What arbitrary rules do I get to impose on you?"

He straightened, holding his hands out as if in deference. "Name them. I'll be happy to oblige any whim that makes you happy."

"Fine. No one is allowed to touch you, either."

"That's an easy one. Done." He closed his eyes, leaning his face into my leg again. "The sight of him touching you with that crop made me insane. I can't get that picture out of my head. I want to rip him apart, the kinky bastard."

I nearly laughed. *James should talk...* but I didn't think pointing that out would help.

I stroked his hair, trying to comfort him. His hair was soft and silky, and so thick, especially for such a light color. I stroked it away from his golden kissed skin.

We stayed like that for several minutes, neither of us saying a word. Princess shifted impatiently but was otherwise cooperative. James began to stroke her neck, making soothing noises, not taking his cheek off of my thigh.

Eventually he straightened, adjusting my hands on the reins, then studying my 'seat' in the saddle. He poked the spot between my shoulder blades with one finger. "Shoulders back," he instructed.

"Perfect," he said when I complied.

"Goddammit," he said suddenly. "He put you on her without a helmet?" He lifted his arms up to me, almost in the stance of coaxing a child into his arms.

I leaned down to him, and he pulled me off of the horse like a rag doll.

He laughed, the moody bastard. "We'll have to work on your dismount. Come. Let's get you a helmet."

We found several, in what he called a tack room. James went immediately to a black one on the wall, fitting it onto my head.

"Feel good?" he asked.

I nodded. He pulled me back out to Princess, who was trotting in circles around the corral. He made a clicking noise at her, and she came to him. She held perfectly still when she was near us, as though waiting for me to mount her.

James glanced around, his brows knitting together. "Where's the mounting block?" he asked, looking at me.

I shrugged, wondering why he thought I should know.

"Where did you mount her?"

I grimaced, seeing where this was going.

"Right here," I said, resigned for another of his outbursts.

His eyes narrowed. "How?"

"Pete lifted me onto her back."

"Mother. Fucker," he said through clenched teeth. But that was all.

He lifted me much like Pete had, but I knew what to do with my legs at that point, so he didn't have to instruct me. I adjusted myself into my seat as they had told me. Back arched, shoulders back, toes in, heels down, thighs tensed. I kept my reins steady but put no pressure on the horse's mouth.

"Beautiful seat. You're a natural. You're going to pick this up in no time. You feel up to walking her around a bit?"

I nodded.

"You want me to lead you, or do you want to try controlling her? You're going to need to be very light on her reins. Shift in your saddle to show her where you want her to go. It's all about the legwork, with the really good thoroughbreds. If you use her reins too roughly she's liable to buck, understand?"

The mention of bucking intimidated me, but I nodded, willing to at least try.

James unsnapped her lead rope and stepped back. He looked a little worried. It wasn't reassuring. "Ok, now walk her around the corral. Hug the edges."

I did, afraid to tug at the reins even a little, sitting forward and leaning how I wanted her to go while gripping with my thighs. She obeyed beautifully, her walk smooth and quick. There was no pain at all in my ribs as she moved, her gait was so smooth.

"Perfect, Love. Are your injuries smarting at all?"

"Not a bit. She has such a smooth walk."

"Yes. She's my best mare. A real prize. Do you feel up to trying to trot?"

I nodded, already wanting to move faster.

"Walk her to me."

I did, and she obeyed perfectly. James patted her coat, then rubbed his hand up my leg, smiling. "We're going to start with posting. This is where you will lift from the horse for one beat, then sit on the next, as she trots. Do you understand?"

I shook my head. I had not a clue.

He put a hand on my butt, the other on my hip. He pushed lightly, and I stood slightly in the stirrups at his touch.

"You'll move with her movement, up and down like this."

He pushed me back down.

"It's rather like being on top when you have sex," he said with a grin. "Just pretend you're making love to the saddle."

CHAPTER THIRTEEN

I blinked at him, wondering if he was being perverted and funny, or perverted and serious.

He grinned wickedly. "That's right. You wouldn't know about being on top. I'll have to let you ride me later, then I can really demonstrate what I'm trying to explain. In the meantime, move all the way forward in the saddle, and keep your feet deep in the stirrups, okay?"

I nodded, obeying carefully.

I yelped in surprise as he vaulted up behind me. Princess shied a little, taking several steps back, but he had her stilling as he commanded her to in a soothing tone. He pressed in close behind me, and I felt his obvious arousal.

I shot him an arch look over my shoulder. "Are you always hard?"

He gave a little shrug. "I can't watch you straddle something and grind yourself against it and not get turned on. So sue me." He gripped my hips tight, grinding against me from behind.

I glanced down at our legs. His dangled behind mine with no stirrups. He somehow made the precarious position look natural.

He slapped my ass lightly. "Pay attention," he commanded. "Look forward and correct your seat."

I wriggled, trying to obey. It was challenging with an aroused James grinding into me. "You're in the way. Or rather, your cock is."

He laughed, rubbing against me. "You'll have to manage to ignore it. I'm up here to show you the rhythm. Like this." He lifted my hips, then lowered them, clicking the horse into the trot. I supposed it was a lot like being on top. Princess trotted up and down, up and down, and James moved me with her momentum.

He was, of coarse, using the demonstration to his advantage, grinding against me every time I touched back down on the saddle. "You could go even higher, and it would still be a good trot. Try it."

I did, and the exaggerated motion felt even more natural to me.

"Okay, now sit deep in the saddle and lean back a bit. We're going to try a sitting trot next. You'll keep in the saddle and just move with her. It's a lot like learning to canter, so you'll be prepared when I start teaching you that."

I did as he instructed, and found the sitting trot a little more challenging. James leaned his chest against my back, hands on my hips. "Just move with her. Accept her rhythm and relax. Yes, perfect, Love."

He leaned in, whispering roughly in my ear. "I'm going to fuck you on horseback soon. You're going to straddle me while I ride, and we can fuck to this rhythm. It's gonna be so hard and rough that you'll be sore when we're done. Would you like that?"

My mind went a little hazy and soft at his visual. "Yes. Can we do that?"

"Oh, yes. But not on Princess. We'll take my stallion, Devil. He's a huge beast of a horse, more than up to the task."

His hand moved to my breast as he spoke, cupping it softly, his fingers finding my nipple as it hardened in response.

It was hard for me to focus after that, and James didn't help, caressing me every time he corrected me.

He called a halt to the lesson some time later. I was aching and needy by then, the last half of the lesson a blur of sensual teasing.

"You're a tease," I told him, my tone breathless.

He hopped off the back of my horse in a smooth motion. He met my gaze with raised brows. "That's a silly thing to say, when I'm about to make you come over and over again. Let's work on your dismount. Swing your other leg over."

I did, standing on just one side of the horse.

He grabbed me, pulling me down the rest of the way. "She's too tall. You'll need a mounting block if I'm not here to lift you. My horses are particularly tall breeds, for the most part. With those long legs of yours, though, you'd be able to mount almost any other kind of horse from the ground." He spoke into my ear after he'd lowered me, pressing into my back. He made the words sound dirty, even though they weren't. The man could make anything sound dirty.

He caressed my breasts from behind, kissing and sucking on my neck. "We're going to fuck like animals in the horse stalls, and you're going to love it."

I gasped. "Aren't there people around? Working?"

"I dismissed them all before I found you. I plan to make love to you in as many areas of this ranch as we can in one trip."

I licked my lips. He'd never used the term make love before. I found it peculiar that he would do so now. "Make love? Isn't what we do called fucking?" I asked him.

"Why can't it be both?" James growled against me.

I didn't have an answer for that. Instead, I thought of another question. The question embarrassed me, but I asked it anyways. My curiosity always seemed to win out on my pride where James was concerned. "How many women have you brought to this ranch?"

"Just you, Bianca. I usually come here to get some peace. The only properties I've ever brought women to were my New York and Vegas homes. Do you want me to buy new beds and such at those homes? Would that make you feel more comfortable?"

I thought he might be crazy, not for the first time. "Are you offering to get rid of anything in your homes that you might have used to fuck other women?"

"Yes."

"I assume everything's been cleaned thoroughly?"

"Of course."

"Well, then that would be wasteful, and silly. Those beds have to be ungodly expensive."

"I think the fact that you didn't answer is an answer in itself," he murmured.

I elbowed him softly. "Your beds look like works of art. I wouldn't want you to get rid of them. I like them. How often do you get new beds just to humor a girl?"

He bit me hard enough to make me yelp. "There you go, belittling us again. You must know by now that I've never done any of this for anyone else. I was a slut once with my body, but I've never been a slut with my heart."

He swung me into his arms suddenly, cradling me. "How are your injuries?"

I was surprised to realize that I had forgotten about them completely. "Good. Great."

"Good. We'll go take one of the trails tomorrow, with Princess and Devil." As he spoke, he carried me into an empty stall. I realized that he'd been serious about where we were going to fuck. I shouldn't have been surprised. He seemed to be a man of his word. Even when he said something I thought was a complete joke, he'd always followed through, so far. I tried not to linger on that thought, since he'd said some pretty outrageous things in just the last day.

He set me down. "Take off your helmet. And your pants," he ordered, leaving the stall.

I obeyed, feeling very odd undressing in a horse stall.

He returned with a huge blanket, laying it on a thick pile of hay. I was just getting to my actual pants, having to first remove my chaps and boots. He lounged on his back on the blanket, peeling off his shirt. He left his pants on, just pulling his breeches down to expose his hard length.

"Come ride me," he ordered, his tone casual. "I want to see what you learned today."

I approached his lounging figure, placing my feet on either side of his hips and lowering myself to my knees. I felt almost more exposed than I did when I was completely naked, with just my bottom half bare.

"Sit on my cock. I want to feel you. Now," he said roughly when I hesitated.

I complied, lowering myself slowly, guiding him to my entrance with my hand. I impaled myself, inch by thick inch, shuddering as I did so. All of his teasing caresses had left me more than wet enough to accommodate his entrance.

"Good," he said, when I'd seated myself to the hilt. "Now fix your seat and post."

I thought he might be joking. I just couldn't tell, but I did it nevertheless. I positioned my knees for best leverage, put my shoulders back, arched my back, and began to post. I moved up and forward, then down and back in big motions. I moved until only his tip was inside of me, then pushed back down in a jerky motion.

I rode him for long minutes, working myself more slowly towards my climax than James usually did. My hands stroked over his magnificent chest covetously as I rode. It felt so good, unbelievably good, but when he was in control, it just did something for me that nothing else could. I watched him as I posted.

He had his hands folded behind his head in a casual pose, his lids heavy, watching me. I thought that this position must not quite be *his* preferred method, either.

"You're bored," I accused him, still moving, my voice a gasp.

He grinned, a wicked grin. I clenched around him just looking at it.

"Never. I would love to do this all day. It just so happens that I also could. It's a lot easier for me to keep from coming when you're in control. I'm sure I don't have to explain why to you."

He didn't. What his control did for me, it did for him as well. In bed, we couldn't have been more perfect for each other.

"Your post is extraordinary, Love. Especially considering your inexperience. Now for the sitting trot," he said.

"Seat yourself to the hilt," he instructed.

I did it on a gasp.

"Now just enjoy the ride." He smiled, and took over the movement, bucking me up and down, his hands gripping my thighs. I caught his rhythm, but that was all. He was on the bottom, but he had suddenly taken all of the control. It was all that I needed.

I climaxed within seconds, crying out loudly enough to disturb any horses left in the stables. I started to go limp.

James slapped my ass, hard. "Keep your seat. I'm not done with you."

And he wasn't. He worked me from below for long minutes, grabbing my hips and thrusting up, again and again. He was so tireless. *Like a machine*, I thought, as he bucked high, bouncing me with the force.

My head fell back, my hands clutching his on my hips. I

couldn't reach anything else at that point in the wild ride. He reached up to pinch a nipple hard enough to bring tears to my eyes. My gaze went to his.

"Don't look away. I need to see your eyes as you fall to pieces." His voice was a harsh growl, his breathing heavy.

"Come, now," he ordered finally, and it was my undoing, as always.

I fell apart, and he came with me, his eyes going to that forbidden place of tenderness that I craved, and feared, and tried so hard not to feel down to my soul.

"Oh, Bianca," he whispered, cupping my cheek as I lowered myself to lay on his chest.

He shifted me so that he stayed inside of me securely. "You're a marvel. I never imagined anyone could be so perfectly made for me."

I shut my eyes, and felt a dreaded tear seep down my cheek. I felt his words deeply, but couldn't find any of my own, so stayed silent.

CHAPTER FOURTEEN

Recovering and getting dressed again was a slow and languorous affair.

James did most of the work, laying me down to get my pants back on.

"I want to tie you to that hook and take you there, but your wrists need to heal from the last time," he murmured as he fastened a chap back on.

I looked up at the hook he was talking about. A bridle hung from it. It did seem ideal for his purposes.

I glanced at my wrists. They were red with conspicuous abrasions. I hadn't been able to put my watch back on. James had packed it somewhere, I knew. I would have to find a way to cover the marks at work. They could raise questions. They stood out starkly against my pale skin.

"I don't mind," I said softly. "I can barely feel them. You could try it. If it got too rough, that's what my safe word is for, right?"

He gave me a wild kind of look. I was already able to read him so well. This look said 'You shouldn't encourage me.'

"You're a dangerous woman," he nearly growled. "I'll be making all of the calls about your safety, since you apparently can't be trusted to judge such things. Your wrists are in bad shape. I went too far the last time, whether you think they hurt now or not. We'll leave them alone until they've healed." He finished the long process of dressing the lower half of my body as he spoke.

All he'd had to do was raise his pants and cover himself, then shrug back into his shirt with a fluid movement. I'd watched each delectable part of his body disappear behind clothes with disappointment. I could have looked at his tan flesh forever.

He smiled, pulling me against him for a long kiss. We walked back to the house with his arm around my shoulder, tucked tightly into his side.

A man in a suit and shades whom I didn't recognize met us at the back door of the house. He nodded at us, opening the door. "Sir. Ms. Karlsson."

"Tell Pete to tend to the horses," James said brusquely. "We are done with the stables for today."

"Yes, Sir. Kent called to check in with you about the investigation," the man said hesitantly, glancing between the two of us. As though not sure whether to speak in front of me, I thought.

"Any new developments?" James asked, his voice cold. This was a subject that didn't improve his mood, I noted.

"Nothing, Sir. Just his daily account of what he and his men have been doing."

"Tell him to send me a report. And notify me if there are any new leads. That will be all, Paterson."

James led me into the house, and Paterson closed the door behind us, remaining outside.

"Is that about my father?" I asked him quietly.

He glanced at me, his face a careful mask. "Yes. Can we talk about it yet?"

"No. There's nothing to talk about. I gave my report to the police, and I won't be so careless again. It was just terrible timing that got him into my house in the first place."

He blanched. "Will you please tell me what happened? I'm trying to be patient, Bianca, but I need to know how he got to you. If only to prevent it from happening again."

I sighed, the pain in his gorgeous eyes affecting me. "Stephan was due at my house. I heard the doorbell ring. I checked the peephole, but a hand was covering it. I was a fool. I actually let him in myself. I thought Stephan was playing a mean joke. Which is so ludicrous, because Stephan doesn't do things like that, even when he's being playful. I undid my security and opened the door, meaning to tell him off. My father had me pinned to the wall before I could even register who it was."

He looked away, his face gone ashen. "He just attacked you on sight?"

His hands had dropped away. He looked so forlorn that I wanted to comfort him. But I gave him his space. And, finally, with a resigned sigh, some answers. "He had seen me in the tabloids. And he thought someone had been investigating him, so he blamed me. He had come to threaten me. The injuries were just his neanderthal way of telling me not to speak to the police."

His eyes shot back to mine, shocked and appalled. "It was my fault. It was my fault you were in the tabloids. And my men had begun to look for him. He laid hands on you because I was careless enough to look for him, and expose you, without protecting you."

I studied him. His tone and his face spoke of a deep self-loathing so misplaced that I didn't even know how to address it.

"Of course it wasn't. It was no one's fault but my own. I know what he's capable of, more than anyone, and I was careless enough to let him into my home. It's not your job to protect me, James. It's my job. Stephan had your same reaction, blaming himself. I don't understand it. It's impossible to take responsibility for things that are completely out of your control."

His eyes were anguished as he told me, "It *is* my job to protect you. You don't have to acknowledge it, but it is. All of my influence is completely worthless if I can't even protect the thing I cherish most."

I reached up and patted his arm comfortingly. "My dad has been like this for my entire life. Will you blame yourself for all of the other times, as well? You must see how illogical that is."

He seemed to get himself under control, schooling his features once again. "We don't have to agree on this, Bianca. But thank you for answering some of my questions."

I thought briefly of all of the questions I hadn't answered. And all of the secrets I still kept. I was grateful that James seemed to drop the subject after that.

"Let me show you the upstairs now. I've made some changes that I think will please you," he told me solemnly.

I smiled at him. "I'd love to see all of it. Your homes are like works of art. You have impeccable taste."

He put his hand on my nape as he led me to a set of stairs. "I have to agree," he said warmly, and I knew he was referring to more than his homes.

He pointed out several guest rooms first, just glancing inside. They were themed in different colors. I thought it was a rather English thing to do. They all had names. The Green Room, The Blue Room, etc.

"All of your homes probably have the same thing. It's so English," I told him teasingly.

He smiled. "You're right. They do." We came to a closed door that he opened with a flourish. "The library," he told me with a smile. "I've made some recent additions. Guess which ones."

I blinked at the massive room. It was filled with sunlight. It was a a room of windows and books. So many books filled the massive room.

"I know e-books are the way of the future, but I can't help it, I still love plain old books. Guess which section I made just for you."

I glanced around, baffled as to how he thought I could know that, with so many things to take in. But my eyes fell on it quickly. One of the dark floor to ceiling bookshelves was filled with content that was just more colorful than the rest of it.

I laughed, delighted and a little embarrassed. "You know, I don't just read Manga," I told him. But I moved to the shelf to study it. It held full collections of all of the favorites that I'd told him about, and several that I had heard of but hadn't yet read. I sent him a warm smile. "Thank you. What a sweet thing to do."

He smiled back. "I can be sweet. You inspire me to be sweet. And you can get whatever you want, for any of our libraries. I added a Romance and Urban Fantasy shelf, as well, though I was just guessing at the authors you might like. You only mentioned that your read the genres, not what in particular." He pointed. "It's over by the window."

I glanced over, blinking at the extent of what he'd done just to please me. There was a small fortune worth of books in this monstrosity of a room, purchased just for me. It was such a thoughtful thing to do. He'd made a few more chips in the thick wall of ice around my heart with the gesture. Little by little, he was making his way in.

I took deep breaths, trying to manage my sudden feeling of panic at the thought. It worked. I was becoming more accustomed to the way I felt about him. I wasn't sure if it was a good thing, but I didn't linger on that thought.

"Thank you. I could spend the afternoon reading, if you need to do some work," I told him politely.

"I have one more surprise for you." He pulled me from the room as he spoke.

I looked at him warily, wondering what he had planned for me next.

He led me into a large room with a bed, though I didn't think it was a bedroom. It was another room of windows, the sunlight streaming in to light every corner. I saw the painting supplies then, lined up along an ornate chestnut table. There was an impressive easel beside it, already holding a large piece of mounted watercolor paper.

I walked to it, speechless.

"The table holds more supplies, in drawers, and shelves. And I had shelving put in along the walls to hold various canvases, so you can keep them organized."

I glanced where he gestured with his arm. One wall was covered with custom made, built-in shelving, with shelves large enough to hold many sizes of canvases and papers. Many blank ones were already stacked there, sorted by size. The room was a painter's dream. It was an inspiration in itself, the large windows giving me an unobstructed view of the majestic Wyoming forest.

There was a large desk in one corner. It held a Mac that had the biggest screen I'd ever seen on a computer.

I pointed at it. "What's that thing?"

He raised his brows, as though I should know. "Those are the best computers for artists. I'm sure you'll find a use for it if you need to pull up a picture, or do any kind of research. There are also several programs you might find useful. I'll walk you through them, whenever you like."

I just nodded, overwhelmed. "It's amazing. Thank you."

He smiled. "So what do you want to do this afternoon? I got to pick horseback riding, and you were more than a good sport about it. Your turn. We could read in the library, or you could paint. Or anything, really. What'll it be?"

I chewed on my lip, my mind already on a picture I'd seen online that I wanted to paint. "There is a painting I'd like to start on, if you don't mind. You could get some work done."

He just nodded. "Okay. We need to shower first, though. I'll work in here with you, if it won't disturb you." He gave me an inquiring look while he spoke.

I just shook my head that it wouldn't.

"Then come." He led me by the hand back to his bathroom.

The shower was a short, if intense, affair. James washed every inch of me, but that was all. I tried to return the favor, but he just kissed me, washing himself. He slapped my ass when I was clean.

"Out," he ordered.

I was dressed before he was dry.

"I need to grab a few things, if you want to go back to your art studio," he told me.

I left the sight of all of his naked flesh with more than a little reluctance.

I went to the computer, sitting down. I hated to have to look at tabloids, but unfortunately they held what I needed for the painting I was planning. It took me a minute to find out how to even go online with the new operating system. I typed in the name James Cavendish with a little feeling of dread.

Looking at tabloids had not been a good idea for me lately, but I really wanted that picture.

CHAPTER FIFTEEN

I braced myself for the onslaught of unflattering pictures and headlines I was about to see of myself. I wasn't disappointed.

A few phrases stood out. 'Cavendish's new Vegas Vixen' and 'Trashy Man-eater' caught my eye as I tried to get quickly to images.

The images didn't hold the picture I wanted, and I sighed with resignation. I would have to delve deeper into the search.

I paused on a picture of James, dated just last week. He was alone, in a suit, looking so much more solemn than he had in any of his other red carpet shots.

I clicked on the picture. It had been taken at a charity event in New York last week. He had none of his usual charm for the camera, instead posing almost coldly. His eyes were impatient, when he usually had a camera-ready smile. I wondered if I had been the cause for his change. If so, the tabloids had probably been running wild with the idea. They hated me, and loved the idea of a love match between James and his best friend's sister, Jules. I tried to just ignore the many old images of James and Jules as I went back to my original search, scanning carefully for what I wanted.

I froze at one particular headline. 'James Cavendish's New Love has Countless Other Men on the Side.'

I clicked on the link before I could think better of it, wanting to see what on earth they could mean. I blinked stupidly at the pictures in the article.

One was of Stephan and I, walking hand in hand on a sidewalk. I recognized that I was in Miami without having to read the article, though I read the horrid thing anyway.

According to the article, Stephan was my long-time boyfriend, and we were scheming to get a piece of the Cavendish fortune.

I scrolled down in disgust, scanning for other pictures. There were several beach shots of Damien and I, and I flushed at some of them. In one, we lounged by the pool. Damien was giving me a very warm look while I lay with my eyes covered by shades, a little smile on my face. It didn't look anywhere near as innocent as it had actually been. Looking the picture, you got the impression that he was staring at my breasts and thinking naughty things about me.

Another was of our walk on the beach. His hand was on my elbow, his eyes tender. The way his face was angled towards me... He looked very nearly loving. I was blushing, as though flustered by him, I thought. According to the article beside it, he was a steamy lover that I'd been stringing along. I flushed with anger at the blatant lies.

They'd even caught a picture of Murphy and I. We were walking beside each other and laughing. The article claimed here that I was a shameless seductress who had too many men ensnared to keep track. I regretted reading the trash before I'd even finished, but finish I did.

I scrolled back up to the shots of Damien and I. They looked so much different than what had actually been going on, and I wondered why. The look on his face, perhaps? Or the dark shades I wore, that made my expression so inscrutable?

I was still staring at the disconcerting pictures when James returned to the room quietly, approaching my desk with his slim laptop in one hand.

He raised a brow when he saw my expression. "Why do you look like a deer caught in headlights, Bianca?" he asked, his voice amused. He glanced at my computer screen as he got closer. I didn't close the window, thinking that hiding what I was looking at would be worse than just confronting it.

James's face tensed instantly when he saw the photos of Damien and I. I was struck with a thought. He had seen these before. He wasn't surprised by the outrageous photos, merely infuriated by them. The conversation we'd had about him hating the beach suddenly made a lot more sense. And his elevated hostility towards Damien.

"Th-this is all garbage," I told him, feeling strangely defensive. "Damien and I were just hanging out. You know that, right?"

He studied me, his face painfully solemn. His entire demeanor had changed since he'd glanced at the pictures.

"Yes," he answered finally. "I know as well as anyone how they can take a made up story and run with it. But it still hurts to see you together like that. Damien obviously cares for you, and wants you. Personally, I think he's in love with you. My only comfort is that if you wanted him, you would have accepted him before you ever met me." He studied my face, his very serious, before he continued, "And I confess, the thought that you'll choose him if you ever decide to go vanilla has disturbed me."

I blinked at his outrageous little rant. "Of course he's not in love with me. You know we've never even been on a date. And I'm not even quite sure just what going vanilla means, but I don't think of Damien as anything but a friend, even without you in the equation."

I wondered, not for the first time, what on earth James could be insecure about. But even the thought was wrong. I just couldn't put James and insecurity together, even with the proof of it in front of me. The whole idea was absurd. No one in the world could compete with him, in any way. *There's no room in perfection for insecurity*, I thought.

He sat down in the other seat at the large desk. He was a good four feet away there, still. He opened his paper-thin laptop, going to work without another word.

"Are you upset?" I asked him quietly, needing to clear the air before I could move on.

His mouth tightened, his fingers already working on his laptop. "I am managing both my unreasonable hurt and my unfounded jealousy. I'll work it out."

I stared at him for awhile, trying to determine how best to proceed. I finally decided that if I wanted to work something out myself, something that nothing could be done about, I would want to be left alone to do so. So that's what I did.

I returned to my search, moving on from the inflammatory article, wanting to forget that the horrid thing even existed. I tried to ignore all of the headlines that drew my unwilling attention, and all of the photos that piqued my curiosity.

I went through webpage after webpage before I finally found what I was looking for. I made a little humph of relief that I'd located the prize.

My noise got James's instant attention. I clicked to print out the picture as he rose, looking over my shoulder from behind.

"What's that for?" he asked.

I turned to smile at him. "I've wanted to paint it from the moment I saw it, a few weeks ago," I explained. "Is that okay with you?"

He blinked at me, but nodded his assent.

It was a picture of him when he was fourteen, at some red carpet function. He was posing for the camera, but it was a far different pose from the polished one he had adopted as an adult. His dark blond hair had just brushed his shoulders even then, perfectly coifed, his dusky skin perfect. His face was solemn and serious, his turquoise eyes haughty and fierce. He had been no more than a child, but the man he would become shone through every arrogant line of his face.

It fascinated me, how his strong character shone at such a tender age. I wanted to make it into a portrait shot that he could hang on some fireplace mantle at one of his many estates. Perhaps it could be a legacy for his children.

"You were like a baby supermodel," I said as he went back to his seat.

He shot me a wry smile. "I detested the way I looked back then. I thought it made my business associates take me less seriously. Typical fourteen-year-old reasoning. It didn't even occur to me that being fourteen did that all on its own."

I studied him, trying to hide the sympathy I felt for a fourteen-year-old James, who'd had far too heavy of a burden to bear.

"I wish I'd known you back then. I bet we would have been friends."

He gave me a warm look. "Me too."

"You weren't homeless, but you didn't have anyone, like I did, to turn to for comfort. I think I got the better deal."

He gave me a sad little smile. "You may be right there."

I took the printout of the photo across the room, beginning a rough sketch, loving all of the new supplies. He'd thought of everything I could possibly need.

"Oh, I forgot," James said. I glanced back at him. He was holding my phone. "Your reception isn't great out here, but Stephan has been trying to get ahold of you. You can call him from my phone."

I realized belatedly that I had forgotten I'd even had a phone since we'd arrived at the ranch.

He carried the other phone to me, already set to dial Stephan. I pushed the button, thanking him.

An excited Stephan answered after one ring. It took me a long moment to piece together his hyper chattering.

I blinked, glancing at James. He was working intently at his computer.

"It even has the white grill and the black racing stripe that I was obsessed with. It's like he took every piece of information he ever heard me say about my dream car and just ordered it."

Stephan had been going on and on about the brand new Dodge Challenger that James had delivered to his driveway for several minutes, before I got a word in.

"That's amazing, Stephan." I listened as he added several excited details. "Yes, James is unerringly thoughtful. I'm so happy for you."

I couldn't get a word in for another solid five minutes while Stephan went on and on about his extravagant gift. Finally, he asked to speak to James, wanting to thank him personally.

James took the phone from me with good grace, smiling as he told Stephan, "It is the best way I could think of to thank you for watching out for our Bianca for all these years. I'm indebted to you." He paused with a laugh as he was obviously interrupted by a frenzied Stephan. "I'll tell you what. Let's schedule a meeting when we're both in New York. I want to discuss a few business matters with you." James listened politely to the response. "That will work fine. Yes, I'll do that. Okay, have a good one, Stephan." With that, he hung up.

I eyed him suspiciously. "What are you up to now?" I asked him ungraciously. But I just knew that he was somehow meddling in my life.

He shrugged. "Stephan is your family. I want to take care of him. And I do feel strongly indebted to him for the way he's protected you. Also, I've found that it pays to be on his good side."

I studied him, wanting to be annoyed at his interference, but I just couldn't. He had found something that made Stephan so happy. How could I help but be thankful to him for it?

"Thank you for doing that for him," I finally said. "He's been obsessed with the new Challenger since it came out. And his obsession for old muscle cars goes way back. There's not a gift in the world that he would love more than what you've done."

He just smiled at me, shrugging like it was no more than the most simple of gifts to give someone their dream car. "And what would be your dream car?" he asked me.

I gave him a warning look. "Don't even think of it. I have a car. I bought it with my own money, and I like it just fine."

He didn't let up, even with the clear warning in my voice. "Eventually, you'll realize that what's mine is yours, and when you do, you can buy whatever you like. I want you to start growing accustomed to the idea."

I took deep breaths as he spoke, trying to calm the panic that bloomed inside of me at his words.

Was he trying to take over my life? It was a dark, terrifying thought for me.

"I can't," I told him on a gasp.

His expression became more closed off, but his tone was as steady as before. "I understand that you need time. I'm trying to give you as much time as I can bear, Bianca."

My eyes widened at his words. Clearly, the man was deranged. "We've only known each other for a month, and most of that time we weren't even in contact with each other. You call that giving me time?"

His expression, his voice, didn't alter. "The lack of contact was not of my choosing. And I've always been decisive about what

I want. When I see it, I take action. This is just how I am. I am trying to be patient, but I have no reservations about what I want from you, what I want our relationship to be. I am trying to respect the fact that you don't feel the same. I'm just asking you to start growing accustomed to the idea of living together."

I took several deep breaths, watching him sitting so calmly behind his desk. "I don't know that I can ever give you what you want. I'm almost positive, in fact, that I can't."

His gaze hardened, but his voice was very even. "And I am determined to convince you otherwise."

CHAPTER SIXTEEN

We didn't speak for a long time after his pronouncement.

I didn't know what to say to him. He couldn't know me well enough to understand how impossible what he wanted was for me. I could give him control in bed, but I was utterly incapable of giving him control over the other parts of my life. Doing so would trap me. And I knew too well that I couldn't be trapped and helpless ever again. It had almost destroyed me as a child. It had most certainly destroyed my mother.

I began the prep-work for my painting, but I felt a little too distracted to work at all efficiently. I sketched for nearly an hour before James spoke again.

"I spoke to the manager of my L.A gallery recently. She's very excited about your debut. She and my New York manager actually had a little tiff over who would get your showing. Due to the desert landscapes, we leaned towards an L.A showing. She will start putting the showing together as soon as you give the go ahead."

I just stared at him, dumbfounded. The idea of showing my work was still a forein concept to me. And so much had happened since he'd had samples of my work shipped to his galleries.

"I don't have to attend the showing, do I?" I asked, the thought daunting and unwelcome.

He looked genuinely surprised. "Well, no. I suppose you don't *have* to. But why wouldn't you want to?"

I gave him an exasperated look. "The press hates me. They will crucify my work if they find out it's attached to me in any way. I would prefer not to use my own name for the work, as well."

He looked troubled at the thought. Those exquisite eyes of his were raw with it. "I'm so sorry you've been dragged into this media circus of a life. It's my fault they hate you. The things I've seen printed about you...it makes me feel murderous."

I held up a hand at his tirade. "Fault isn't the issue. We need to deal with the issues at hand, not whose at fault. And you have to admit that my showing won't be helped by the media attention my name and appearance would bring to it."

He flushed a little, though I couldn't tell why. "Please just consider attending. You deserve to take pride in your work, and to get credit for it. I would love it if you would allow me to escort you to the event, but by all means take some time to think about it. I'll have Sandra prep your work and hold off on the date until you decide what you want to do."

I nodded that I understood, but still dwelled on it as I worked. If I was brave, I would just go through with the ordeal. It wasn't as though I'd be forced to read the horrible reviews about my work.

I was so distracted that I made a mess of my initial sketch, finally having to just toss it and start over. I could hear James talking quietly on the phone or I would have turned on some music to relax. Finally, I put in some headphones and played the music on my phone, tucking it into the pocket of my jeans. The picture started to come together after that, the sketch much closer to the image I had in my head of what I wanted.

We worked for hours like that, in relative peace and barely speaking. We worked for so long that I even began the painting process, which sometimes took me several sessions to advance to. I liked to have a very good sketch, usually, before I broke out the paint.

I wasn't sure what it was, but suddenly, I just felt a change in the air, a shift of energy. The hair on the nape of my neck stood on end, and I turned slowly to look at James. He had his phone to his ear, but he watched me. His eyes were...haunted, as though he'd just learned of a loved one's death.

I moved to him, removing my earbuds. He just watched me, not taking the phone from his ear.

"Thank you for the update." He just listened for a long time. "Yes, it is. Keep looking into it. And double your search efforts." He hung up after that, but watched me almost warily.

I perched on the desk facing him, his laptop near my hip.

"What's happened?" I asked, knowing with a certainty that something had.

"My investigators just found out from the police that your father has a warrant out not just for assault and battery, but also for murder." He just stared at me for a long time, a torment in his eyes that was becoming familiar to me. *Those dear eyes.*

I cupped his cheek, bracing myself. "Yes, I know," I told him reluctantly.

"I let a murderer lay his hands on you," he told me in an agonized whisper.

I cupped his face in my other hand, as well. "That's an unreasonable way to look at it. I've known he was a killer since I was fourteen, long before I knew you, and he's laid his hands on me many times since then."

He blinked at me, as though my words were beginning to register past his shock and fear.

"You knew he had killed someone?" he asked.

120

I nodded, my mouth tight, my chest aching. "I'm the one who reported him to the police, though I was nearly a decade too late. It was my mother that he killed. I was the only witness. I was standing close enough to touch her when he did it. I lied to the police for him for all these years. But after this last attack, I realized that I couldn't live like that anymore. I can't run anymore, even if it means he kills me, too."

His eyes were so panicked and vulnerable that, unwillingly, I felt my own fill suddenly with tears. It was hard to believe I'd gone years without crying before I met James. But the things he made me feel had opened a floodgate, and the damned thing wouldn't close.

I continued, wanting to get it all out. "I felt so guilty, for all of these years, for dishonoring her memory, for helping her killer run free, but inside I was such a scared child that I just couldn't go back to the police. After he killed her, they just took his word at face value, never even interviewing me in a separate room from him, and I knew that he would kill me if I told. I was absolutely certain that not even the police could stop him. Even years later, when I hadn't had contact with him at all, I tried to go to the police, but just got cold feet every time."

I brushed his hair out of his stricken face with a soft touch, wanting to comfort the things I saw in his eyes so clearly. It was such a reflection of my own torment. His soul was a mirror of my own. Perhaps his insane claim that we were made for each other wasn't so very far off the mark. I had known him for such a short time, but sometimes I felt I could read him so perfectly, so naturally, that it astounded me.

"You can't bear the burden of protecting me from my father," I told him gently. "No one can. And you couldn't have known that he would seek me out to threaten me to stay silent, because you didn't know about my mother, of course. But you are responsible for helping me to find the strength to finally tell the truth. Thank you for that."

It nearly broke me when one lone tear rolled down his cheek. "It just keeps hitting me, over and over again, that I really did come close to losing you forever. I can't bear the thought." His voice was a rough whisper. "And he's still out there, loose, so you're essentially in as much, if not more, danger than ever. I'm glad you got to finally tell the truth, but it still terrifies me what that truth might mean for you."

I traced the tear down his cheek, catching it right at his perfect jaw. He didn't seem bothered by the tear. He was so much braver than I with his feelings, I knew, but he still managed to surprise me with his depths.

I tried to put myself in his shoes briefly. If his uncle was still alive, and capable of hurting him, even killing him, but just lay in wait for the right opportunity...It would make me insane. But could James feel for me what I felt for him? I just couldn't picture it, even though he obviously felt at least *something*.

Neither of us seemed capable of working after both of our emotional outbursts.

We ate dinner in silence. It was a spicy chicken chili. I ate quickly, polishing off the comfort food without tasting it properly.

We went to bed early, James mentioning that we needed to rise early to get a proper ride in, beating the worst heat of the day.

I got ready for bed with little comment. I felt as though I hadn't slept for days as I lay on his exquisitely comfortable bed and closed my eyes. I sighed in contentment when I felt James wrapping himself around me.

I swiftly drifted into a deep and peaceful sleep.

CHAPTER SEVENTEEN

James woke me up with a light kiss on the forehead. I blinked awake, surprised to find him already dressed in clean riding clothes and leaning over me. He began to dress me without a word.

My riding clothes were much different this time. My tight pants were made up of a thin black material, not much thicker than tights, and reached just past my knees. I took note of the fact that he didn't bother with putting any panties on me.

He worked snug, thigh-high black chaps onto each of my legs slowly. I touched the soft suede material, running my fingers over it.

He was arranging the chaps over my riding boots when he spoke. "The full chaps are normally worn with jeans. I'll pack a pair, for the ride back."

I digested his words, my mind going to dark, sensual places with it.

He pulled me to my feet, dragging my thin shift over my head in one smooth motion. He ran his tongue over his teeth as he studied my naked torso.

I had to stifle the urge to cover my bare breasts. Clearly, I was not as comfortable with casual nudity as Mr. Beautiful.

He zipped me into a thick sports bra, pulling a tight, thin shirt over my head.

He braided my hair, keeping his hands, disappointingly, to himself. I was still turned on at his every motion.

I closed my eyes as he spread sunblock over my face very carefully. The man thought of everything.

He slapped my ass, hard, when he finished. "Let's go for a ride, Love," he told me with a wicked smile, taking my hand.

The horses were saddled and ready when we got to the stables. It was the first time I got to see James's stallion.

He introduced me to Devil by handing me an apple, and a warning. "Careful, he bites."

I fed the huge beast carefully, admiring his exceptional coat. I ran my fingers over his blue-black mane. His coat was a blueish gray color, so dark it shone in the sunlight like blue fire. His fur got much darker at his face, nose and feet, almost black-tipped. He seemed like a stallion out of a fairy tail, his coat too astonishingly colored to be real.

"He's amazing," I told James, running my hands along his smooth neck. Another horse butted my back from behind. I laughed when I saw that it was Princess.

"She's jealous." James wore an indulgent smile as he ran a hand along Princess's neck.

I had thought she was an exceptionally tall horse, but she was almost short compared to Devil. I patted her, as well.

James handed me another apple to give to the friendly palomino.

Pete was nearby, but kept a careful distance. He had obviously been the one to saddle the horses for us, but was wise enough to stay away from his boss after the episode of the day before.

He had merely nodded politely as we had passed him in the stables.

I had nodded back with a small smile.

Nevertheless, James's hand had tightened significantly at the small exchange.

Impossibly jealous man, I thought to myself, but kept my own council.

"Devil is a rare blue roan thoroughbred," James told me, feeding a carrot to the oversized stallion.

"I didn't even know that horses could be blue," I told him with a sheepish smile. I really didn't know a thing about horses, I was quickly realizing.

"Normally it's just an expression for a bluish tinge to a horse. Devil is a truly unusual shade, though, almost more blue than gray."

"An outrageously beautiful horse, for an outrageously beautiful man," I told him with a smile.

He tugged on my braid, tilting my head back. His eyes were hot as they looked into mine. "Whatever keeps you around, Love," he said, fitting a sleek black helmet carefully onto my head. I saw with no surprise that it exactly matched his own.

He worked black leather gloves onto my hands, patiently working them on, tightening them at the wrists.

"You know, I'm fully capable of dressing myself," I told him, but I knew it was pointless. I knew that he loved to tend to me, no task too insignificant for his attention.

He just smiled in response, kissing my leather clad knuckles. He worked on his own gloves next, and I watched, transfixed, as he worked them onto his powerful hands. His fingers were long and elegant, but so very strong. I watched his tan hands disappear into the black leather, and flushed, remembering the feel of those gloved hands punishing me.

He saw my stare and gave me a wicked smile. "You

remember these?"

I nodded, still watching, captivated, as he worked on the gloves. Even his hands were an obscenely tempting sight to me.

"I love your hands. So much." My voice was already breathless.

He threw his head back and laughed. I was captivated by the sight. Even his smooth, golden throat was perfect, and I wanted to bury my face there.

I had to stifle the urge. He was obviously on a schedule this morning.

He gave me the warmest smile as his laughter faded.

He gave me a short, sweet kiss, and lifted me by the hips to mount the Princess. I mounted how I had been taught, swiftly trying to position myself into the seat correctly.

"Perfect," he told me, unhooking the lead rope attached to Princess's bridle and roping it over the fence post.

I felt a wonderful little thrill as I got to watch the amazing sight of James vaulting up onto Devil in one smooth motion. He was such an elegant man, but his strength was astounding. Muscles bunched under his tight shirt, his breeches snug enough to show the cut of his thigh muscles as he moved.

He passed me on his horse, pausing to finger my collar, apparent just above the neckline of my top.

"I should get a lead rope for this, as well," he murmured, clicking his horse to go.

"Follow me," he ordered, as he rode to the gate that Pete had just opened without a word.

I followed, Princess moving into a brisk walk with the slightest pressure of my heels.

He led me into the thick woods, the barest hint of a trail guiding our way.

I admired the scenery as we walked, trying to move with the horse and keep my seat nice and smooth. It was so peaceful and calm there. The trees covered us in cool shade, and it was early enough that the weather was perfect for a long ride.

The forest always made me feel that I had been transported to another world, another time. The solitude, the serenity, had my mind drifting into fantasyland. The pine trees were incredibly tall there, the foliage thick and little purple wild flowers dotted the ground whimsically.

It was almost jarring when we passed out of the thicker forest and onto a trail pronounced and wide enough to be a small road. James stopped there, waiting for me to rein in beside him.

He sent me a sidelong, wicked look. "How do you feel? Are you sore?"

I just shook my head. I sucked in a breath as he brought a gloved hand to the waist of his skin tight pants.

He laid his reins on his horse's neck, giving a firm command for Devil to stay. Then he proceeded to undo the thick buttons on his pants, folding them down and under his thick manhood. It jutted up proudly, already so thick and hard that my mouth watered at the sight. He shrugged out of his shirt in a smooth motion, tucking it into one of his chaps.

I just drank in the sight of his gleaming golden flesh, always amazed at his perfection. The muscles of his chiseled bronze abs were visibly working as he sat his horse. Somehow, his legs being covered, and being on horseback, made his nudity all the more obscene. And unbelievably hot.

He gave me his wicked grin, and I nearly melted. "Come here," he ordered.

I obeyed, my horse sidling towards him eagerly.

He snatched me up, swinging me to straddle him in a seemingly easy motion. My eyes were on the hard play of muscles in his magnificent arms.

He perched me just in front of him, almost on Devil's neck.

"Don't move," he ordered, pulling a rather large pocket knife from his boot. He worked me onto his thighs, until I was just inches from his jutting cock.

I sucked in a startled breath as he used the knife on the waistband of my pants, cutting towards himself. He cut to a few inches above the saddle, putting the knife back in his boot. He ripped my pants the rest of the way off. The initial sound of ripping made Devil start, but James calmed him with a few soothing words, still ripping away, until I wore only the chaps. My sex looked profoundly bare and obscene, surrounded by black suede chaps and nothing else, my top half still completely covered.

James reached behind me, rearranging the reins, untying them to make them longer, and wrapping them around his right arm. He was giving Devil free rein, controlling him with his legs, as he'd said he would teach me to do.

He used firm hands on my hips to lift me up and poised me on the tip of his erection. He touched my sex with only his cock, moving his hips in small circles to spread my growing moisture onto his eager tip.

I moaned, jerking my hips. I wanted him to impale me so badly, just a quick thrust to ease the ache.

He did, his head jerking back to look up at me, his jaw clenched at the excruciatingly tight fit. He thrust straight to the hilt, and I melted around him.

"Oh, James," I cried out with feeling. Even with him full inside of me, I still ached. My hips jerked in a request for movement.

James clicked, and Devil began to walk. James moved with him, an expert rider, each movement of his hips a little thrust inside of me. My legs almost dangled behind his, my body had submitted to him so completely.

We watched each other as he moved inside of me, the movements half thrusts that left me gasping for more.

"Do you want a posting trot, Bianca?" James asked, his voice a growl.

I thought of the exaggerated movements of a posting trot. *Oh God, yes, I wanted that.*

"Yes," I moaned.

"Beg me for it," he said, in a strangely calm voice. *How was he not more winded?*

"Please, Mr. Cavendish, bring us to a posting trot."

He just tsk'd at me impatiently. "That was a sad excuse for begging, Bianca. Now you only get the sitting trot." He clicked Devil into a trot, keeping his seat. He sat the trot so smoothly, it barely increased his thrusting from the walk.

I moaned at him in distress, gripping his shoulders now. I needed more. I needed the deep thrusting that I had so quickly grown addicted to.

Our eyes never strayed from each other, his intense turquoise gaze imprinting itself on me inexorably.

"I beg you, Mr. Cavendish," I tried again. "Please, fuck me at a posting trot. Please, please, please."

His eyes smoldered at me, and he clicked the horse into the faster trot. "*That* is the tone I was looking for. Hold on, Love."

He lifted me higher, his posting trot thrusting him into me with the longest, hardest strokes. I was close to screaming within seconds of the new rhythm.

"Come," James growled, his eyelids heavy as he watched me. He impaled me hard and to the hilt as he spoke, and I fell apart in his arms. I was gasping, back in the ride again as he pulled out of me, dragging along each sensitive nerve. I was in a fever dream as he continued to thrust. I came again to his harsh command. And yet again, before he found his own rough release, shouting my name, his eyes going from hard and commanding to tender as the rapture took him.

He kissed me, still buried deep inside of me, as we floated back to reality, Devil slowing to an aimless walk.

I broke the spell several minutes later when I pulled back from his long kiss. "Have you ever done that before?"

His eyes shuttered, and I knew I wouldn't like his answer. "Made love on horseback?" he asked.

My eyes narrowed, taking immediate exception to his wording. He seemed to me to be splitting hairs.

"Fucked someone on horseback," I corrected.

He flushed, and my vision went a little red, knowing his answer. "I've fucked a woman on horseback before, but it wasn't like that. It was far more technical, almost clinical. It was more about seeing if it could be done, for me, than the actual doing. And I was barely an adult at the time." He studied me, his eyes wide as he read the iciness that was blooming there. "Please don't try to demean what we just shared."

I heard his words as if at a distance, my mind suddenly recalling an appalling little detail I'd read in a tabloid, about James and Jules both coming from affluent English families who both shared a long history as avid equestrians.

"Was it *her*?" I asked in a whisper, my eyes narrowed.

He squeezed me more tightly against him, as if sensing a threat. He buried his face in my neck before he spoke. "Who are you referring to?"

I stiffened even more. "Jules," I said, my voice going glacial.

I felt him sigh against me. "It was. But it didn't mean anything. Please don't use her to keep me at a distance."

I tried to move off of him, but he had me at a severe disadvantage, and he wasn't letting me go.

Instead, he clicked Devil back into a brisk walk.

CHAPTER EIGHTEEN

He began to move inside of me again, his erection swiftly growing and hardening, as though it were a parlor trick.

I gasped, slapping at his shoulders. "You can't use sex to subdue me," I told him. I was hurt and angry, but also unwillingly and wildly aroused.

"You can't withdraw from me every time you get mad or jealous. We need to talk this out. I'm not letting you go until we do."

I pulled on his hair, hard, but my hips were already moving unbidden with his thrusts. "You call this talking?"

"I call this making love, and yes, talking." He tried to smile at me. I yanked on his sweaty hair. He winced, but made no move to stop me.

"Why do you keep calling it that? Why do you keep calling it making love?"

He gave me a smoldering look. "You know why. You keep trying to belittle what we have, but you need to understand that it's as new to me as it is to you. I have a past. A wildly sordid past. I can't change it. I would if I could. You are going to run into a lot of my ex-lovers. That's an unfortunate fact. It will be a lot less painful for you if you can just get it into your head that none of them were anything but a fuck to me. And fucking was nothing to me before I met you. Sex was a bodily function to me before I met you. That's why I call this making love. It means something to me."

"I've never even had a girlfriend before you, never even considered the idea. I'm sure it sounds callous, but no woman has ever been anything to me beyond a fuck, a sub, or a friend, occasionally all three, though never all of them for long. They all knew the score. I was brutally honest with every single one of them, without exception. *You* are the one that I want, the one that I need. So getting upset about my past, or feeling jealous of women I've been with, is unwarranted."

He never stopped moving as he spoke, and I felt emotionally charged.

"Unwarranted?" The word burst out of me, angry and wounded. "I've years worth of pictures of you going out with Jules. How can you expect me to dismiss that out of hand?" I gasped as he thrust harder, a deliberate motion, his eyes intense. "Unfair," I muttered. "And you are hardly one to talk. I was a virgin when I met you, but you're still jealous of every man I speak to. *That's* unwarranted."

He lifted me up and down for several long, fast strokes before he spoke. He was playing me like a drum, I knew. It was very hard to stick to my point when I was insanely turned on, and in the middle of getting thoroughly fucked. "When I was about eighteen, the paparazzi were hounding me relentlessly, printing silly stories that drove me crazy. They were hiding in the bushes when I left school. It was out of control."

I tried my hardest to focus on his words, but he wasn't helping, still moving inside of me tirelessly.

"You know how I need control," he growled.

He thrust harder, clicking Devil into a hard trot. He clicked again, and the motion took us into a canter. This movement was unfamiliar to my limited riding skills, and I clutched at James's shoulders in panic. His thrusts were more measured at this pace. I was falling apart almost instantly.

"Come," he ordered roughly. It took me over the edge. He slowed back to a walk, but still didn't stop.

"You know how I need control," he repeated. "But the things they were doing were completely out of my control, and I realized one day that the press was like a garden hose," he explained.

I blinked at him, dazed and confused. "A garden hose?" I asked.

He gave me a gentle smile, enjoying the complete loss of my composure. "A garden hose. If you turn it on too lightly, you can't control the flow. It just drips where it will. But if you turn it to full force, you can control the flow, sending it wherever you want. So I began to court the paparazzi, rather than ducking away. I encouraged their attentions by charming them, and publicly, becoming an open book. Or rather, making it appear that way. Jules was my best friend's sister, and occasionally, a very casual lover of mine, and we'd been friends for awhile. We were seen out and about together, since we traveled in the same circles. I quickly noticed that she loved the attention, encouraging rumors about us shamelessly, even leaking lies to the press about us."

His eyes were solemn and serious on my face as he continued, "I see now that it was stupid to let her take it so far, but at the time I couldn't see a problem with it. Other women thought she and I had an open relationship, so no one tried for anything more with me. It saved me from worse misunderstandings, for a time. I see that it looks bad, but I want you to trust me that that's all it was. Jules is not someone you need to worry about."

He began to move in earnest after that little speech, and he undid me yet again, bringing me to release at a trot. I sobbed his name, gripping his hair in tight fists. He came with me that time, his eyes going so soft that unwanted tears pricked my eyes.

He slowed Devil to a walk. He leaned me back slightly, his eyes moving down to where our bodies joined. He ran his tongue over his model perfect teeth as he studied the sight. My own gaze followed his. The sight that greeted me made my barely steadied breath catch.

I was still impaled on him, my moisture mixing with his on the thick base of his shaft as he shifted me slightly up and back.

His voice was low with pleasure when he spoke. "You're so full of my semen right now. You're stuffed full of my cock and my cum. I want to keep you like this forever. I might have gotten you pregnant just now, if you weren't on the pill."

His words made me stiffen, the sensual haze lifting from me in an instant. I tried to shift off of him. He had to help me lift off of his semi-hard length.

He pulled me flush against him, his cock between us. "Wrap your arms and legs around me tightly. I'm going to dismount. Too much more of this and I'll make you too raw to fuck for days."

I did as he said. "I thought it was making love," I told him archly.

He sent me a censorious look. "Sassy girl."

He set me on unsteady feet, leaning me against Devil when I swayed.

"Get your balance. I need to catch Princess."

He fastened his trousers while he walked away. Princess was still visible, though she was quite a ways behind us. It seemed she had been trailing us, albeit slowly.

I hadn't noticed, for obvious reasons.

Devil didn't protest as I leaned against him heavily, watching James stride to Princess purposefully, vaulting onto her back in that smooth motion that seemed impossible, given the height. He rode her back to us at a smooth canter, stopping smoothly beside us and dismounting with the grace of a panther.

He studied me from head to foot, his eyes lingering appreciatively on the sight of my bared sex. He moved to a pouch on his saddle as he spoke. "I take it from your reaction that you don't want children any time soon." His tone was almost idle, as though it were the most casual topic in the world.

I looked at him incredulously. "Or ever. I'm way too fucked up to ever be a mother," I said, my tone final.

He didn't take the hint. "Why would you think that? Because of your childhood?" He turned to look at me as he pulled a rolled up pair of jeans from the pouch.

"Yes, of course, because of that. My mind is too clouded with dark things. Mother's are supposed to be, I don't know, happy, and full of love. They should be able to give and receive love, and I'm not sure I'm capable of that." I flushed at what I'd revealed. I was embarrassed by how screwed up I was, but he needed to know.

He moved to me as I spoke, cupping my cheeks, his eyes impossibly tender. "Oh, Bianca, that's just not true. You think only the people with perfect childhoods should be parents?"

I mulled it over, finding the answer easily. "Of course not."

"You probably think someone like me should never be a father."

I blinked, mortified that he would think such a thing. "Of course not. I think you'll be great at it, when you have children. You're so patient, and controlled."

He stroked my cheeks, giving me a look so intense that I had to fight the urge not to look away. It was so much like trying to stare into the sun. "So will you. But if you never want to have children, I can live with that, as well."

My heart stopped, just stopped, then began to pound as though I'd just run a marathon. "What are you saying?"

He kissed me, a long, heated kiss. "Nothing. You just aren't ready to talk about this. I don't want to scare you off again."

I took deep breaths, trying not to panic at what I knew he'd almost said.

He shrugged the whole thing off, slinging my jeans over his shoulder and digging back into the saddlebag. He pulled out some packed wet cloths, unbuttoning his trousers to wipe our mingled fluids off.

I watched him touch himself, biting my lip. How could I still want him with such desperation when he'd just had me, again and again? I didn't know, but there it was.

He disposed of the wipe in a small bag, taking out more wipes to clean me. His gaze was scorching as he cleaned me, eyeing me from top to bottom in a sexy once over.

"Keep looking at me like that if you want to get fucked against a horse," he warned.

I looked away, moving against his searching fingers as he cleaned me. He smacked my bare ass roughly with his other hand.

"I'm trying not to fuck you raw. Don't make it harder." His tone was so stern that I just got more turned on.

I closed my eyes, still biting my lip.

He growled, dragging me over to a tree. He placed my hands against the rough trunk. "Don't move an inch. You need a good spanking. You're just lucky that you need to ride back, or I'd spank you raw, you little minx."

I arched my back, my body running the show.

He growled again, and began to spank me, his leather-clad gloves smarting at the first blow.

I moaned, shifting around. He stopped after ten, breathing hard.

He was entering me without warning an instant later, cupping my breasts, his breath rough and heavy in my ear. "Just one quick, gentle ride. I can't fucking think straight, I want you so bad. Don't move, this needs to be quick and soft."

I let out a ragged laugh at his description of being fucked against a tree by his impressive cock 'gentle' and 'soft'.

It wasn't the jarring ride I usually craved. He moved in and out of me smoothly, crying out in my ear as he came, too fast for me to even keep up.

I was shocked at his release. He usually went for so long before coming himself. But, of course, he didn't leave me unsatisfied for long. He was turning me, kneeling in front of me, ripping a glove off impatiently with his teeth.

He buried his face between my legs with a rough moan, and I screamed as he purposefully made me come, using his tongue and fingers and just the barest hint of teeth, my hands gripping his silky hair all the while.

He cleaned us up again after that, shaking his head ruefully all the while. He had to strip off my chaps before he worked me into my panties and then tight jeans. They were new, but still fit perfectly. I wasn't even surprised by it anymore. He worked the chaps back up my legs swiftly and efficiently, as though he'd done it a thousand times. I tried my best not to dwell on that fact.

"I never thought I'd have the urge to fuck someone to death," he muttered.

I giggled.

He gave me a little smirk as he led me back to Princess. He helped me mount, and I turned quickly, wanting to see him execute his own perfect mount once again. He did so effortlessly, taking the lead as we headed back to the ranch.

"Did you need to get back to Vegas today or tomorrow?" James asked, glancing back at me.

I grimaced, thinking about it. "Tonight. I'd hate to push it and hit bad weather."

He sighed with resignation. "Okay. We'll have lunch and head out."

CHAPTER NINETEEN

We were heading back to Vegas in way too short a time. So much had happened in our short reprieve.

James had weakened my resolve to keep my distance in that way he had, with his persistence and his willpower. He was not a man to be deterred. And for whatever reason, he seemed resolute in his desire to be with me. And wanting me for something more permanent than I'd ever thought he would even consider. Living together didn't terrify me, as marriage did, but I couldn't say that I was even approaching comfortable with it.

We were both quiet for the drive, and then the flight. I didn't mind. I had a lot to think about, and James seemed lost in his own thoughts, not even getting his laptop out to get some work done on the flight.

"We'll stay at your house tonight," James said, as we touched down in Vegas. It was the first thing he'd said in an hour. I studied him. He seemed a little distant, a little sad.

"I'm having some work done on my place," he explained. "I'll finally give you a tour of the property sometime next week."

I just nodded, but he hadn't been asking me a question.

We went to bed early that night. James could see that I was exhausted from the riding and the traveling, and oh yeah, the phenomenal fucking.

He did his kinky little exam of my body. It had become a habit of his. I felt well enough, mostly tired, and a little sore, but he insisted on checking every inch of me. He softly kissed shadow bruises still on my ribs and back, the abrasions on my wrists and ankles, and even turned me around to check my butt, for soreness from the saddle. He studied my sex last, his eyes heavy-lidded as he touched me ever so gently, fingers sifting through my folds.

"You've got to be the kinkiest wannabe doctor on the planet," I told him with a half smile.

His mouth turned up faintly at the corners. He took it as a challenge. The comment seemed to inspire him to be kinkier.

He'd brought a glass of ice water into the room, and he grabbed it from the beside table, taking a long drink. One of his hands still held my inner thigh, keeping my legs pushed wide apart and my body pinned to my spot right at the edge of the mattress.

He bent, burying his face between my legs. I gasped as he pushed an ice cube inside of me with his clever tongue. He lapped at me like a cat for a moment before straightening again. He took another long drink, repeating the process. My hands fisted in his silky hair, begging him silently for release, but he took his time. He stroked me, and licked me, and sat back, just to look at me, again and again. He pushed a finger into me, thrusting, but I wanted more.

"Please, James, I want you inside of me."

He bit the bottom lip of that pretty mouth, but didn't respond, just kept up the process.

I was shivering, chills wracking me from both desire and the delectable feeling of cold ice inside of me. He had shoved five cubes in deep.

He took another ice cube and began to run it along my belly, circling my navel in almost lazy motions. Next he ran the ice up along my ribs, then traced my sternum. My nipples were already pebbled long before he'd paid them any personal attention. I shivered and shuddered as he finally circled a quivering nipple.

The ice wasn't the only cold thing he'd brought into the bedroom with us, I realized after endless minutes of his teasing. His very demeanor was cold tonight, his eyes icy as he worked on me slowly, torturously.

"Am I being punished?" I asked him finally, when he held back from letting me come, pulling his busy fingers out of me just short of release.

He smiled, and even the smile was cold. "Not exactly. This is only a lesson, Bianca. I'm doing this to you for one simple reason. Because I can. This is what it means to be my submissive."

I writhed at that, his calculated actions bringing out a shivering fear that, perversely, made me want him even more.

"Will you be fucking me tonight? Or is this all a tease? Because you can?"

In answer, he buried his face between my legs again, his tongue circling my clit, his fingers going back to work inside of me. I felt the ice cubes clink together, and I moaned, right on the edge of orgasm. He straightened, leaving me bereft.

He stood, stripping out of his boxer briefs in one smooth motion. He was hard. At this point, I would have been more shocked if he wasn't. He stroked himself, looking down at me with that hard, stony expression. I bit my lip as I watched him stroke himself, once, twice. I was sobbing on his third stroke, drawing my legs up to my chest, wanting to touch myself, anything to ease the ache that the ice inside of me only antagonized. I pushed my legs down, lifting my hips into the air in a silent plea.

He stopped abruptly. "No," he finally answered. "I'm punishing myself tonight, so I won't be fucking you. Only you get to come tonight."

He bent down, and began the torture all over again. He'd said I could come, but he hadn't said when, and he left me wanting for long minutes that felt like hours.

The first ice had melted, with new cubes replacing it, before he finally sucked me into a climax so hard that I sobbed out his name at the end, tears running down my cheeks.

He tried to hold me afterwards, and I turned away, trying to roll out of his reach. But my bed wasn't that big, and he was determined. He swatted my butt for the effort.

"Don't turn away from me," he said in a hard voice, pulling my back against him.

I tried to fall asleep, but he began to touch me again, kneading my breasts until I was arching my back, brushing my backside against his stiff length.

"You can take me there," I told him, brushing my backside against him again. I hated that he was denying himself, whatever the reason.

He purred against me. "No release for me, not tonight. I keep pushing you too hard, even though you're injured and unaccustomed to this. I need a torturous night to reflect on my sins. Keep teasing me. I deserve it."

I stopped rubbing my butt against him, not willing to help him in that regard. He bit my neck, one hand snaking down to stroke my sex. "You don't want me to suffer, Love? You don't agree with the punishment I've chosen for myself?"

"No," I said on a gasp.

He plunged his large fingers into me, starting up an exquisite rhythm.

"I want to bring you pleasure, not punishment," I told him.

He grunted. "Well, it's not up to you, is it?" he asked, his fingers quickening, bringing me to orgasm quickly this time, a stark contrast to what he'd done to me the first time.

He kept his fingers inside of me, a hand gripping my breast, and his stiff erection still pressed firmly against my butt.

"Go to sleep, love," he whispered harshly in my ear.

I was so exhausted that I actually did.

James woke me in the morning in much the way he'd put me to bed, his hand stroking me, his other kneading at my breast. He was sucking on that perfect spot on my neck, his rigid cock grinding against my butt in rhythm to his fingers.

"Are you awake?" he asked into my ear.

"Yes. Please, I need you inside me. Please don't deprive yourself again." I arched my back as I spoke.

He shifted me onto my back, but stayed on his side. He dragged me around until my wet entrance was pointed at his stiff member, throwing my legs over his hip. My head was nearly hanging off the side of the bed.

One of his arms was used to prop him up, but his other hand was free to roam over my body. He lingered on my breasts, plucking at my nipples.

"I'm going to have special rings designed for these," he said, and rammed into me.

I didn't have a chance to ask him what he meant. I was too busy gasping as he began a jolting rhythm, still pulling on my breasts.

"I'll make them match your collar and your earrings. I want you dripping in diamonds. I'll decorate all of your chains with them. Before I'm done with you, every part of your body will be stamped with my ownership."

My hands fisted in the sheets. It was all I could reach in this position. I used my legs to move with his thrusts, and he groaned in approval.

He had us both coming in swift moments, impatient from his night of torture.

"Did you get any sleep last night?" I asked him as we lay panting, spent.

"A little. Though every time I drifted off, I woke up trying to violate you in your sleep. I need to rethink that punishment, I think."

I shifted until I could kiss him. It was a long, sweet kiss. He was surprisingly passive for it, as if he was curious to see what I would do.

I pulled back, touching his cheek. I knew my tenderness showed in my eyes. "Get a little more sleep. Please? At least rest while I go try to scrounge up breakfast."

He must have been exhausted, because he nodded, closing his eyes. He didn't open them as he raised my hand to his lips, kissing it softly.

I rose, pulling a sheet over him, and impulsively kissing his forehead before throwing on my tiny, nearly transparent shift. I grabbed a thong from my drawer full of the lacy things, even knowing I would be changing again soon, since I needed to shower after breakfast.

I padded into the kitchen, getting out anything I could find that went well with eggs. I cursed when I heard the loud sound of the garbage truck driving down my little street. I had already forgotten to put out my trash can the week before. I really needed to get it out to the curb before the truck passed my house.

I wouldn't normally go out front in my tiny slip of a nightgown, but I didn't have a spare moment to change.

Besides, I'll be quick. I told myself. I just needed to drag my one full garbage can out of the garage and onto the curb, then dart back in. And this was Vegas. See-through clothing was hardly unheard of, even in public.

I moved into the garage, punching the button to open my garage door. I was already dragging the can underneath the door when it was only halfway up. I was relieved to see that the garbage truck was a few houses away. I had made it in time.

I didn't notice the strange man blatantly photographing me until I was at the curb, lining up my garbage can.

I saw him, and just froze while he took shot after shot of me.

I wasn't galvanized into action until he looked up from the large camera, leering at me. "Thank you, Ms. Karlsson. Looking hot this morning."

He was a paunchy man, in his late forties, I guessed. Just the look on his face made my stomach churn. I was turning to rush back into the house when all hell broke loose.

A large man in a suit grabbed the greasy photographer, handling him roughly at the same time that the garage door into the kitchen burst open, a frantic, boxer clad James sprinting out. I heard clicks behind me, the photographer somehow managing to get a few shots of James, even while being restrained by a man much larger than himself. It was almost impressive.

I watched James's face as he took in the mess, watched it change from frantic to livid in a heartbeat. He looked like he wanted to murder the man as he strode to me, glaring at the paparazzi the entire time. He stepped in front of me, blocking me from view.

"Get inside," he said through gritted teeth.

I had seen his face. I couldn't imagine, from his look, that he didn't plan to do the man violence.

"Come inside with me, please," I pleaded with him, my voice pitched low.

"Go, Bianca. Now."

I hugged his back, not wanting him to get into trouble for some scumbag photographer.

"You look like you're going to attack him, James. I don't want you to go to jail." Even as I spoke, I heard a few more clicks from that damn camera. The man was fearless.

"I would rather fucking go to jail than let him leave with those pictures of you. Now go inside."

"Your man over there can handle it," I said, my cheek against his back. "And who will protect me, if you're in jail? Would it be worth it, if something happened to me while you were gone?" I felt horrible saying it, and I knew it wasn't even a sound argument, but I was desperate to get him to walk away, and I thought it would at least get his attention. Some scandalous pictures of me were not my biggest concern.

He shuddered, and I felt a rush of relief. He turned into me, still using his body to block me from view, and ushered me back into the garage.

"Get those fucking pictures off of his camera, Stimpson, or it's your fucking job!" James barked over his shoulder, not slowing.

"What the fuck were you thinking?" James burst out the second he'd shut the door from the garage into my kitchen. "Do you like giving the world a fucking show?"

I stiffened at his words, raised nearly to a rage-filled shout. I didn't respond, raising my chin and walking woodenly through my house and into my bathroom.

If he was going to take his anger out on me in a way I couldn't handle, I supposed it was better that I find out sooner rather than later. I tried to stay calm, but my whole body was shaking as I waited to see what he'd do next.

I tossed off my scanty clothes before stepping into the shower, turning it on, the cold spray hitting me for several seconds before it began to warm.

I just stood under the spray, unmoving, for several minutes. It was a long time before James joined me. I felt him more than saw him, since my eyes were closed.

He hugged me very carefully from behind. My first instinct was to pull away, but I let him hold me. I could feel him trembling, and the thought of hurting him, when he was as vulnerable as I, was abhorrent to me.

"I'm so sorry, love. Of course you were just taking out your trash, like a normal person. I shouldn't have taken my anger out on you. I'm sorry I raised my voice. I would never put my hands on you in anger. Whatever demons I may have, I don't have *that* in me. But I saw that scared look on your face when I raised my voice. I hate myself for putting it there."

I didn't say anything, but I didn't push him away, either.

He washed me, his touch gentle. "Will you come to the hotel with me today? You can do a spa day while I get a few things done." As he spoke, he lathered my hair.

I sighed, feeling weak from the morning's drama.

Why not do a spa day? I asked myself, seriously considering the idea. I never got to do things like that. I didn't have to work until evening, and James would spend ridiculous amounts of money on me, spa day or not. It was really a drop in the bucket at this point.

"You can invite anyone you want. They'll give you the royal treatment, as well as any of your friends. Just invite Stephan, and tell him to get the word out. You could have a flight attendant reunion at the spa, if you want. My resort has one of the best in town."

I caved at the plea in his voice. He was like a child, grasping for a way to make amends.

"Okay," I finally said. I sounded like a brat to my own ears. "Thank you, James. That's considerate. *You're* considerate."

Wet lips kissed my cheek almost sloppily. It was so unlike him that I let out a little giggle.

"Thank *you*. Nothing makes me happier than taking care of

you, in any way that I can." His voice was a raw whisper against my skin.

I turned and hugged him, his vulnerability almost palpable to me at that moment.

"You make me so happy, Bianca. I was just angry with myself, that I'd failed to protect you, yet again."

"Oh, James. What am I going to do with you? A few stupid pictures aren't going to hurt me."

"When I heard the garage door opening, my heart stopped. Just the thought of you being outside by yourself, when your father is still on the loose, makes me panicky."

"I obviously wasn't alone, with that bodyguard out there. Seems to me like you had your bases covered."

He stiffened up at that. "What took him so fucking long to react? That's what I want to know."

I kissed the center of his chest, right in that little indent between his well muscled pectorals. I loved that spot.

I filled my palm with shampoo, reaching up high to lather his honey-colored hair. I smiled at him as the motion dragged my chest against his. He bent down to give me better access, leaning his forehead onto my shoulder. I washed him as he had washed me. It was the first time he'd allowed me to tend to him as tenderly as he so often did to me. "Do you mind me touching you like this? Is that why you avoid letting me do this to you, usually?"

He shook his head, his eyes closed. His voice was a rasp in my ear. "Not you. I love any touch from you. It feels caring, and I want that. I want so much for you to care for me."

My heart hurt a little at his words. I wanted to reassure him, but the words were a lump in my throat.

He just hugged me tightly, not pressing me for the words. If he had wanted a woman who could express her feelings easily, I supposed he wouldn't have chosen me.

"Move in with me." His words were quiet but heartfelt.

I sighed. He was an undeniable force. A few short days, and it was nearly impossible to tell him no. "How about this? We'll spend more time together. If we're in the same city, we'll have sleepovers, just like we've done the last few days."

He just about squeezed the breath out of me. "Thank you," he rasped, and began to kiss me. His hands were everywhere, his mouth hot, as he backed me against the shower wall. When he felt my hot center and found it wet, he lifted me against him, impaling me brutally.

"Tell me if you're sore," he said roughly.

He leaned my back against the tiled wall and began to thrust.

I was sore, deliciously sore, but I wouldn't have told him so for anything. Then he might have stopped the heavenly orgasm that built as he pounded into me. I watched his lovely face, as he had taught me, as he moved, my hands grasping his shoulders. His face was wet, his golden skin so perfect. I thought he looked like an angel, with his wet hair trailing into his face.

"You're so beautiful," I told him quietly, but he still heard me over the spray.

He clearly enjoyed my admiration, his body shuddering in preparation for his climax. I felt him shuddering down to my toes, and it tipped me over the edge.

I cupped his cheek as we came together. It was so intimate that it should have made me cold, or uncomfortable, or even repulsed, but it didn't. More and more, I was craving this intimacy, not running from it.

CHAPTER TWENTY

After we'd showered and dressed, I found my phone, intending to text Stephan about the spa day.

James held up a hand. "Let me talk to him."

I wrinkled my nose. He tapped it.

"Why do you need to tell him?" I asked, suspicious.

"Why not?" he asked.

I dropped it, seeing by his innocent expression that I would have better luck asking Stephan what James was texting him.

"I'm going to cook some eggs for breakfast, unless you object," I told him, pulling on an old sundress. I figured I'd get dressed for real after we ate. I didn't even bother with underwear.

He gave me a heated kiss. He tasted unbelievably good. He always did. I sucked at his hot mouth, and he groaned, pulling away. He smiled and slapped my ass.

I beat a hasty retreat. At this rate, we would fuck each other until we starved to death.

I was walking to the kitchen, phone still clutched in my hand, when it began to ring. I glanced at the face. I recognized the number, since I'd missed several calls from the same 702 number over the past month.

Impulsively I answered. I didn't like mysteries, and I wanted to know who kept calling me so persistently.

"Hello," I said into the phone.

There was no response on the other end, just silence with the faintest hint of soft music in the background. Three heartbeats later the phone disconnected from the other end.

My brow was furrowed as I set my phone on the counter and began to cook breakfast. The calls were strange, but hardly something to let myself be bothered about. I resolved not to let myself dwell on them.

I made a huge portion of eggs and whatever else I could find that went with them. Peppers, onions, ham, smoked turkey, with some extra sharp cheddar to top it off. It was a better breakfast then I'd thought I could come up with, so I was rather pleased with the effort.

James ate a ridiculous amount of it. His plate had to be filled with at least five eggs worth, but he cleared it in short order. He ate it as though he'd never had such fine food in his life, when the reality was, it was just what I could scrounge up, since I was often out of town. Still, I appreciated his enthusiasm.

I shouldn't have been surprised to find new additions to my closet, both for me and for James. It was stuffed full, whereas before it had been rather sparse. I sent him an arch look as I noticed the change. He didn't even seem to notice, looking through my new clothes. He pulled a pair of tiny white cargo shorts off of a hanger, handing them to me. They were shorter than anything I owned. He picked out a little gold tank top with geometric designs printed across it in black and white. He handed it to me without a word.

I raised my brows at his arbitrary choices, but I put them on without a protest. I could at least see how they fit, and how they looked.

The shorts were very short, but stretchier than they looked, and oddly comfortable. I hadn't ever owned a pair of white shorts that I could remember. I checked my panty line carefully, a little worried that my pink thong would show through, but the material seemed solid enough. The top was comfortable, hanging rather loosely to my hips. I decided I liked James's choices as I studied the outfit in the mirror. It was flattering but tasteful. Well, as tasteful as short shorts could be.

I was nearly done with my easy hair and minimal makeup by the time James emerged from the closet, dressed and looking fabulous, as always. His attire was different than any I'd seen him wear before. He wore white linen shorts that clung to his hips deliciously. My eyes lingered there the longest. He wore a loose, brilliant blue dress shirt, sleeves rolled up and open at the collar. The color set off his eyes and his tan to perfection.

I was surprised that he was dressed down. I didn't imagine that anyone at his resort had ever seen him in anything but a three-piece suit. He looked like he was about to go on vacation in the Hamptons, not spend a few hours working.

"That looks nice," I told him as he approached my vanity, hovering behind me. "I'm surprised to see you in anything but a suit, though, for the hotel."

He just shrugged, studying me with that razor focus of his. He reached past me, digging into the silver box of jewelry that had followed us from Wyoming. I'd taken off my collar before showering, and he clasped it back around my neck without a word. I fingered it as he reached back into the box, pulling out a pair of huge, princess cut diamond earrings I'd never seen before. He put them on me without a word, pressing against my back intimately.

"It's all too much, James," I said, but didn't take them off. He seemed to need to do this, to shower me in gifts. I should have put up more of a fight, I knew, but his warm gaze stopped me. It pleased him to do this, and it killed any urge I had to stop him when I realized just *how much* it pleased him.

He reached into the large jewelry box again, pulling out a good-sized black jewelry box. I pursed my lips, knowing he had done yet another outrageous thing.

He opened the box, showing me matching diamond cuffs. The were thick, twinkling with more tiny diamonds than I could even guess at. It didn't escape me that they looked like jewel encrusted shackles.

He studied my wrists, running a light finger over the abrasions still visible there. "These will have to wait a few days, I think." He snapped the case closed, putting it back.

He pressed a palm flat against my stomach, pressing me harder against him. His other hand snaked down to my inner thighs, pressing past my scanty shorts and panties. It was shocking how fast and easily he could access me there.

I sucked in a breath as he worked a long finger into me. I sought out his hot gaze in the mirror.

He watched his hand as though transfixed. "My dresser is getting you more shorts like this. Not only do your legs look phenomenal, I can also do *this* anytime I please. Gotta love that kind of access."

Regrettably, he extricated his finger rather quickly, kissing the back of my head. He sighed heavily before moving away. He went back into my closet, returning with two pairs of shoes that I hadn't put in there. He slipped on a pair of white loafers that set his golden skin off to perfection, handing a pair of bright blue wedge heels to me. I saw immediately that they matched his shirt.

In spite of myself, I smiled.

"It seems you know the contents of my closet better than I do nowadays, Mr. Cavendish." My tone was arch as I bent down to fasten the heels onto my feet. They were comfortable for three and a half inch heels, I had to admit.

He didn't respond, just smirked, waiting for me.

"How did you get so much stuff into my house without my noticing?" I asked.

He pursed his lips, taking my arm and leading me out of the bedroom, making a beeline for the front door. "Stephan let my dresser in. When will I be getting my own set of keys?"

I stiffened. It didn't escape me that he had somehow turned the conversation around on me. "Why would you need them?"

He sighed, aiming a hooded look at me as we walked out the front door. I didn't even question that we would take his car. I couldn't picture him in my own small car.

A new, creepy photographer had taken up residence on my sidewalk. However, he wasn't snapping pictures when we walked out. He was far too occupied arguing with an intimidating Clark. Clark shifted in front of the man, blocking us from his view as soon as we were spotted. I couldn't imagine the man got any clear pictures of us as James ushered me swiftly into the car. Clark didn't get out of the man's face until we were safely ensconced.

"Very good, Clark," James said as Clark slid into his seat.

Clark nodded and began to drive. "I fired Stimpson, Sir. I'm very sorry about what happened this morning. I thought he was more reliable, or he never would have gotten the job."

"Thank you," James said, clutching my hand tightly. "Was he at least successful at retrieving all of the pictures taken?"

Clark's voice was quietly furious when he answered. "He claims he did, but it's impossible to say. I only have his account of events."

James's grip tightened almost painfully. "I should have handled it myself," James said darkly.

He closed the privacy screen after that, brooding quietly for most of the drive. It wasn't until we were nearly at the hotel that he spoke. The impressive resort was visible from far away. I watched it as we drew closer and closer.

"Have you been to the property before?" he asked.

"I haven't."

I remembered all of the buzz when it first re-opened two or three years ago. It was one of the swankier casinos on the strip, with five star restaurants and a nightclub hotspot that was quite famous, and I had heard a lot of people mention the large shopping mall attached to it. But I rarely went on the strip, and when I did, it was usually to meet with friends, and never at the more overpriced hotel/casinos.

He kissed my hand. "I'll have to show you around on the way to the spa. Stephan said he'd meet you there. It sounds like he got quite a few friends to come, considering that it was such short notice."

I smiled, thinking of Stephan's reaction to a spa day. It sooo wasn't his thing. "Did he gripe about the spa?"

James grinned. "He did. But I told him you missed him, and it was enough. Has he never done a spa day before?"

I shook my head, laughing. "Neither of us have. That sort of thing is ungodly expensive."

We pulled up to the huge entrance that read Cavendish Hotel&Casino as he spoke. "Well, you'll be getting the royal treatment today, I can assure you. And you can go every day of the week, if you want to. I will inform the staff that you have carte blanche status."

I didn't bother to protest. I knew I wouldn't be making much use of that extravagance. I felt spoiled enough just going today.

He led me through the shopping mall first, as that was where we had entered. He wrapped a possessive arm around the back of my waist, his hand gripping my hip warmly. I put my hand over his as he ushered me around, giving me a short but thorough tour of the shops. He introduced me to several managers throughout the mall, but I knew I wouldn't remember hardly any of their names.

Only the female owner of the casino's famous tattoo shop stood out. She had dark hair streaked with blue and a pouty red mouth, every inch of her exposed skin covered in ink. And she had a lot of of exposed skin. She wore a half shirt and cut-off jean shorts that were so short they made mine look overly modest.

She smiled at me warmly, but I stiffened immediately at the sight of her. I had seen her and James photographed together in several pictures online. It was rumored that they'd had a steamy affair. There was a reality TV series filmed at her shop, I suddenly recalled reading. Her name was Frankie, and I tried not to be openly rude to her, but it was a struggle.

James embraced the woman, showing an easy affection with her that made my vision go a little red and hazy. He introduced me simply by name, not giving me a title or explaining our relationship. We moved on quickly.

I was tense and stiff after that meeting. I knew it was unreasonable to be jealous and moody after that, but I still couldn't shake it. James led me through the shopping mall and the restaurants, through the expansive casino, and lastly, through the hotel portion and into the spa.

I was happy to see my group of friends as James led me into the swanky waiting lounge that led to the salon and spa.

It *was* an impressive group on such short notice. But then again, *who would turn down a free spa day*?

Stephan was waiting in the luxurious waiting area, flanked by a laughing group that consisted mostly of girls. The only exception sat rather close beside him. Javier looked happier than I'd ever seen him as he laughed at something Stephan had said.

Marnie, Judith, Brenda, and Jessa flanked the cute couple, chattering excitedly.

Marnie and Judith jumped up, squealing in delight when they spotted James and I. They hugged me, thanking James as they did so, talking over each other and giggling all the while.

I glanced at James. He smiled indulgently, waving at Stephan, who waved back with a nod, as though answering a silent question. The two men in my life seemed to be developing their own language of sorts. Perversely, I found that fact both heartwarming and disconcerting.

James addressed the group. "Please, everyone, enjoy yourselves. Don't hesitate to avail yourselves of any of the spa and salon services that you wish to. It's my treat, of course."

He just smiled and nodded when all six of them thanked him at nearly the same time.

He turned to me, leaning down to kiss me softly on the cheek. "I'll miss you, Love. Take your time. I'll be awhile. If you need to get ahold of me, call my cel," he whispered the words into my ear softly, then departed.

CHAPTER TWENTY-ONE

No one even bothered to wait for James to get out of earshot before they started talking about him.

Everyone seemed to be in agreement. James was dreamy, and sweet, and fabulous in every way imaginable. I took all of their dreamy gushing and good natured advice with a wry smile.

Stephan rose and kissed my cheek, smiling. "You're glowing. Things going well?" he asked, his voice pitched low, but I still heard him over the loud women, who were still extolling James's obvious charms.

I just nodded.

"Are you glad that you finally agreed to see him?" he asked, his voice almost chiding.

I shot him a look, but knew he had a point.

A spa hostess approached me, looking harried. "I'm so sorry, Ms. Karlsson. We are ready for you now. I apologize for the wait. Which service would your party like to begin with."

I just blinked at her for a long moment. I didn't even know what services there were, and I hadn't even been waiting for more than maybe five minutes, tops.

I looked to my group for help. "What first?" I asked them. I figured someone there had to have a preference.

Judith didn't hesitate. "The deluxe package how it's listed should be perfect. Massage first, I think."

The hostess nodded, looking relieved. "Yes, right this way." She led us into another waiting area. It was even more posh than the first one, with stone walls and opaque glass throughout. There was a tea bar, but before we could serve ourselves, the hostess introduced us to our own personalized attendants. Mine was a delicately petite asian girl named Mina.

She seemed anxious and nervous as she asked me what I would like to drink. "I can get you literally anything, Ms. Karlsson. Please don't hesitate to ask."

It was an intimidating request. I would rather have just had a menu. "Tea, please."

She named off ten different teas that the spa boasted. "I'll take the youth-berry oolong infused with lemongrass. Plain, thank you," I told her.

She seemed relieved, as though she'd been worried I would request something more complicated. She brought a tea service tray to the table in front of me, and prepared my tea as though it were a ritual. I thought it was charming. I told her so.

She looked up, beaming at me. "I trained in Japan, when I was little. You should see my mother. Her tea service puts mine to shame."

She finally poured the impressively prepared cup of tea, then left briefly, returning with trays of food. There was fruit, vegetables, tiny sandwiches, hors d'oeuvres, and cheese and crackers. She brought tray after tray, and I took little samples from each.

All of my friends were getting the same treatment in comfortable seats around the stone lined room. *It was almost like being inside of a luxurious cave*, I mused.

I heard Judith telling the room at large that the cucumber sandwiches were divine. I ate the one I had grabbed. It was pretty tasty, I had to admit. And the tea was to die for, smooth without a hint of bitter.

Mina brought a tray of tiny muffins, truffles, and fruit tarts. I took one of the fruit tarts, thanking her. I ate lightly, sampling more than eating. I had a nervous stomach, since I didn't know what to expect from the spa day, and surprises made me nervous. I was even bad at relaxing at a spa. The thought was somewhat disheartening.

After we had snacked and drank, we were escorted into a large massage room. It was another modern cavelike design, with frosted glass obscuring us from each other for the massage. We could talk, but we didn't have to all get naked together. I was relieved.

Mina explained to me how I should prepare for the massage, then left me to it. I undressed, putting my clothes into the large locker provided in my massage nook. It felt wrong to take my jewelry off in public, and leave it in a locker, but I did it, not knowing exactly what we were in store for. I got quickly under the white sheet in only my thong, as Mina had instructed, lying on my stomach.

I saw white shoes approaching me from the hole in the table my face fit into.

"Ms. Karlsson, I'm Jen, I'll be massaging you today," a very soothing voice told me.

Jen went through all of the techniques she offered, and I requested the deep tissue. She set to work immediately. She was good. I'd never had a massage like that before, never had a professional of any kind, and it felt divine. Everyone must have been having a similar experience, because shortly after the service began, no one said a word, not even Marnie or Judith, who were notorious for never being able to shut up. There were some appreciative groans heard throughout the hour, but that was all.

We all wore matching plush terrycloth robes as we followed our respective spa attendants to the next service. We used separate rooms for that one. The facial also lasted an hour, and my face felt clean and fresh when it was finished.

All of the girls met up in a modern, stone-walled room that housed a collection of pools designed to look like a modern twist on a natural hot-spring. Stephan and Javier had to go to a separate pool, since the pools were not co-ed, though we were the only occupants of this one.

We soaked for a long time, and I mostly listened to the chatter with a half-smile.

"How cute are Javier and Stephan together?" Judith was asking the room.

I silently agreed. It wasn't just that they were good-looking. The way they looked at each other, even casually, was good for my soul. I wanted so badly for them to work, I was almost afraid to hope for it.

"Do you approve, Bianca? Does Javier get your stamp of approval?" Marnie was asking me, snapping me out of my musings.

I wondered why everyone thought that I was Stephan's keeper. The idea was bizarre to me. I would never tell him who to date. From my point of view, I always just wanted his dates to like me, and not mind me being around a lot, since that was usually how it went. "To be honest, anyone that Stephan wants gets my stamp of approval. I just want him to be happy."

For some reason, that got soft 'ahs' all around. Then the topic moved to how cute Stephan and I were.

"You guys are related somehow, right?" Brenda asked. She was the one in the group that had known us the shortest amount of time. "Stephan told me you were family."

I smiled. "Not by blood, but in every way that counts. He's

like a brother, and my best friend. If that's not family, I don't have a clue what is."

Another round of 'ahs' made me smile. The talk soon turned to James, of course.

"Is it serious, Bianca? It seems really serious." This came from Judith, who had no qualms about prying.

I had a hard time with girl talk, with opening up in general, but I wanted to try. "I don't know. It feels that way, but it's still so new." I took a deep breath, continuing. "He wants me to move in with him." I was surprised at myself for revealing that, but I wanted their opinions.

Every single one of them gasped, hands flying to their chests. It was comical.

"What did you say?" Jessa asked. She was the first one to recover, from the looks of the other ones.

I shrugged. "I told him we needed to spend more time together before I could consider something like that. He's not easily deterred, though. He had a stylist, or dresser or whatever you call them, buy me a wardrobe for each of his houses, so he already has me kind of moved in, even though I never agreed to it."

More comical gasping and some stuttering at that one.

"That's crazy, right?" I asked, hoping to hear a sensible opinion.

I didn't get one. Even sensible Brenda thought he was romantic, and hopelessly in love with me.

I didn't tell them that he'd never said he loved me. *It will hurt to say it out loud*, I thought.

"You guys would have supermodel babies," Judith said on a sigh, in fantasyland.

Jessa was watching me closely, and seemed to see something on my face at Judith's words. "Oh, my, god, have you guys talked about having kids?"

I grimaced. "He mentioned it briefly. He dropped the issue when he saw that it made me want to run screaming. It's all way too fast, right? It's crazy to move so fast in a relationship, right?" I asked, again looking for a voice of sanity.

"Martin said he knew he was going to marry me on our very first date. He said he just knew, like something in his mind clicked. He said I was the missing piece in his life's puzzle. He pursued me until I saw it, too. And that was twenty years and two kids ago, so it worked out for us." Brenda smiled as her story got 'ahs' around the room.

Okay, even I could admit that story was pretty sweet.

"James strikes me as a man who knows what he wants," Brenda continued. "I don't see him changing his mind, either, not with the way he looks at you."

Okay, I am not going to get any sobering advice from this crowd, I decided.

Next we moved on to manicures and pedicures, the guys joining us again. They weren't a cute couple, I decided, watching them. They were beautiful, Stephan so muscular and golden, Javier so, well, pretty, and elegantly built.

"Me and Marnie are official losing it, guys," Judith told us all.

"Did we ever even have it?" Marnie asked her, mock despair in her voice.

"What happened?" Jessa asked, laughing at the outrageous women. They were like a comedy duo, playing off of each other for an entertaining routine.

"We tried to get a guy to do a three-way with us, and he *turned us down!*" Judith's voice was bewildered.

I giggled a little. The unexpected turn of conversation had surprised it out of me.

"Captain Damien?" Stephan asked them sympathetically, but he couldn't quite hold back his smile.

Marnie and Judith were in pedicure chairs next to each other, and they nodded at the same time, as though in sync.

"Don't take it personal, girls, he's hopelessly in love with Bianca," Javier said, his first words in a while.

Stephan gave him a look, and Javier winced at me sympathetically.

My face flushed. I hoped he was joking, or at least mistaken.

"That's not fair!" Judith told me. "You have Mr. Beautiful. Give us Damien!"

I wrinkled my nose. "Damien is just a friend. He's not in love with me." My voice was almost apologetic. I looked to Stephan for support. "You talk to him all the time, Stephan. Tell them he's not into me."

Stephan grimaced. "I've told him, over and over again, that you're not interested in him like that, but he at least has a very enduring crush."

"What do you mean by enduring?" I asked him, my eyes narrowed on him.

"Two years or so. And he stopped dating, and hooking up, at least six months ago, so that you would take him serious when he asked you out again. He thought that the fact that he's a slut is what was keeping you from seeing him as more than a friend."

I was shocked. All of this had been going on without my knowledge, and Stephan decided to tell me about it when we were getting our feet worked on by strangers, and in front of five of our friends. I gave him my best 'WTF' look.

It grew real quiet after that, the others sensing the sudden tension between Stephan and I. It was a good ten minutes before they all started chatting again, but I stayed silent, brooding.

I didn't understand why Stephan had kept it from me, but I supposed it was an awkward thing to bring up, when he'd known how I clearly felt.

Stephan sat next to me when we got the manicures. He

looked pretty cute, a big muscular guy in a soft robe, getting his nails done. I was smarter than to point it out, though.

He gave me a searching look. "I'm sorry. That came out at a bad time, but when you asked so directly, I couldn't deny it. That was just the first time it came up, yanno?"

I could see his position, and I nodded. "Yeah, it's just awkward. But it's awkward for you, as well. I just don't understand what I could have done to give Damien the wrong idea. It makes no sense."

Stephan flushed a little, and I studied him, fascinated. "From what I've gleaned, your disinterest is just more of a turn on for him. I think he likes unreadable, mysterious women, and you're the ultimate when it comes to that. The problem is, it's because you genuinely aren't interested in him. But that just doesn't seem to faze him. He thinks he just needs to wait out your relationship with James, and that you'll come around eventually."

I sighed. "Well, what a waste of *his* time. I wish someone could talk some sense into him."

"Believe me, Buttercup, I have tried."

We were escorted back to the refreshment waiting area. Mina offered me more snacks and drinks. I took more tea, trying jasmine oolong that time.

We changed back into our street clothes before being ushered into the salon portion of the spa. I took very careful inventory of my jewelry as I put it back on.

I went for the full hair treatment as well, needing a trim. My hairdresser was pleasant and friendly. She immediately started trying to talk me into some highlights.

Mina interrupted her, her tone apologetic. "Mr. Cavendish left instructions *not* to color her hair," she explained, then moved away.

The hairdresser looked nonplussed. She seemed to shake herself out of it. I almost wanted to tell her to give me the highlights, anyways. *Who cared*? It was just hair. But I would feel terrible if it somehow got her in trouble, so I left it alone. James was her boss, after all.

She indicated a spot on my forehead. "What about short, straight bangs for you? It would set off your eyes, and your hair is straight enough to pull off the style that's really hot right now."

I gave a little shrug. "Do whatever you think would look flattering. My hair only ever stays straight just like this, so keep that in mind. I usually just trim it, and keep it like this. I wouldn't mind a change, as long as it doesn't require a long time to style."

She nodded decisively, seeming to know just what she wanted to do. I closed my eyes and let her work.

I was rather pleased with the finished product, despite my apathy. It was flattering, and it did bring out my eyes, the short bangs making them seem bigger in my face.

Everyone seemed to agree, and I flushed a little at all of the compliments thrown at me.

We got our cosmetics done next. The woman who did my makeup tried to instruct me as she did so, handing me a large bag of cosmetics when she finished. I liked what she had done, the effects subtle but flattering, the smoky eye not too heavy on my pale face, as I would have thought. I thought it went particularly well with my new haircut.

We were ushered back to the tea room again to finish up, the hostess asking me if they could provide any other services.

I checked the time on my phone, surprised to see that it was nearly time for us to start heading home to prepare for work that night.

"No, thank you."

"I hope you were satisfied with our services, Ms. Karlsson."

"Very much so. We had a great time. Thank you." As I spoke, James walked into the room, as though he had timed the entire thing down to the minute.

He grinned wide when he saw me, looking happy and...mischievous. I knew instantly that he had done or was planning to do something outrageous.

"What are you planning?" I asked him as soon as he was within earshot.

His grin just widened, and I got a little worried.

He glanced around at everyone, smiling warmly. "How was it?"

He got flooded with enthusiastic answers, all positive, of course. Who could complain about a free spa day? He seemed pleased, though, that everyone had enjoyed themselves.

"I got you something," James told me, that happy smile never leaving his face. He was positively beaming.

I bit my lip, tilting my head back to look up at him. I was scared to ask. "What is it?" I asked, not even trying to hide my worry.

He laughed. "I'm not sure I can do it justice by explaining it. I'll have to show you. And your friends, too, I think. I did promise."

I was perplexed when he started to unbutton his shirt, still grinning, his eyes glued to mine.

"What on earth are you doing?" I asked him.

Someone, I thought it was Judith, hooted in encouragement.

Was he giving me a striptease? I wondered, genuinely confounded. And unwillingly turned on.

I gasped, my heart stopping when I saw the blood red letters inked on his perfect chest. *Right over his heart,* I thought. He had marred his perfect skin for me. I felt tears prick my eyes.

The room around us went straight into chaos mode, Marnie and Judith shamelessly screaming and jumping around like maniacs.

I heard a disgruntled, "What the fuck, man?" from Stephan.

I took deep breaths, my eyes glued to the *Bianca* written in small letters cleanly over his heart.

"It's fake, right?" I asked him. "It's a joke, right?"

His smile didn't falter as he wiped a horrifying tear from my cheek. "Why the tears?"

"Your perfect skin. You shouldn't have marked it for my sake. You have the finest skin on earth. It seems like a shame," I told him, my voice whisper soft.

That surprised a laugh out of him. "You'll get used to it. I think you'll like the other one better," he told me.

"Please, tell me the other one is on your dick!"

I sent Judith a stern look for that one. She just dissolved into helpless giggles.

James bit the bottom lip of his pretty mouth, turning to show me his back.

CHAPTER TWENTY-TWO

The tattoo was etched directly over the clean slab of his right shoulder blade. And, like the man himself, it was exquisite.

I stood, brushing close to him to study it intently. Tears ran liberally down my cheeks, embarrassing but irrepressible.

It was a portrait of my face, my hair flowing out to shape into lilies that formed a perfect frame, as though it were a painting. He had taken one of my self-portraits and etched it permanently into his skin. It was the sweetest, craziest, most romantic thing I'd ever witnessed, and I didn't know what to make of it. I loved the tattoo on sight, though, loved having my painting turned into something so wonderful. Even the lilies used to frame the portrait had been copied from my work, I recognized. I was suddenly glad that I had spent so much time on the paintings he'd used, trying to get all of the details just so.

James was shooting me expectant looks over his shoulder, his face as happy and carefree as I'd ever seen it. "Well, what do you think?"

"Oh, James," I said, my voice catching. "It's exquisite. It's more colorful than any tattoo I've ever seen. I've never seen one that looks like this. It's more like a painting than a tattoo. Why does it look so different?"

"I didn't use any black ink for outlining. I used lighter colors for that. And with James's dark skin, I was able to use white ink for the skin color, which gave it a very painting kind of feel. He's one of the best canvases I've had the pleasure of working on. I'll have to thank you for helping me finally get my hands on him. Obviously, you inspired his sudden interest in ink." I hadn't seen her approaching until she spoke, but the tattoo artist, Frankie, was suddenly beside me, pointing out details of the tattoo on his back, standing nearly as close to him as I was. I stiffened.

I knew it was illogical, and unreasonable, but realizing that another woman had done the tattoo, one he was obviously fond of, made me a little crazy. That red haze I was beginning to recognize as jealousy was now a pernicious film over my vision.

"Can I cover it now, James? Have you finished the show and tell?" Frankie asked him, sounding sassy but playful, her smile very warm on him.

He grinned at her, still looking over his shoulder, letting me look my fill.

I still studied the incredible portrait. I wanted to run my fingers over it, but even with my limited knowledge on the subject, I knew it was too new for touching. My hand gripped the top of his shoulder instead, as I leaned in very close and studied it intently, trying to ignore the woman standing too close, and too familiarly, beside James and I.

I was smiling in the picture, a slight, sort of enigmatic smile, my eyes heavy-lidded and mysterious. She had even matched the blue of my eyes astonishingly well. She was very talented, I had to admit. I had never even known a tattoo could look like that. Most of my friends had one or two, but they were usually outlined in heavy black, or else entirely black. What Frankie had done looked so much softer than that. It was hard to even think of James's marking as the same thing.

"It's beautiful. You're very talented. I didn't even know that a tattoo could look like that," I told Frankie, trying to be civil, but my voice was stiff and a little cold.

James seemed to notice my tone, his eyes flying back to my face, studying me intently, his happy smile wilting a little, his eyes becoming solemn.

I felt instantly contrite. Just the wrong tone of voice, and his ridiculously happy mood seemed to have been subdued.

I tried to give him a smile, but I could feel that it looked forced. "I'm finished looking at it, if she needs to tend to it," I told him, stepping back from him.

Frankie stepped in instantly, rubbing a clear gel over the entire inked surface. I watched her hands on him, and felt the strangest urge to move between them.

I moved away, turning my back to them.

Frankie's voice was still friendly as she addressed me. "You're very talented. I just did my best to do your picture justice. It was a real treat for me to get to work on a picture like that, on a body like James's. Talk about a work of art." Her voice turned over the top flirtatious on the last sentence, and I knew she was talking about his body.

I counted to ten, hating myself for being so weak and so insanely jealous.

I heard Frankie giving James care instructions briefly.

"So, um, nice meeting you, Bianca. I'll see ya around," Frankie said, her voice still friendly, but a bit uncertain.

A brief glance at my group of friends showed most of them looking at me, wide-eyed, as though they weren't sure what to make of my behavior. I couldn't blame them. I felt ridiculous, but I still couldn't look at James, worried that if Frankie was still near him, I would do something completely insane.

Stephan was the only one of the group who seemed oblivious

to my strange reaction, his intent glare focused narrowly on James.

I just tensed up more when James hugged me from behind.

"We need a minute, guys. Thank you all for coming on such short notice," James addressed the group, politely but briskly, his tone a courteous dismissal. He gripped the back of my neck, in that dominant spot, leading me into a room.

I recognized the room immediately. It was the faux hot springs room. One of the attendants followed us in. "May I help you with anything, Mr. Cavendish?" she asked, her voice nervous.

"Yes. Please make sure we're not disturbed until we've finished in here."

They were at my back as they spoke, and I looked resolutely at the low pools, a hot blush coloring my face. I knew what would be assumed, of course. I didn't even know myself what James had planned.

"Of course, Sir. Please let me know if I can further assist you."

I heard the door shut just as she finished speaking. The sound of the door clicking closed echoed in the huge room.

James was silent for a long moment, his hand heavy on my neck.

"You seem tense," James told me in a sort of offhanded way, his voice almost disinterested. He removed his hand, and I heard clothes rustling behind me. I held my breath, trying intently to hear what he was doing.

"Take off your clothes, Bianca," he ordered, still in that offhanded way.

I did, my hands shaking a little. I didn't know why I was so nervous, I'd had sex with him more than once that very day, but I was nonetheless. I just never knew exactly what he had planned.

"Go sit on the edge of the pool. Put your legs in the water, just up to your knees," he told me, still in that disinterested tone.

I sat at the edge of the water, leaning back on my hands, watching him.

He was completely naked as he took the steps into the shallow pool. The water came just to his hips, his arousal clearly visible above the water. I trembled, biting my lip as I watched him.

He dipped into the water, just up to a spot right below the tattoo over his heart, standing up straight again almost immediately. All of the wet spots on his body were slick and dripping. My mouth watered. He ran his hands over his slick torso, watching me as he touched his abs and stroked his chest. The plastic covered patch over his heart was the only thing he left untouched.

He glided towards me, hips moving directly between my knees when he drew close. "What does it do to you, when you see someone else put their hands on me?" he asked. "Even the most casual touch. Does it make you crazy? Do you feel like you might do something insane, or even violent? Does it make you sick, deep in your stomach? Does it make your chest hurt, and your insides clench? Does a red haze overtake your vision? Do you lose all ability to be civil, or even form a coherent thought?" He moved against me as he spoke, his mouth speaking directly into my ear, his tone so cold it made my whole body shiver with a delicious kind of fear. He was in a mood, and he had plans for me. I just knew it. And it was nothing I could predict.

"Answer me," he said, biting my earlobe with enough force to make my back arch, pushing my breasts into his slick chest.

"Yes."

"Yes to what? Which of those things happens when you see someone else's hands on me?"

"All of it. I can't even trust myself, it makes me so crazed. I don't recognize the person I become when I'm jealous. It's nothing I've ever had to deal with before. I hate it."

He was adjusting my body as I spoke, bringing my hips to the very edge of pool, which made my words even more breathless and desperate.

He poised himself at my entrance. "Good," he said, his voice still cold, but with anger now. He entered me, having to work himself in slowly at that angle, my hips right on the edge of the pool.

"Why is that good?" I asked him on a little moan, my eyes going to his as he penetrated me. I had been well conditioned. My eyes couldn't seem to look away from him now when he was inside of me.

"I want you to feel what I feel. I want you to know what that does to me, what it's like to feel jealous and covetous. And now you do."

One of his hands, which had been at my hip, moved up to my neck. He circled it, squeezing lightly.

"Grab my wrist with your hands," he ordered.

I obeyed.

"If you look away from me, I'll let up," he told me. "But I want you to scratch me while I choke you. I want you to try to rip my hand away. I want you to struggle, but don't look away unless it's too much. That will be your safe word, since you won't be able to speak."

I nodded, trembling and watching his beautiful eyes.

He used his other hand to push my legs wider apart as the hand at my neck began to squeeze. He thrust slowly in and out of me, but they were heavy thrusts, and so deep.

My hands began to tug at his hard hand at my neck, and I dug my nails into that thick wrist, hesitant at first, but as the pressure increased, I raked at him desperately, lightheaded with the sensation. My head fell back, and he perched me back like that, his hand squeezing and releasing in time to his heavy strokes.

My vision started to get a little hazy, and that's when he

would let up, beginning the drugging process all over again. I hadn't realized my neck could be such a source of intoxicating pleasure, not in that way. My very pulse seemed to throb in time to his rhythm inside of me. I did what he told me and struggled against him, particularly his hand and wrist, but not one inch of my body wanted him to stop. The choking and the struggling was a marvel to me.

I saw with clarity that I loved to struggle against him, loved to fight him wildly, my efforts not even straining him, not even slowing his purpose. His sheer strength floored me. I relished it.

His grip tightened as he began to pound relentlessly.

My vision went spotty, and I came so violently that I wasn't sure how long the orgasm lasted, and I wasn't certain if I had blacked out for a fuzzy moment.

When I focused again, James had his choking hand gripped in my hair to hold me in place as he rubbed out the last of his own orgasm inside of me. He was making these deliciously shivery little involuntary thrusts, his neck arched back. His eyes found mine again, his heavy-lidded and sated.

"Was it too much, Love?" he asked, his voice low and hoarse. "You were having such a fit, I couldn't tell if you passed out." As he spoke, he hugged me against him, tilting my head back to look at him from where I was pressed to his chest.

"It was...exquisite. It was fucking perfect, James."

He swallowed hard, studying me. "It would have been, if we could keep eye contact at the end doing that. But I probably don't have to ask if choking is on your 'yes' list. I think I can figure it out. I need to be very careful with that. You're so delicate, and I have the urge to be...overzealous when I get your neck in my hands."

He pulled out of me suddenly, shuddering as he did so. I was right there with him.

"We need to get moving. We need to rush, actually." He

tugged me into the water, dragging me to the steps with a firm grip on the the ring of my choker.

He dried us both with businesslike efficiency, leaving the spa's plush towels on the floor.

"Get dressed quickly," he told me.

CHAPTER TWENTY-THREE

We dressed quickly, rushing out of the resort. James held my nape, steering me out of the vast property. I was completely lost by the time we reached the casino. The place was colossal.

James's car was waiting when we got to the valet station, Clark ready with the door open wide. He inclined his head to us politely, his face warm and smiling. I thought the stoic man might be softening towards me. "Sir. Ms. Karlsson."

James was silent until Clark got behind the wheel and started driving, rather speedily towards my house, before he leaned in close to my ear to speak to me. We were sitting very close, but not touching, which was unusual for James.

"So, when do I get to pierce these?" he asked quietly. As he spoke he reached up a hand, pinching first one nipple and then the other. He quickly withdrew his hand.

My mind just went sort of...blank. It had hovered around in the back of my mind in a sort of disjointed way when I'd seen the tattoos, but it was still a shock to hear it out loud. I mulled it over, thinking about the ink he'd gotten on his beautiful skin. If he wanted so badly for me to do this thing, why not? I couldn't say that I would like the piercings, but I couldn't say that I wouldn't, either.

"I thought that was all a joke," I told him, but I didn't say no.

"I wasn't joking, obviously. But if that's really what you thought, I won't make you do it. And I am certainly willing to wait until you're ready. There's no reason to rush it."

I thought about it, really thought about the deal we'd made. I had told myself that he was joking, but had I really thought that he was? If I was honest, I had known on some level that, though he was being playful, he always did exactly as he said he would.

I met his gaze steadily. "I'll do it. I think I tried to convince myself that you were joking, but I'm beginning to understand you enough to know that you always do as you say."

He pulled my head back lightly by the hair, and began to kiss me, an open-mouthed, hot kiss. He took his time before pulling back. "Thank you for being honest. But you still don't need to do it. I wouldn't force you, even if the thought appeals to me strongly."

"I'll do it. I said I would. And, though I can't deny I've never thought of doing something like that, it appeals to me simply because you want it so badly. I can't seem to help myself. I want to please you. I *love* to please you."

He reacted strangely with a sharply indrawn breath. He leaned his head back against his seat, shutting his eyes, his face a little drawn.

He found my hand and squeezed it in his. "Thank you, Bianca."

An unexpected laugh escaped me suddenly. He opened his eyes, giving me a puzzled look.

"Sorry," I told him, smiling warmly into his eyes. "You just looked so relieved that I would pierce my nipples and it struck me as funny. That's such a strange thing to be relieved about."

He smiled at me, but it didn't reach his eyes. It was a sad

kind of smile, and I felt my own fade a little. "I *was* relieved, but not about the piercing. Don't get me wrong, I'm very happy about that. But it was what you said that eased my mind. The thought that you love to please me, it gives me hope. If you truly love to please me, you won't leave me. You'll stay with me, and live with me. If not now, then eventually. I can at least hope to talk you into it."

I flushed. I still thought moving in with him was ridiculous, but I could see that I had already softened towards the idea, and for just the reason he had latched onto. I loved to please him. But more, I loved him. I wondered if I would have the courage to tell him. *Not anytime soon.* It was still a shock to me to even think it, to even realize it fully. How had this happened so fast? But how not? With him being so charming, and so perfect, so heart-achingly beautiful, but tarnished in all of the right places, and in all of the ways that I understood so well, how could I not love him?

"Did you like Frankie?" he asked. The change of topic made me flush, but for a different reason. *And why did he sound so smug when he asked that question?*

My mouth tightened involuntarily. "Have you slept with her? Because *you* seem to like her," I told him, trying to pull my hand away.

He gripped it more tightly, still with that smug smile. "No. She's a very close friend of mine, though, so I would like you to get along with her."

I felt my face turning red. I looked away from his infuriating face. "I doubt I will. She likes to touch you, and talk about your body."

"Would it make you feel better to know that she's a gold star lesbian, and a dominant herself? She and I are as about as platonic as a male and a female can be."

I blushed impossibly harder, feeling silly and ridiculous suddenly. Because it did make me feel better to know that.

Worlds better. I was a fool.

"What is a gold star lesbian?" I asked him.

"Never been with a man, never even thought about it. *She* liked *you*, I could tell. I should probably be the jealous one, with the way she was looking at you. But I'm not. She's too good of a friend. She may be envious of what we have, but she would never cross a line. She knows that you're important to me."

"I-I wouldn't-even if she wanted to," I stammered, feeling flustered at where the conversation had gone.

Did he think I would be submissive to any dom? I didn't understand that, and I was just too embarrassed to ask. I wasn't just interested in James because he could dominate me. I wondered, for the first time, if he felt that I used him for only that aspect of himself. I wanted to ask him, but the words just wouldn't come out. I never felt used by him, and I had just assumed that a man so perfect and confident couldn't feel used. Not by someone like me.

He kissed my hand softly as we pulled up to my house. "I know. But in some circles, having a dom so much as approach your sub is a huge breach of conduct. It's not something you have to worry about. And I don't feel threatened by Frankie. It would please me if you two could be friends, actually. Would you be willing to go have dinner with her sometime? The three of us, I mean."

I felt a little mortified. I had very nearly been openly rude to the woman. "If she still wants to, I would be willing to. I feel like a fool. I was so jealous of her. I thought for sure you two had been lovers."

He just smiled that smug smile again as he ushered me out of the car. "She won't be fazed by that. I'll set it up."

I had only thirty minutes to get ready once we walked in the door. I hurried, packing up my suitcase before moving to get dressed.

I had just slipped off my bra, grabbing the one I preferred for work, when James pressed up behind me. He had already changed into dark blue slacks and a pale blue polo that hugged his chiseled torso distractingly. He had been ready before I'd even finished packing. He gripped my breasts, kneading at the supple globes. He moved his fingers to my nipples, twisting them almost cruelly.

I gasped, arching my back. He released the captive flesh abruptly. I felt him digging into his pocket, still pressed hard against me. I looked down at my quivering breasts while he fastened nipple clamps to each hardened crest.

He slapped my ass, hard, before stepping away. "Okay, get dressed. And don't even think of taking those off. I'm driving you and Stephan to work. He's already ready and waiting."

"Won't you be late for the flight if you drop us off first?"

He just gave me a look. "I'll make it. But you need to quit arguing and get dressed. If I have to take the time to spank you, then we'll both be late."

I scrambled into my clothes, double checking my suitcase to make sure I had everything.

"Remember, you don't need to pack for New York anymore. You're all set up there, and you can buy anything you want, if I overlooked something. By the way, I was a little distracted, but your hair looks lovely. I like the cut. It brings out those devastating eyes of yours."

I shot him a look. He thought *my* eyes were devastating? The irony wasn't lost on me, his exquisite turquoise gaze captivating me at a glance.

"Thank you. Thank you for the spa day. It was a very nice treat for my friends and I."

"Anytime. You can take them as often as you like. The staff knows that you have carte blanche status. You don't need an appointment, or even to call ahead, though it's never a bad idea to give them a heads-up. Everything that's mine is yours, love. I mean that in every sense you could imagine. Feel free to test it."

I straightened my tie as he spoke, feeling the clamps on my heavy breasts acutely.

I moved to my vanity, clasping my watch over the angry marks on one wrist. I studied the other one, wondering how to cover it. It really wasn't even uncomfortable. It just looked rather conspicuous. As I studied it, James circled it with long fingers, reaching into my silver jewelry box. He pulled a smaller box out of it that I hadn't even noticed before. He opened it, showing a platinum bracelet that closely matched the band pattern of the rolex he'd given me.

"You're shackled and collared, my love," James said as he fastened it onto my wrist. They did indeed look like shackles, I thought, as he led me from the house, pulling my suitcase. "Do they chafe your wrists too badly?"

"No, not at all. My wrists aren't bothering me at all."

"Good. I have plans for you. We get to spend some time in our playground tomorrow, before we have to get ready for the gala."

I had nearly forgotten about the gala. He had swept me up so thoroughly from the moment we had reunited, I had forgotten about everything save for my Mr. Beautiful.

Stephan started in on James almost the moment we all got into the car. "Bianca thought that tattoo and piercing thing was a joke. You can't hold her to it, James," he said, looking ready for an argument.

James smiled. Contrarily, it was a rather fond smile, and all for Stephan. "I wouldn't dream of it, Stephan. Bianca, would I hold you to doing something like that, if you didn't want to?"

I shook my head, giving Stephan an exasperated look. I was blushing involuntarily. I sooo didn't want to talk about things like that with Stephan, especially not in front of James. "Stephan, he knows I thought it was a joke. Please don't get upset about it. James is crazy, that's all."

Stephan gave a very heartfelt sigh of relief. He had been dreading the confrontation, but had obviously felt a strong need to say something. "Okay, okay. Sorry, I just saw those tattoos, and remembered what you two had said at the bar. I didn't know you had it in you, James."

James grinned, hugging me to him. He kissed my forehead rather sweetly. "I didn't, not until I met my perfect Bianca."

CHAPTER TWENTY-FOUR

The flight was an agonizing ordeal. Every time my aching breasts pulled or strained at the clamps, which was constantly, I thought of James, and it left me yearning and hot but still with a job to do.

It was a full flight, the only empty seat the one next to James, as was his habit.

I rushed and served and passed him again and again, my sensitized breasts sending little jolts right to my sex every time I so much as thought of him.

He barely glanced at me, working on his laptop. He didn't even look up as I asked him direct questions, just gave brief answers, his bored gaze on the screen of his laptop. He was the disinterested master tonight. It made me want to scream, I was so agitated and keyed up. I wanted to hit him, I was so frustrated. The fact that he wouldn't even look at me drove me crazy.

It was nearly two hours into the flight before the cabin began to get quiet and sleepy. Most of the first class passengers were drinking heavily, so I had been on my feet in the cabin, serving almost constantly.

Stephan headed back to help coach as soon as our regular

service was done. Javier was on the flight as a passenger, though he hadn't been able to snag a first class seat. Flying non-revenue, we only got first class seats when there was space available. He had been lucky to find a seat at all, since the flight had been overbooked. That would have been a waste, since he had taken days off to join Stephan on our layover.

My passengers were all taken care of, most falling asleep or already there. A few alert faces could be seen, but I was suddenly too desperate to care, my usual professional reserve escaping me in a brash moment.

I sat down in the empty seat next to James. I leaned over the console that separated the two seats, grabbing his wrist, pulling it from the keyboard of his laptop. Finally, he looked at me.

His gaze was amused, and I wanted to scream. "No touching, Bianca. That's an order."

I dropped his wrist like it was on fire, breathing heavily as I glared at him. His smiling eyes were wickedly infuriating. I tried to compose myself, tried to smooth my features. I knew I failed. "Please, Mr. Cavendish, I'm desperate. Why are you ignoring me? You've put these...things on me, and I can't think of anything but you. Meet me in the restroom. I need you to touch me."

He shook his head, still just looking amused. "Not tonight, Bianca."

I clasped my hands together tightly, nearly overwhelmed with the urge to touch him. "Are you punishing me?"

He ran his tongue across those perfect teeth. My sex clenched, and I felt a rush of moisture between my legs. "No. Just teaching you. Sometimes we have to wait for what we want. I have been extremely lax in this part of your instruction, but you need to learn."

"I'm so wet, James. And I think if you just keep talking, your voice alone could make me come. Please."

His eyes turned a little hard. "You won't entice me into changing my mind, you little vixen. You'll be punished if you try that again."

I wanted that punishment, wanted it badly, but I wanted to please him more. "I can't bear this. What should I do, Mr. Cavendish? I could go into the bathroom and pleasure myself. It's not what I want, but I think it would help."

His eyes narrowed into an almost mean glare. "No. You're not allowed to touch yourself, either." His eyes moved to a spot behind my seat. "You need to move, Bianca. That seat is spoken for."

I got up, moving away, feeling baffled and bereft. I noted absently that Javier took the vacated seat, giving me a polite nod. I nodded back, moving away as Stephan stepped in close to them, thanking James for relinquishing his extra seat.

That was nice of him, I thought absently. James began to chat amiably with Javier, not sparing me another glance.

I went into the galley, not knowing what to do with myself. I took off my serving vest, leaving just my white dress shirt and tie. My nipples stood out like sore thumbs with the clamps on them in such a thin shirt. I decided I didn't care. I wanted James to see how conspicuous they were, how impossible to ignore. He had left me wanting, and seemed unaffected himself. I wanted to affect him.

I returned to Javier, asking him politely if he needed anything. I felt James's gaze on me then, since I had interrupted their polite small talk.

"Just a bottle of water, please. Thank you, Bianca," Javier said with a smile.

I smiled back, not looking at James. I turned away, heading back to the front of the plane.

"Bianca," James called, his voice very casual.

I looked at him over my shoulder, my brow arched.

"Put your vest back on, Love. Now." James gave me a bland smile, as though he hadn't just given me an arbitrary order in front of Javier, in front of strangers.

I fumed as I went back into the galley. I hadn't gotten around to putting my vest back on when Damien stepped out of the cockpit to use the restroom. He stepped into my galley when he saw me, smiling warmly. I had seen him briefly on the crew bus, but we had been in too big of a hurry to chat. His smile dropped a little when he saw that I was visibly agitated.

"Everything all right?" he asked, concern in his voice.

I just nodded, meeting his eyes while I took deep breaths. I should have realized that the action would accentuate my conspicuous breasts, but I didn't, not until his eyes roamed there, widening when they saw the outline of my clamped nipples. I didn't think he could see the actual clamps, but I really wasn't sure. I thought he must have just seen my over exaggerated nipples. Whatever he saw, it seemed to freeze him in place. He couldn't seem to look away from my chest.

He put a hand on my shoulder, licking his lips nervously. "Can I help you with anything?" he asked in a low voice.

I just shook my head, still looking at him. I didn't remove his hand, didn't think of it. My mind wasn't working right. I knew that James wasn't touching me, but all I could think about were his hands on me. So while I knew that it was Damien's hand on me, it felt almost as if James was touching me. And besides, it was only my shoulder he was touching. But I was in a state.

"Kindly remove that hand, Damien. Shouldn't you be flying the plane or something?" James asked, stepping into the galley. His voice was cold as ice. I didn't have to look at his eyes to know that they would be the same.

Damien pulled his hand back, eyes wide, looking as though he'd been doing something much worse than just touching my shoulder. He mumbled an agreement, backing off and going into the lavatory.

I felt more than saw James moving to me. He plucked my vest from where it hung on an open cabinet, holding it out for me to slip into. I did so without a word, not looking at him.

"What was that, Bianca? Do you want him? Explain it to me." His voice was still so cold. I was intimated and...embarrassed.

"I-I don't want him. I think he was just caught off-guard. And I...I was just distracted, thinking about you. I know he was standing right in front of me, but I couldn't seem to focus on him."

James gripped my hair at the nape, the only place he touched me, pulling my head back to look up and squarely into his eyes. They were more shuttered than I would have guessed. Whatever he was feeling, I couldn't have guessed it from his face.

"I told you this wasn't a punishment, Bianca, but it is now." He pulled my hair hard enough to make me gasp. His voice was strangely blank. "It will be better or worse, depending on your answer. Were you trying to make me jealous by letting him touch you, or are you drawn to him? Do you want him, just a little?"

I mulled it over, wanting to give him the most honest answer, dreading the punishment, when it was this overwhelming depravation. "I was too involved with my own thoughts to react to what he was doing. I think I would have reacted, would have pulled away, if he had touched more than my shoulder, but he didn't, so I didn't. I just don't think of him like that."

I was relishing his hands on me, even with this limited contact, as I continued breathlessly. "He doesn't feel like a threat, and I've never even thought about having sex with him. I couldn't tell you why. I can see that he's good looking, and I value him as a friend. He's funny, and charming, and nice, but I've only ever had platonic feelings. Perhaps it's something like how you feel about Frankie. For all I know, he's another submissive. That may be why I could only see him as a friend."

He studied me for the longest time, his eyes still shuddered, but if I had to guess, I would say that he was feeling hurt and worried.

"I like your answer," he finally said. "I can't tell if I believe it because I want so desperately to, or because it's the truth. You'll still be punished, but I won't draw it out like I was planning to when I saw his hand on you. Don't let it happen again." With that, he walked away.

The rest of the flight was long and James wouldn't so much as spare me a glance. When he deprived me, he deprived me of everything, even his beautiful eyes, and that intense regard that I had come to adore and depend on so helplessly. I hadn't realized how much I craved even his stare, how it made me feel less empty, less cold. He was the sun, and when he turned away, I felt so cold and empty, so achy and wanting.

I hadn't realized it before. Is that why I was getting this lesson? Had he known the extent of his affect on me, and known how to show me just how much I needed him to want me, needed him to show me.

The depravation of his physical affection affected me first, but I thought that the emotional withdrawal from him was by far more devastating. And I wouldn't have realized it, wouldn't have realized how generously he had always tended to my emotional needs, until he had set my body on fire and withdrawn from me completely. It was a revelation.

He was a generous man. I had never doubted it. But I had never given him credit for being so generous with his emotions and feelings. They were things I never would have realized I needed so desperately until he'd lavished me with them, and then suddenly taken them away. How long would I feel the loss? How long would he put me through purgatory? It had only been hours so far that he had left me wanting, but I didn't know that I could bear much more of it.

I wanted to bask in the sun again.

CHAPTER TWENTY-FIVE

"We're going directly to my house," James told me as he walked with my crew through the airport.

He wasn't touching me, but pulled my bag. He would barely look at me, though his tone and posture seemed relaxed.

I had gone past the point of only wanting him to make me come, to ease the ache that traveled from my tortured nipples and directly to my sex. Now I wanted his affection, his attention. I wanted him to hold me. It made me almost angry, that he would make me so needy with so little effort on his part. But even anger didn't change the wanting.

It took me a moment to process his words. We were trailing behind my crew. Melissa cast me sharp glances, as though we were slowing them down. I ignored her. It seemed the best way to deal with her in general.

"I could get into trouble for that," I told him, my voice pitched low. "We're supposed to ride with the crew to the hotel, and check in there."

"I spoke to Stephan. He looked it up in the manual. The exact wording is, 'at the discretion of your lead'. Stephan is your lead. He gave you the thumbs up. You're coming with me."

I didn't argue, didn't respond. I wanted to get to his house. I didn't know what he had planned, but I was sure that the sooner we got there, the sooner this torture would end.

I waved goodbye to most of the crew at the curb, only giving Stephan a quick hug and kiss.

"Call me if you need anything, Buttercup," he said into my ear, then let me go.

I scooted in close against James, nearly touching hips when we got into his town car.

I spoke into his ear, since the privacy screen was down and I didn't recognize the driver. "This is more than delayed gratification. You're depriving me of every part of you. You'll barely look at me."

"Not in the car," he said, looking out the window and dismissing me.

I felt stung.

"What is the punishment for touching you?" I asked him after several minutes of complete silence. I was past the point of only wanting to please him. If it was a punishment I could stand, I was willing to risk his displeasure. He had brought me to that point.

"A simple one. If you touch me, I won't touch you," he said, his tone idle.

It was like a slap in the face. I averted my face, tears stinging my eyes. It felt like a rejection, something I'd never experienced even a hint of from James.

It was a long and silent drive into Manhattan. The clamps on my nipples were a constant ache. I had resorted to trying to hold perfectly still, since every movement further agitated the sensual torture.

I wanted to say mean things to him, hurtful things that might goad him into touching me, but I refrained. I didn't want to cause him to stay this withdrawn from me. I knew that the more I cooperated, the sooner I would get *my* James back.

Finally, the unfamiliar driver dropped us off in the underground garage I'd been in once before, on my first visit to James's Manhattan penthouse.

He took my suitcase out of the trunk, inclining his head at us. "Sir, Ms. Karlsson. I'll be here at 9:00 p.m to pick you up for the charity event."

James just nodded, dismissing the man. He pulled my suitcase to the elevator, still barely acknowledging my presence.

I lowered my chin, my posture rigid, standing very still in my work heels. My gaze seemed glued to his navy dress shoes. They were sexy. I thought sullenly that even his feet held a sort of elegance.

The elevator car arrived, the door sliding open silently. James stepped inside.

I hesitated, still just watching his feet, wanting some sign from him that he even remembered my presence.

He sighed, the softest sound, and reached a hand to me. I watched, transfixed, as his hand went to the collar of my work shirt. He used one finger to fish out the hoop at my throat. He managed not to touch even an inch of my skin, pulling me forward by just that diamond-studded circle. He led me into the car, keeping his finger crooked into my collar as he slid in his card, pushed the button, and we began to ascend.

"My perfect little submissive," he murmured, and that was all. I sopped up even that little bit of his jaded attention.

He led me into his opulent home by that one finger on my collar. I was as lost in the maze of rooms as I had been the first time, as he led me to the kitchen. He only let go of the collar when we encountered an unfamiliar woman prepping food next to the oversized stovetop. She was plump and middle-aged, with light brown hair and kind brown eyes that I noticed the moment she turned to greet us.

She smiled. It was a good smile, warm and sweet. "Mr. Cavendish, Ms. Karlsson, good morning. How was your flight?"

"Very good, thank you. Bianca, this is Marion. She's our new housekeeper and cook."

I blinked my eyes a few times, wondering if I was seeing things when she bobbed us a little curtsy. "I'm looking forward to working for you, Ms. Karlsson. It's nice to finally meet you. Please let me know if you need anything. Anything at all."

I processed their words, the way they both implied that she was somehow working for me. It was a baffling development, but I didn't comment.

"I'm making you vegetable omelets with feta, as you requested, Mr. Cavendish. Is there anything I can do for you?"

"We will be in the dining room, Marion. Just serve the omelets when they're ready. That will be all." James held the door open for me, and I moved into his grand dining room. He pulled a chair out for me and I sat. He took the seat next to me at the head of the table. He stapled his elegant fingers together on top of the heavy table.

I watched those hands as I spoke. "What happened to the other housekeeper?"

"I had to let her go. She proved to be...unprofessional. She seemed to think that, because she had worked for me for eight years, she could interfere in my personal life. I found some of her actions and words unacceptable."

I mulled that over for awhile, still watching his hands. Even those hands were like eye candy.

"She seemed like an unpleasant woman, though she and Jules appeared to be close," I said absently. "She was pleasant enough to her."

I watched his hands squeeze together very tightly as I spoke. "Yes. And that was the problem. She let her into my home against my wishes, and then she made the fatal mistake of insulting you, Love. I fired her that night."

I took a deep breath, savoring that light endearment. I was starved for his affection.

Marion served us quickly, withdrawing with a smile. We ate the delicious omelets in silence. James finished before me. I could feel him watching me as I took a drink of water. He stood the instant I swallowed my last bite. He led me by the collar through the multi-floored penthouse, heading to his bedroom without further ado.

I was more than happy to go. I had been living in a world of tortured anticipation since he had pinched on my nipple clamps, just waiting for him to get me alone like this.

He took me into his colossal bedroom closet.

"Take off your clothes," he commanded, shrugging out of his shirt, his back to me. I obeyed without a word, taking off everything but my jewelry. He took off my watch and cuff, putting them on a little tray on the huge dresser in his closet. My eyes had moved to his feet as soon as I was undressed. He was barefoot now, wearing only his slacks. I thought about how even his tan feet were sexy.

He threaded a silver chain through the hoop at my collar. It attached to each of my nipple clamps, raising my nipples.

I winced, rubbing my thighs together restlessly.

He fastened a sheer black half-slip over my hips. I had worn it just once before, in his playground. It covered nothing, but the sight of it turned me on. It made my body look sinful, with just that touch of black. I bit my lip, arching my back a little.

To say I was turned on was a vast understatement. I was so far past that point. I raised my gaze just enough to see the hard ridge pressing against the front of his navy slacks. I moaned at the sight of it.

"Don't try to tempt me, Bianca. You'll be punished for that.

Is that what you were trying to do?"

I shook my head, out of my mind with wanting him.

He led me by my collar to the elevator that went directly from his bedroom and into his private playground. I mewled at the cruel pressure that pulled at my nipples. He slapped my ass hard as we descended to his 4th floor. For making the noise, I thought.

He pulled a length of black cloth from his pocket, stepping behind me in the elevator. It was a blindfold, I realized, as he covered my eyes, tying it firmly in the back. The material was silky and luxuriously soft.

The elevator stopped, and he pulled me forward by the collar. Our footsteps seemed loud in the hallway, but the padded flooring once we got into the playroom made a softer, muffled sound. He led me only a few steps into the room before stopping.

"Get on your knees," he told me.

I obeyed, raising my chin. I heard him move away.

I heard him opening drawers across the room. Some sort of machinery whirred softly, the sound of chains clinking together following immediately, and I had no idea what would make such a noise.

I sat back on my heels, my hands flat on my thighs. I began to rub them slowly over my own skin as I waited, anticipation and fear a palpable feeling along my skin. As my hands rubbed, I shifted my arms, moving them against my breasts, pushing the round globes closer together to rub against each other, craving contact, even if it was just the contact of my own skin on itself.

"Stop that," James snapped from across the room. "If you pleasure yourself, then that's all you'll do. All you'll get is a dildo to relieve your ache, if you keep that up. Which would you prefer? My cock, or a dildo?"

I gasped, and stopped moving, though I wanted more than ever to move after hearing his words. "Your cock. Oh god, I want your cock, James."

"It's Mr. Cavendish, or Master, in here, Bianca."

"Yes, Mr. Cavendish."

There was a noise, like chains clinking together, and then he was pulling me to my feet by the collar. I gasped at the rough pull on my nipples. They seemed to be getting more sensitive, not less so, the longer those mean clamps stayed attached.

He pulled me across the padded floor. He pulled me maybe twenty feet before stopping abruptly. Finally he touched my skin, pulling my wrists together in front of me. The action rubbed my breasts together, and my back arched. He placed something soft around my wrists, closing it with a loud metal clink on first one wrist and then the other. Padded handcuffs, I thought.

He moved very close to me as he reached above me, pulling down a metal chain that clicked loudly with each link. He dragged the length along my cheek, my collar, against the side of one breast, and finally to my joined hands. He attached the chain rather noisily to the handcuffs, stepping away. I heard the links clinking again as the cuffs were raised above my head agonizingly slowly. My arms pulled up high until I was stretched taut onto the balls of my feet.

"Grip the chain," James told me.

I tried, but obviously did it wrong, because he adjusted my hands until I had a firm double grasp on the chain that held me up. He jerked suddenly on my neat little work braid, arching my head back. It pulled at the chain between my clamped nipples, as everything seemed to.

I whimpered loudly.

"I want you to be silent," James told me, his voice a hoarse rasp. "Don't make sexy little noises. Don't beg me to stop. Be as quiet as you can, unless you need to safe word."

CHAPTER TWENTY-SIX

I gave a little nod, since I couldn't speak. I felt him move away. He was gone for long minutes, and I felt bereft. I couldn't move or speak, because he'd ordered me not to, so only my mind was active. It was the most torturous part of all, as I imagined what he would do to me, what he was planning, and all I could do was wait.

Soft music began to play, the notes of a dark song drifting through the room. It had an ominous tune.

I didn't even sense him move but just suddenly felt something soft brush across the skin of my back. A feather, I realized, as he trailed it down my spine. He removed it, but it was instantly replaced by something else, something rougher, with thin strands that caught at my skin as he stroked it where the feather had been. The feather came back, stroking along my butt and down my thighs.

I shivered as he softly stroked it over the back of my knee and down to my foot. He moved the feather back up my body via the other leg. It covered every inch of the back of my body before he pulled back. The rougher object began to move across my skin, mirroring the feathers trail exactly. Where the feather had made me shiver all over, the rougher trail made me writhe, fighting to keep from making noise.

The rough little tails were absent, and the feather was back, brushing just below my shoulder blades. It lingered there, slowly whispering over that skin oh so carefully. The feather pulled away and the instant it left my skin he struck, flogging me with those rough little tails viciously.

I bit my lip so hard I tasted blood, my back arching, spine bowing.

He struck again and again, only striking those tender spots that the feather had paid such special attention to. My heart was trying to pound out of my chest, and tears ran down my cheeks silently but freely before he stopped.

I felt him unclip the tiny slip at my waist, felt it drop to the floor, the feather lightly caressing my naked ass. I wondered if he was timing the feather contact to the timing of the flogging. It seemed that way to me, and it was a torturous realization, because he lingered for the longest time on my rear, that soft feather relentless. Of the two touches, I thought the feather was the cruelest.

The feather's absence was immediately replaced by the sharp bite of the tails. It went on and on, striking again and again, and I began to move with the strikes, circling my hips, the pain taking my mind to a little fuzzy place, and I thought I would come if he so much as touched my sex.

I heard his ragged breaths when he replaced the tails with the feather on my thighs. When the feather touched my inner thigh, a scant breath from my sex, I nearly came. I didn't know if I could stop myself when the tiny whips replaced that cruel feather. I wondered, very briefly, if I would be punished for that.

My breaths were so ragged that I worried I would be punished for the noise when the tails replaced the feather, slapping at my sensitive thighs relentlessly.

My back bowed, my feet pushing on my toes as the whips hit that spot on my groin, and I came, gyrating on my chain and biting on my bloody lip. At least I had kept silent, if you didn't count my loud panting breaths.

"Fuck," James panted, and that was all. He replaced the little whips with a feather on my calves. This was a shorter touch, and a shorter flogging.

He seemed to finish with my back, stepping away. I felt him studying me for impossibly long minutes. My release had been involuntary, and done very little to ease the ache. My pulse still beat in time to the blood pounding in my veins and every inch of me wanted him inside of me, against me, touching me. My hips made little circling thrusts as he watched me.

Finally, I felt him moving to the front of my body. He studied my front for nearly as long as he had my back.

Abruptly, he released my breasts from the mean little clamps. I took deep breaths, counting to ten, trying to keep the noises in my throat. He began to move the feather along my front, starting with my cheek. He circled my lips with the feather.

He stopped abruptly, walking away. I wanted to scream at his abrupt absence, but he returned almost instantly, placing some type of strap against my mouth.

"Bite down on this if you need to," he ordered. "Don't bite your lip anymore. You'll need stitches if you keep that up." I bit it. It was an instant relief to have something firm to bite down on.

He started in on me with the feather again, covering the front of my body with those soft caresses. He mirrored the movement with the tiny whips. The pattern was already familiar, but still I agonized over what he would do next. The feather was back again, and I knew what to expect when the whips had a turn, every touch telling me sadistically just where and for how long I would get the attention of those mean little tails.

He softly caressed my upper thighs first, using his foot to

part my legs, snaking that little feather in dangerously close to my wet core. I felt the feather drag a little through the moisture there, and heard James suck in a gasp. But there was still no pause as he pulled back the feather and struck with the whip in almost the same motion, as though they were two sides of the same object. I wondered, rather distantly, if they were.

He struck my thighs again and again, stopping abruptly, but I knew that if I had been counting, it would have timed the same as the feather.

My head fell back, and I sucked in harsh breaths when the light touch made contact with my breasts. He caressed the fleshy globes for long moments, thankfully only briefly teasing at my tortured nipples. When he began to whip me there, I shuddered, my body on the brink of release when he stopped.

He stared at me for the longest time, until I heard him unzip his pants.

I wanted to sob in relief just at the sound.

He moved to my back. "That's enough of a lesson and a punishment, I think," he said, his voice rough and affected. Just how I wanted it.

His smooth chest moved against my back as he leaned into me from behind. "Grip the chains more tightly," he told me, his hard hands settling on my hips.

I obeyed eagerly.

"Arch your back. More."

I felt the tip of his cock at my entrance. It poised there for long moments, quivering against me. He entered me, but not how I wanted, not with a hard thrust, as I was wishing for. He worked his large length inside of me, inch by thick inch, working into my tight wet sheath agonizingly slowly. I wanted to cry. I wanted to beg.

His mouth moved to my ear. "Now you may beg me," he whispered, as though reading my mind.

I did beg, sobbing as I did so, the strap falling from my mouth, his permission acting as a floodgate. I begged with heartfelt feeling. He pulled out of me slowly when I'd finished. His mouth moved to the spot between my neck and shoulder, right on the tendon, that perfect sensitive spot, and he bit down savagely at the same moment that he plunged into me, hammering into me with the hardest, fastest thrust. It was a wonderful, brutal angle, my hips held immobile in his hands. I had no way to move with him or away from him, even my toes lifted slightly off the floor.

He bottomed out in me, reaching the end of me with a vicious twist of his hips.

He was making this perfect little noise low in his throat, deep but almost helpless, as though he couldn't believe what was happening every time he slammed into the end of me. The third time he made that noise, I came, screaming.

He didn't stop, still pounding , one hand snaking from my hip and up over my tortured breast. It hurt, my skin raw, but that pain seemed to jolt directly from my breast to deep inside my sex, where his stiff cock still worked furiously.

The second release caught me like that, a mix of pleasure and pain, jolting through the parts of my body that he played like an instrument. I was perfectly tuned, but only to his expert touch.

His thrusts stuttered for a moment, the hand at my hip sliding forward from my hip and his finger began to circle my clit. He resumed his pace, the arm now anchored over me from waist to pelvis and his other hand still a vise on my breast. His hardness rocked into me with that furious pace.

He slammed, slammed, slammed, his breathing harsh and ragged enough that I could hear it over my own uncontrollable mewling.

"Come," he ordered roughly.

I shuddered as the waves of pleasure took me for a third

time. He allowed himself to come with me that time, and I felt him shuddering and pouring inside of me, making those sounds I loved deep in his throat.

His hard arms wrapped around my waist, his cheek touching the top of my head.

Was the tender lover back? I wanted that, had never wanted it more. I needed some reassurance that this coldness that had overtaken him wasn't permanent. Only a night of it and I felt emotionally bereft. But he released me quickly, pulling out of me, and I heard the chains clanking together as my arms went a little slack. It put me more solidly onto my feet, but my knees gave way almost instantly. The cuffs caught me right away, since he'd only lowered me a few inches.

"Get your balance back. Get some weight onto your feet," James ordered, lowering the chain a few more inches.

I put more weight on my feet, catching my balance slowly, shifting from foot to foot until I felt like I could stand without aid. It took awhile.

He unwound the chains above me until I was taking all of my weight. He unlatched my cuffed hands. I didn't have to hold my own weight for more than a split second before he swept me off my feet, cradling me like a child as he carried me across the room.

I stroked my cheek along his bare, sweaty chest. He felt divine. He smelled divine.

He laid me down on a firmly cushioned surface. It felt like being on an examination table at the doctors office. I hadn't seen anything like it the last time I'd been in his playground, but I'd only been there once before, and I'd been more than a little distracted at the time

He drew my cuffed hands above my head, fastening them there. I tested the restraint. I didn't even have an inch of slack. He fastened my feet to the bottom of the table, parted slightly. He used soft straps of some kind on each of my ankles, though I couldn't have said what they were. I was still blindfolded, and it wasn't anything he'd ever used on me before. I tested those restraints as well. There was no give at all. He definitely couldn't fuck me in this position. My legs wouldn't part far enough with the way I was bound.

I writhed a little at that realization, suddenly afraid of what he *did* plan to do.

He slapped the front of my thigh, hard. "Don't move," he ordered, his voice all dominance, with no hint of affection.

My tender lover was still missing. I didn't think there was anything that I wouldn't endure to get him back.

CHAPTER TWENTY-SEVEN

A little shriek escaped my lips as I felt cold metal grip one of my nipples firmly.

I felt James untying my blindfold, and suddenly I could see again. He had what looked like tiny smooth metal forceps holding my nipple captive. The end was a small hoop that fit perfectly around my hardened nipple. He reached into a drawer inside the table with his free hand, pulling out a marker. He bent close to my chest as he carefully marked my nipple on both sides.

His hands were covered in latex gloves that I hadn't heard him put on, though he must have done so sometime since he had bound me to the table. His eyes were intent, studying the marks he'd made. Finally, he put the pen away, pulling out a thick needle with a sharpened end. I could see that it was hollowed out in the middle, but I was still surprised at how big it was, how intimidatingly thick.

He smiled slightly as he saw my eyes widen as I studied the needle. "You ready to be pierced?" he asked, his voice wicked.

I studied him. He still wore his slacks, though the top button was undone. He was shirtless, and I could see my name in crimson over his heart. Somehow, I had almost forgotten about his new tattoos. The crimson lettering was startling and lovely against all of his golden skin.

He had his hair tied back, the first time I had seen him do that, so he could work on the piercing without his hair in his eyes. Some people were more beautiful with hair framing their faces, but it didn't matter with James. He was exquisite even without all of that caramel hair falling artfully into his face. His face was just too perfect for it to affect his looks either way.

"You're so beautiful," I told him. I couldn't seem to keep it in.

He sent me a very hot glance. He loved my admiration, I could tell. Even in this cold mood, he wasn't immune. "You think flattery will distract me?"

I blinked at him. It wasn't flattery. It was fact. "You're magnificent."

He didn't respond, just pulled my nipple taut with the tongs, digging the thick needle into my skin. I held my breath, waiting for him to drive it in. I couldn't seem to look away.

He surprised me when he pulled back, opening the drawer underneath me and dropping the needle and forceps inside. By the look on his face, he'd surprised himself.

He stripped off the latex gloves, tossing them aside. His eyes were on my breasts as he bent down to me, sucking on the abused nipples. He did it with singleminded focus, drawing on the flesh like his life depended on it.

I writhed beneath his ministrations, though my movements were hampered considerably. My head was bent forward as far as it would go and I watched him. His eyes were closed as he suckled there. His hands cupped my breasts from the sides, pushing them close together. He moved to my other breast, opening his eyes to gaze up at me, watching me as he very deliberately lapped at the flesh and then sucked so hard that a shudder went through my body, the sensation causing a shock of pleasure to shoot directly to my core.

He didn't lift his head when he spoke, his breath punching at my skin, his eyes steady and heavy-lidded on mine. "I'm going to drink your milk like this when you breastfeed our children." He bent down and began to suck again, drawing at it with hard suction, as though the large globes were already filled with milk. His words made my sex clench.

I told myself to reprimand him for saying something so outrageous. To imply that we would have children was stepping over a line, and saying that he would nurse on me like a babe, well, that was just wrong, but my body didn't care. It thrived on any kinky thing that came out of his mouth.

He straightened. My hips were making little twisting motions even as he pulled away. He watched them, his eyes almost lazy, the lids were so heavy.

"I can't pierce you yet. I won't be able to suck on your nipples, or even play with them, while the piercings heal. That will take months. I just can't bear to do it yet. Perhaps in a week or two." He released my ankles as he spoke, and then my arms, swiftly releasing my cuffs. It always amazed me how quickly he untied my restraints, as though he'd been trained to do it. For all I knew, he had.

He cradled me against him. "Put your arms around my neck, Love," he murmured, striding from the room.

Even his voice had changed. It had softened between one moment and the next. The tender lover was back. My James was back.

"I missed you," I murmured against his sweaty chest.

He gazed down at me, and I could see real surprise in his eyes as he stepped into the elevator car. "I can't shirk my duties to you, as your dom. I know what you need, Bianca. And I need you to know that no one else can give it to you like I can." He punched the button, and we began to ascend as he spoke.

I wanted to respond, but he gripped my hair and leaned down to kiss me. It was a desperate kind of kiss, not altogether practiced. He ate at my mouth like he was starving for me, as though the distance he had put between us had affected him as well. He licked at my mouth, sucking at my injured bottom lip.

It hurt, but I didn't mind hurting, and I kissed him back with all of the pent-up longing he had built in me over the cold evening. There was so much I wanted to tell him, about my feelings, about his, and I tried to put it into the kiss. I was much better at communicating my feelings to him in this manner.

The elevator stopped and he stepped off, still kissing me, as he strode to his beautiful bed. He laid me on it, pulling away to push his slacks off impatiently. It took the briefest moment, and he was back, arranging me in the middle of the bed.

He parted my legs wide, moving his hips between them, lowering his chest to mine. He was propped up slightly on his elbows, and he moved those elbows almost into my armpits so he could cup my face as he stared down at me.

His eyes were so tender and soft that an embarrassing tear slid down my cheek. His thumb caught it, and he pressed his thick arousal against my sex, pressing that first perfect inch inside of me. He entered me very slowly at first, though I was slick from arousal and the shared fluids from our last bout of fucking.

"I missed you," I told him again, and he groaned, moving into me more forcefully, but with the smoothest strokes.

"I'm glad," he told me with the softest smile. "I'm relieved that you want more than just the dominant side of me."

I wanted so badly right then to tell him that I loved him, but the words wouldn't form past the lump in my throat. I kissed him instead, gripping my hands in his silky hair and pulling him down to me.

He seemed pleased with that, kissing me back with a moan.

His thrusts increased into that steady pounding that he'd taught me to love, and I melted under him, an exquisite orgasm building inside of me. I cried out into his mouth as I came, and he joined me, his own cries just as loud, just as desperate, as mine had been.

"You're mine," he told me, but it was a tender admission that time.

He crushed me under him when we'd finished, as though he didn't even have the energy to roll off of me, when he was the most inexhaustible of men.

I didn't complain, even though it was a bit of a struggle to breath like that. But I liked his weight on top of me. I relished it. When he did finally roll off of me, it was only to lay plastered to my side, a heavy arm thrown over me.

We didn't speak for long minutes, and I felt a sleepy fog invading my senses. But something was nagging at me, a persistent thought that I wanted to clear between us before exhaustion took me.

"Do you feel used by me?" I asked him suddenly.

He rose on an elbow to meet my eyes squarely. His studied mine, looking sad. It made me feel a little sad just to see it.

"I don't," he said after a long pause. "I worry that you don't care for me, not like I care for you. I worry that you aren't able to return my feelings. And I realize that, for the first time in my life, I would let you use me, however you wanted, if it came to that. If that's all I could get from you, I would take it."

I stroked his cheek, feeling an almost uncontrollable need to reassure him. "I do care for you. It scares me sometimes, the way I feel." My voice was a whisper. It was all I could manage.

His eyes closed and he pressed his cheek into my hand, looking relieved but still almost anguished, all at once. It was hard to look at him, his face was so raw with emotions.

"Then live with me," he said softly. "Be with me. Swear you'll never leave me."

I sighed heavily, but I knew him well enough to know that he couldn't help but be so demanding. I'd given him a confession of sorts, and it was his first and strongest instinct to press forward and use it to his advantage. I had known, just known, that he would. When I gave, he took more, it was what both drew me to him, and terrified me about him.

"We need to be rational adults about this, James. Let's start by trying to be together, trying to spend time together, when we can. I think that's a good start. So, yes to the 'be with you' part. We'll see on the rest."

He arranged me against him for sleep, spooning me from behind, both of us lying on our sides how we slept. "Move in with me. We'll be traveling so much that I'm not sure you'll notice the difference, but say you'll live with me. Just give me that much, and I'll relent from pressing you for more, for the moment."

Shockingly, his persistence actually just made me smile. That's when I knew that I was well and truly sated. Or perhaps that was just an excuse for my sudden weakness. I made a conscious effort not to analyze it to death, and just thought about his request. What would it mean, to live together? *It wasn't a permanent step, right?* I could always withdraw, if I panicked.

"I'm keeping my house. I worked my ass off for that house, and I'm keeping it," I told him, shocked even as the words left my mouth, because I knew how he would take them, and it was, amazingly, actually how I meant them.

His arms squeezed me almost painfully from behind. "Of course. We can stay there when we're in Las Vegas. Whatever you want. I'll sell the other house in Vegas, if you prefer, though we should probably keep it for the stables, if you want to keep riding."

I felt such a relief at my own acquiescence, at the world of relief that I heard in his voice and felt in his body, that it floored me. I had wanted this just as much as he had, I realized. I just hadn't allowed myself to admit it.

"I do want to keep riding," was all I said.

"Yes. Thank you, Bianca. You make me so happy. I never knew life could be like this," he murmured into my hair. His voice was thick, as though with tears. I wasn't brave enough to look back and see.

"So now you can't propose, or do anything else crazy, since you said you'd relent if I agreed to live with you."

He stiffened slightly as I spoke, and I was right there with him. My words had been a joke, because of course he wouldn't propose, but they had made him tense up. *That* made *me* tense up.

"How long do I have to wait, then?" he asked, his tone earnest. "Give me a time frame, and I'll respect it."

The word 'forever' wanted to shoot out of my mouth, but I counted to ten, trying not to panic. "I can't give you a time frame, James. I can't even talk about it without having a panic attack. Let's just enjoy the living together part, ok?"

He nuzzled against my hair, burrowing deep until he'd moved all the way into my neck. He kissed me there. "We'll talk about it another time. I'll give you time to grow accustomed to the idea."

My exhausted body began to drift off, but not before I had the clear thought that he had somehow managed to get me to agree to one huge concession and still insisted on gaining some ground on yet another.

Impossible, dominant man.

CHAPTER TWENTY-EIGHT

I blinked awake slowly. James was still spooned tightly behind me. And he had apparently been the thing that woke me up, as he murmured softly into my ear. He was saying sweet little things, an apology in his soft tone. "I'm sorry, my love. I'd let you sleep longer, I'd stay like this forever if I could, but I have to go to this thing, and I can't bring myself to leave you. Please wake up."

"I'm awake," I told him in a voice rusty from sleep.

He kissed my hair. "Good." He sat up, slipping away.

I made a loud sound of protest at his absence.

He laughed, and it was a carefree, happy sound.

I felt my face soften, my whole body softened, and a tender smile took over my face. Hearing such a happy sound come out of James made me happy. How not? I couldn't imagine being immune to him.

I sat up sluggishly, watching him stride naked to the door of the bedroom. I was naked myself, and couldn't even bring myself to cover up as I sat up, sitting cross-legged and just watching him move.

He opened the door, bent down and picked up a large

covered tray. He shut the door again with his foot, carrying the tray to a large heavy dresser and setting it on top. He took off the lid, picking up two large plates and moving back to the bed. He handed me one, sitting close to me, cross-legged, to dig into his own.

It was a small portion of lightly seasoned salmon with a small cucumber ginger salad on the side. James scarfed it down in a few large bites, and I didn't take much longer to finish mine.

"This feels decadent, eating in your bed," I told him between bites.

He took my plate from me, smiling. He fed me the last few bites himself. "Our bed, love. Everything is ours now, remember."

I gave him an arch look. That was something I didn't think I'd ever really agree with. What was his was his. I felt no ownership for any of it, and couldn't imagine a time when I would. But I knew it was pointless to argue with him, and I really wasn't in the mood to, so I kept my silence.

James discarded our cleaned plates on the tray, covering it and shoving it back out of the room.

He dragged me into the bathroom, and then the shower, speaking more to me with smiles than words. He washed me as he washed himself, as though I was an extension of him. He even shampooed our hair at the same time, lathering my hair and then his. It was a strange thing, having someone tend to me like that, but I knew it was his preference, and I was growing to love it, as I loved everything he did to me.

He even lathered up my underarms and legs, shaving me expertly, bending down under the showers hard spray, without a qualm, to shave my legs. He even had and used the razor I preferred. The man didn't miss a trick.

It was a quick shower, though it felt luxurious. He toweled us both dry afterwards, touching all of the marks he'd made on my body as he did so. He had insisted on leaving my choker on, even to shower, and he dried it carefully and thoroughly.

His eyes were enigmatic. If I read him right, he both loved and hated the marks he'd made on my body. The angry little marks both fascinated and worried him. He pulled me to the bed, laying me down to rub nearly every inch of me with a creamy lotion.

"This is not the thing to start if you want us to leave your house tonight," I told him rather breathlessly.

He smiled wickedly. "This is actually me *not* starting anything. And it's our house."

Impossible man.

He even dressed me, though not in much. He slid me into a tiny black thong, a strapless black bra, and a very short, very sheer black slip. He put on the large diamond hoop earrings that matched my collar.

"Did you see the changes I made to our room since the last time you saw it?" James asked as he pulled the slip over my head. He pulled on a pair of low slung black athletic shorts, his chest bare.

I glanced around. I hadn't noticed much of anything since I'd come to his house. I had been more than a little distracted, with eyes only for James.

I saw my paintings almost immediately, once I started looking. He had two of my self-portraits beautifully framed and hanging facing his bed. I didn't know how I hadn't seen them before then. They were the most conspicuous pictures on his wall, positioned for a clear view from his bed.

"They kept me company when I was missing you. Your larger self portrait is hanging above our fireplace in the main living space downstairs. The others are in the bedrooms of our other properties. And the nude is in our playground."

"I didn't see it," I told him. That was understandable, I supposed, since I'd been blindfolded for most of our activities.

"You will next time. And I replaced the mattress and all of the bedding. You said you didn't want me to replace the beds, so as you see, they stayed. Also, if you didn't notice, most of the playground was redone."

I took some deep breaths, trying to process his actions. It was all very sweet, and my heart felt like it was twisting in my chest to think of all he had done for me, but my first instinct was to panic.

I counted and breathed and tried to react calmly and reasonably. "That was very thoughtful, James. You didn't have to do all of that."

"I wanted to. We need to get moving. First, we're meeting with the dresser so you can pick out a dress. You'll get your hair and makeup done while she makes any adjustments that might be needed." As he spoke, he pulled me from the room.

I dug in my heels almost immediately. "You aren't wearing a shirt. There are people in the house? You'll give someone a heart attack like that, James."

He completely ignored me, and I got quickly distracted as I caught a glimpse of the tattoo on his back. It was still so shocking to me, and so lovely. A thought occurred to me. "Are you just showing off your new tats to anyone you can?"

He flashed me a grin. It didn't tell me much of anything. He was just happy in general, and he wasn't putting a shirt on anytime soon.

We stayed on the third floor, but walked down the long hallway. He pulled me into the room closest to the stairs. It was a very sparsely furnished guest bedroom decorated in blue. There were racks of dresses everywhere, nearly overwhelming the large room.

"James, is that you?" a voice called from what must have been the closet.

"Yes, Jackie," he called back.

A small, black-haired woman walked out of the closet, clutching hangers full of colorful dresses in each hand. She grinned at us.

She was beautiful, with sleek, long black hair pulled back from her stunning face. Her dark eyes were almond shaped and vibrant, with heavy violet eye shadow that brought out her olive skin to perfection. Her lips were pure crimson and the shade suited her coloring. She was one of those people who could have been just about any race, but whatever it was, it was lovely.

She wore cute little eyeglasses on her nose that were so attractive that you had to wonder if they were just a fashion statement, or if she really required them. She wore an impeccably fitted emerald green sheath with a bright blue belt. Her shoes were five inch stilettos and hot pink. She wore a necklace of deep jewel-toned stones, with heavy gold hoops in her ears. Both of her wrists were heavy with intricate metal bangles.

She looked fashionable and intimidating, and though the outfit somehow worked beautifully, I could tell at a glance that she was a woman who wasn't afraid to try and fail at fashion. I was betting that she would think that not trying was the only way to fail. Her outfit was timeless elegance but still managed to be trendy. I was impressed. I would have been happy to achieve either of those things. It was ambitious to try for both.

She eyed me up and down without shame as James introduced me. "Jackie, this is Bianca. Bianca, Jackie. She's responsible for all of the new additions to your wardrobe."

She smiled at me rather expectantly. "What do you think? It's okay if you hate it all. I just need feedback, so I can get an idea of what you *do* like. James here is my favorite client of all time. He lets me dress him however I like. Can you imagine? It's every stylists dream, a supermodel of a client who will wear damn near anything I pick out." She eyed me critically as she spoke, as though mentally taking my measurements. She even began to circle me. I thought she was a strange little woman.

"I, uh, haven't had much of a chance to look at it."

She nodded, pursing her lips. "Well, when you do, any feedback would be good. It will give me some direction for your sense of style."

"Bianca likes the preppy look for men, Jackie," James told her. "Keep that in mind when you're shopping for me as well."

She snorted. "And so it begins." She sounded very put out by his request. "I'll keep it in mind."

I shot him a baffled look. Where did he come up with this stuff?

He shrugged at me, smiling a little. "You forget that Stephan and I talk."

She was still circling me, studying me rather unnervingly. "James had you right on, size-wise. A size 5/6 in the waist and hips, and a 7/8 in the bust and shoulders. You have a body that's fun for men to play with, but not too fun to dress. Your legs are a plus, though. There's nothing I love to dress more than a killer set of legs. If you lost about ten pounds, though, you could have model proportions. That would be ideal. Something to think about."

Some part of me agreed with her about the need to lose ten pounds, but it still stung to hear it. It was petty, but I had gone from kind of liking her to thinking she was awful in a few short sentences.

"Jackie," James said, a cool warning in his voice. "She doesn't need to lose a pound. If you talk her into a diet, I *will* fire you."

She just grinned, uncaring about the warning and my stiff expression. "Okay, okay, just a mild suggestion."

She laid the colorful armfuls of fabric onto the bed. "Based on your body type and skin tone, I picked out five dresses that I thought had the best shot of suiting you. Try them on, if you please, or anything else you see that catches your fancy." She seemed to dismiss me completely after she finished speaking, approaching James with wide eyes.

She stabbed the red ink on his chest. "When did this happen? It has to be brand new!"

He just grinned, turning to show her his back. She was struck speechless at the sight.

I turned my back on them, grabbing the dresses on the bed and heading into the closet to try them on, while they continued to chat.

You wouldn't have known it was a guest room if you were going by the closet. It was the size of a guest room all by itself, with mirrors lining every wall. I assumed this was the room where he usually worked with Jackie, going by the clothing, both male and female, lining the walls, tags intact.

I hung Jackie's choices on a bare stretch of racks, eyeing them up dubiously. They were gowns. I liked skirts and sundresses well enough if they were cool and comfortable, but I felt overwhelmed even trying on the gowns I was looking at now.

I took a deep breath, plunging in. I wouldn't let someone like Jackie see that I was intimidated by the clothes, or any of it, for that matter.

I grabbed a plain navy gown first. I could see by the cut of the top half that I wouldn't be wearing a slip with it, so I slipped out of it before working the silky material over my legs, hips, and finally my bust. It was a strapless gown, with a long slit up the side. It zipped in back, and I couldn't manage on my own. I almost took it off just because of that, but with a sigh, I stepped out of the closet to get a hand.

Jackie was still studying James's shoulder tattoo when I stepped out of the closet. He shot me a admiring smile. "That looks great."

I gave him a rather weak smile. The more I got ready for the gala, the more I felt a little overwhelmed by my misgivings. This was not my world, I didn't want it to be, and I didn't know if I could fake it, even for James.

"Can you zip me?" I asked him, my voice very stiff. He did, after all, have a strange woman running her fingers along his back.

He moved to me, completely ignoring Jackie's demand for him to hold still. He held the back together, zipping me in with more ease than I would have expected. The dress didn't have a bit of give in the silken fabric, and I'd thought it would be tighter.

I turned to the huge mirror mounted on the wall, approaching it to eye the gown with a critical eye. James followed me, watching my face more than anything. I thought he could sense my uncertainty.

I thought the dress looked nice enough. "It fits," I said flatly. "And it's actually long enough. That's pretty impressive, I suppose."

Jackie made a little humming sound in her throat. "They make them long like that, for heels. Looks like you'll need at least a three inch heel to pull that one off. It fits well enough. A little plain, but it fits."

I headed back into the closet, biting back a comment about the fact that she had been the one to pick the thing out.

I chose a pretty lavender gown next. The top was a halter, and it didn't take long to realize that I couldn't wear a bra with the neckline.

I usually wouldn't be caught dead going braless in public, but I tried it on, just to see. The way it tied gave the top a surprising amount of support in the bust area, and the silk was soft against my skin.

It was fitted, but not tight, from neck to about mid hip, where it fanned out in fluffy layers of chiffon, a high slit showing a lot of one leg. Jackie liked her high slitted gowns. It was ultra-feminine but still sexy, and I loved it instantly.

James blinked at me as I walked out, his jaw going just a touch slack. I was gratified. I decided instantly to wear the dress. Jackie's input be damned.

Jackie whistled. "Very nice. I almost want to save that one for a bigger event."

"No. I'll wear it tonight," I told her. I needed all of the confidence boosting I could get for the night, and James looking at me the way he was looking at me did exactly that.

He swallowed, then licked his lips. All of his nervous tells. It made me smile.

"You look beautiful," he said, with feeling. "But it seems a little revealing. Do you think it'll pick up as see-through with the camera flashes, Jackie?"

She gave him a 'do you think I'm an amateur?' kind of look. "It wouldn't be in the pile if it did." She turned back to me, her voice brisk. "Now to accessorize. You can go start getting dressed yourself, James. I got this."

CHAPTER TWENTY-NINE

Jackie pointed me in the direction of shiny navy wedges with a peep toe and a four inch heel. They were more comfortable than they looked, though that wasn't saying much.

"Does the navy go with the lavender?" I asked dubiously.

She gave me a very exasperated look. "Would I pair them if they didn't? And James is wearing this amazing all navy tux. It's very fashion forward. Only a supermodel like James could pull it off. And he mentioned that he likes you guys to match, so I think he'll like the shoes.

Eyeing myself up in the mirror, I had to agree that the shoes went well. I would have never guessed the the dress would pop even more with shiny navy shoes, but *I* was no stylist.

She sighed, looking at my jewelry. "James obviously wants you wearing that choker and earrings. While they're lovely, I had other accessories in mind for that dress. Oh well. Sometimes I must compromise my vision. A girl's got to eat." As she finished speaking, James was striding back into the room, a jewelry box in his hands. He was still shirtless. He set it on the bed without a word, just smiling as he strode back out.

Jackie sighed again, opening the box. Her eyes widened. She shot me a speculative glance. She took two thick diamond studded cuffs out of the box, walking to me. She snapped them on my wrists, making no comments about the abrasions that they covered. She circled me, pursing her lips as she tugged at several spots on my dress, adjusting it just so.

"It doesn't need alteration, since you're so damned tall, so that saves time." She grabbed a smooth white robe off of a rack, holding it up for me. "So you don't mess up the dress while you get hair and makeup done. We have a minute to talk."

I thought that sounded ominous, but I met her gaze squarely.

She arched a brow at me. "James and I go way back. We went to school together. I'm his stylist, but it's not because I need the money. I love fashion, but I come from money myself. I've had to dodge my fare share of fortune-hunters, but it's nothing compared to what James has to deal with."

She eyed me from top to bottom, but it only made my spine straighten. "You're attractive enough, but I must admit, I don't get it. Is your vagina gold plated? He's been chased by supermodels and playboy bunnies. He fucked a lot of them, hell, most of them, but he never even talked about having a girlfriend. Not once. Now you've moved in with him, and he's acting like he's a one woman man for life all of a sudden. I'll admit, I'm intrigued and mystified by the change in him, but I don't understand any of it. How did you wrap him around your little finger, Bianca? And how do you feel about him? As one of his few close friends, I'd like to know your intentions."

I returned her narrowed gaze with an icy one of my own. If I'd had any doubts before, I knew it now; Jackie and I were not going to be friends.

"If you and James are such close friends," I began coldly, "you should be having this conversation with him, not me. You're a virtual stranger to me. I won't be discussing my feelings, or my intentions, with you."

She just sighed, as though I'd disappointed her. "I was too direct, wasn't I? Now you don't trust me. I'm blunt, Bianca, but we don't have to be enemies."

I just gave a little shrug, wanting to end the awkward and personal conversation as quickly as possible. "Hair and makeup?" I asked coldly.

She sighed again. "Follow me. They've set up a room for it."

She led me to a large room one floor down. It had glass walls, and I thought it must have been some sort of entertainment room before they'd taken it over. There was a huge flatscreen TV mounted on the wall, and several reclining chairs pushed up against the wall, as though to make room for the salon-like setup. Two ladies were waiting and chatting, looking antsy as we entered the room. There was a barber shop chair set up in front of a a table loaded with hair products and cosmetics. It was intimidating to imagine the setup was all for my benefit.

A thin, dark-haired girl strode towards me, smiling. Her heavy chestnut hair hung in waves nearly to her waist. Her nose dominated her thin face, but in an attractive kind of way. It was somehow a distinctive nose, rather than just large. Her big, dark eyes helped. And her artfully applied makeup, with smoky eyes and plum colored lips.

"I'm Amy," she said. "I'll be doing your makeup. It's very nice to meet you, Ms. Karlsson."

I shook her hand, thinking that her amiable approach had to be the polar opposite of Jackie's. "Nice to meet you, Amy. Please, call me Bianca."

The second woman stepped forward, her smile just as friendly as Amy's. "I'm Ariel. I'll be doing your hair. Nice to finally meet you, Ms. Karlsson."

I shook her hand, smiling. The friendly women were already

helping me shake off the awkwardness that was Jackie. "Bianca, please. Nice to meet you, as well."

They sat me in the chair, tripping over each other to discuss my hair and makeup, then giggling at each other. They were obviously friends.

I made it easy on them. "You're the experts. I trust your judgement, so fix me up however you think is best." I'd never spared much time or thought on my appearance, and I didn't intend to let my strange new lifestyle change that.

This seemed to please them both, and they set to work. I closed my eyes, just letting them. They worked on me, blowdrying my hair, and applying my makeup for maybe ten minutes before I felt James enter the room. Both women paused for scant moments before resuming their ministrations. I guessed that he'd waved them back to their work, sitting somewhere to watch. I felt Ariel begin to play with my hair, pulling it back and twisting it.

"Leave her hair down," James said from somewhere to my right.

Ariel let it fall without a word, smoothing it out.

James wasn't quiet for a full minute before speaking again. "Are you ignoring me, Love?"

Impatient man. "If you didn't notice, Amy is applying makeup to my face. I'm trying to hold still."

He made a little noise of displeasure in his throat.

"You can open your eyes, Bianca. I can work around it," Amy told me. I could tell she was just trying to appease James, since I could still feel her working on my eyelids.

"It's fine. I'll hold still until you're done," I told her.

It was maybe thirty seconds before James spoke again. "Did you like the cuffs?" he asked me.

"They're lovely. Thank you," I told him.

Amy and Ariel began to ooh and ah over my diamond jewelry. "That is luxe. Who did you borrow from? You'll need a bodyguard for this kind of jewelry." Ariel's voice was awed.

James answered for me, but I felt my cheeks redden. I had tried very hard not to think about how much the jewelry he gave me was worth, but her comment made it harder to ignore.

"I actually had it all designed for her," James told them. "It's her own personal collection."

More oohs and ahs. "What a generous boyfriend," Amy said, her voice dreamy.

"That's nothing. I haven't even begun to gift her with my mother's jewels. She left me a queen's ransom's worth," James said, a clear grin in his voice.

I thought the two women were going to swoon as they rushed to tell him how wonderful he was. He *was* wonderful, but I couldn't bring myself to be pleased with the prospect of more extravagant gifts. They still just made me uncomfortable. And if he wasn't joking, if he really did intend to give me some of the jewels his mother had left him, well, that was even more disconcerting. It seemed like such a huge step. You didn't give a woman things with such sentimental value unless she was your wife, or you were certain that she would be. The thought still made my blood run cold. Would he really push this issue so soon after I had agreed to live with him? I still couldn't believe we were moving so incredibly fast, and yet he only wanted more. I tried not to panic at the thought.

"She even left me her five-carat princess cut diamond engagement ring, surrounded by sapphire baguettes. Don't you ladies think that would look particularly lovely on Bianca's left hand?"

I felt myself get a little light-headed, but the ladies went crazy, gushing over how romantic he was. I told myself, rather desperately, that he was only joking, that he was just having fun at our expense, but I was beginning to know him well enough to be worried.

"Just take deep breaths, Love. You'll grow accustomed to the idea, once the initial shock wears off," James told me, his tone rather casual considering the topic matter.

The ladies giggled, as though he were joking. If only.

"James," I began.

"Deep breaths," he said again, the clear smile in his voice infuriating. But I took a few deep breaths, and it did help a little.

Amy and Ariel finished my hair and makeup within seconds of each other, almost as though they had it down to a science. They seemed to be used to working together, so I wouldn't be surprised if that was the case.

"Thank you, ladies," James said, his voice a touch husky.

I knew that tone. It wasn't fit for company. It was way too tender and affected for that.

"You can open your eyes, Bianca. Tell us what you think. We can change anything you don't like," Amy said, her voice endearingly earnest.

I looked. I was...stunned. I looked more lovely than I had thought makeup could make me. My eyes were lined in a soft brown, my lashes sooty and black. My lids were a pale lavender near the brows, with a more vibrant violet along my lashes. The color brought out my eyes startlingly, the liner making them look huge in my rounded face. Just a touch of bronzer on my cheeks had me glowing, and a soft, shiny pink lip made my lips look plump and kissable. My hair was straight and smooth, the short bangs working with the makeup to bring out my pale aquamarine eyes.

"Wow," I managed to get out.

"Exquisite," James murmured.

My eyes traveled to him when he spoke. He had turned one of the reclining chairs towards me, and was lounging in it comfortably, one perfectly tailored leg crossed over a knee, shiny navy shoes gleaming in the light. They were the mens version of my shoes. I knew he'd get a kick out of that, if he hadn't noticed already. Hell, I got a bit of a kick out of it. He looked amazing, of course. Jackie had been right about his tux being fashion forward. It was sleek and navy, more fitted than a normal tux, showing off his stark muscular build to perfection. Even his sleek dress shirt and bow tie were a dark navy that caught the light a bit more than the rest of the ensemble. It was something you would normally only see on a runway at fashion week, because no one who wasn't a damned supermodel could pull it off. The dark navy set off his dark tan, his turquoise eyes shining vibrantly against the dark contrasts. His hair was slicked back just a tad.

I pointed at him. "Did it really only take you ten minutes to look like that? That is so unfair."

He looked at his watch. It wasn't one I'd seen before. I had quickly caught on that he liked to collect watches. Expensive ones, of course. "Love, it only took you forty-five minutes, so you can't really complain, either. That's unheard of for a red carpet event."

I waved a hand at the women hovering behind me. "It took a team to get me ready that fast, Mr. Beautiful."

Amy and Ariel giggled at the name.

James smirked. "Every woman attending tonight had a team getting them ready, love, and I guarantee that no one other than you only took forty-five minutes, team or no."

James politely dismissed my 'team' of beautifiers, and I thanked them again.

When we were finally alone, he pulled me to my feet, whipping off the white robe that protected my gown. His eyes were hot as he just stared at me, studying me from head to toe. He smiled when he saw our matching patent-leather navy shoes.

"I take it you like me all dolled up like this. Are you going to try to have those two follow me around to achieve the affect more often?" I asked him, only half-teasing. There was no telling what the crazy man would do.

He ran his tongue over his teeth, a gesture that always drove me wild. "To tell you the truth, I like you best bare of makeup and everything else. I've never met a woman who looked more beautiful without a thing on. But I have to admit that I love the idea of shoving you in the face of the press when you look so polished and lovely, and when they've printed so many unflattering things about you. It will make them all look like fools, after some of the nonsense that's been posted."

I gave a little shrug. I really couldn't let the things being said about me get to me, or I'd never leave my house again. I thought that it was a little naive for James to think that he could change anyone's mind after the things that had been said about him. I certainly wouldn't be holding my breath.

CHAPTER THIRTY

Jackie reappeared as we were almost to the elevator, handing me a tiny navy patent-leather clutch. It was cute, but I hated having something on me that would take up the use of my hand for the entire night, so I declined. She looked baffled by the refusal, looking at the clutch in her hand as though it had done something to warrant the rejection.

I looked at James. "Do I need to take anything?"

He considered. "Only what you would consider essential. If you don't have anything you want to bring, then you certainly don't have to."

"But it completes the ensemble!" Jackie said.

I just looked at her. If she was paying attention, she could have seen in my eyes that I just didn't care that much about 'completing the ensemble'. She finally got the idea, moving out of our way, though the look she gave me was less than friendly.

"Will you be attending tonight?" James asked her as he led me into the elevator by a hand on the small of my back.

She shrugged. "I may come to hound the red carpet press about who I dressed tonight. Free publicity and all that."

James just nodded, pushing the button.

Jackie hurried into the car. She seemed to have just realized that she was leaving, too. She pushed the button for the fifteenth floor. She saw my look.

"I live in this building, as well," she explained.

Well, that was handy, I thought.

She got off on her floor with a dismissive little wave.

"What do you think of Jackie?" James asked as soon as the door closed.

I gave him my little shrug that drove him crazy. I was going for nonchalant, but I ruined it with a dumb question. "Have you slept with her?"

He didn't get offended, as most men probably would. He never seemed to mind my inquiries about his past affairs. He didn't *like* my questions, but he seemed ever willing to give me answers. I appreciated his candor, even if I didn't always like his answers.

"I have not. We have always been strictly platonic, and we've been friends since high school. So what did you think of her?"

I grimaced a little, but not so he could see it. "I'm trying hard to reserve judgement, at the moment. She told me you've been friends for a long time, but she seems to be nurturing a vague dislike for me. The feeling is very much mutual, so far."

His hand gripped my hip almost painfully. "Why? What did she say to you?"

I shot him a look. "She thinks I'm after your money, I guess. It's what you can expect everyone to be thinking and saying. I'll have to get used to that kind of nonsense, I suppose."

He used the tight grip on my hip to push my other side into his rigid stomach. He spoke very close to my ear, as though we weren't alone in the elevator. "You don't have to put up with that. We can fire her. You can fire anyone who doesn't suit you, for any reason."

I placed a hand on his chest, right on his heart, where my name was branded. I looked up into his beloved eyes. "That's not necessary. You've obviously been able to maintain a good working relationship with her over the years. Maybe just don't have her shop for me anymore. I don't want anything else, anyways. It's all too much, James."

"I will have a word with her, Bianca. If she disrespects you again, I'm firing her. She will get a clear warning, but only one."

I rubbed that sweet little spot on his chest. "People will be thinking that, James. We need to be prepared for it. It's a conversation that I will undoubtedly be having again and again. There's no way for me to prove to the world that I don't want a damned cent from you."

We arrived at the lobby floor, and he hugged me into his side, a hand going to the hoop at my collar to hook in that familiar finger as we made our way through the swank lobby and to the waiting town car. In the scant space from the building's doorway to the car, three flashbulbs snapped at us just getting into the car. James ushered me in without a word, crowding in behind me. I scooted across the seat to give him room, but he just followed me, plastering me to his side as the door closed behind him.

He kissed the skin just behind my ear as he spoke. "And yet, it's all yours, love. Every damned cent. I want to lay the world at your feet. There's nothing I wouldn't do for you. You know that, right?"

I rubbed my hands over him comfortingly, hearing a strange vulnerability in his voice. I stroked his knee, and found my favorite spot on his heart, running my hand over it again and again. "I don't need any of that, James. I've grown to need *you*. I love your honesty, and your tenderness, and your dominance."

I took a deep breath, suddenly panicky about the things coming out of my mouth. I had never said anything quite so revealing to him before. "But I don't need any of that other stuff," I said firmly.

"Nonetheless, you have it," he murmured, burying his face in my neck. He began to suckle me there, and I melted. He pulled back abruptly. "I don't want to muss you up for your first red carpet."

I was breathless when I responded. "At least I'm not nervous now. I can't even remember why I should care enough to be nervous. I only care about getting you to touch me again."

He threw his head back and laughed. It was his happy laugh, and I felt my whole body get soft, my smile as our eyes met unmistakably tender. I didn't think there was much I wouldn't do to make him that happy. And yet I had done so little to make him so. It seemed miraculous to me that my every small gesture seemed to affect him so.

He was still giving me that boyish smile as the car stopped. The gala was apparently very close to his home.

James handed me out of the car expertly, his hand falling swiftly to my waist. He ushered me through the press as though it were a dance, the cameras snapping at us in quick succession. I plastered my most polished smile on my face. It was a photo-ready smile, if a touch cool. I had perfected it at a young age. Growing up fast and painfully had taught me that smile. Yes, it was polished, but I had earned that polish.

A few photographers shouted out some rather rude comments, but we both ignored them. They were acting that way for a reaction, and it was the last thing I would give them. My smile never even slipped.

James kissed my forehead when we finally made our way into the grand entrance of the building. "You're a natural. Those bloodhounds can take some getting used to."

My mind had already moved past the strange red carpet experience when I saw a doorway into some kind of elaborate ballroom. "Oh, James, I don't know how to dance. I didn't even think of it."

He kissed my forehead again, and I caught the edge of his smile at the top of my vision. "You only need to dance with me, Love. And we know all too well that if I lead, you know how to follow, even without experience."

I tried to tell myself that he may well be right. Perhaps it would just be that easy. I felt the nerves clench in my stomach nonetheless.

A seemingly endless stream of introductions and polite mingling began almost immediately. I gathered from some of the pleasantries exchanged that this was a gala that his mother had been involved with before she'd passed. She had made the charity rounds, I learned, donating generous amounts of both her time and money. James had mentioned briefly that it was a fundraiser for cancer research at a prominent New York hospital. I tried to say the right things when addressed, but I felt quickly out of my depth. I had never been to anything like the gala before, and I was overwhelmed by all of the affluent company I was suddenly keeping. It was daunting, to say the least.

James, for his part, was a perfect date for such an event, including me in conversations that really had nothing to do with me, and keeping a warm hand on my hip, often sending warm, reassuring smiles my way. He seemed content just to have me at his side. But I just felt awkward, as though I had no purpose there. The introductions quickly became a blur for me. Most of the people I met hadn't left enough of an impression to put a face with a name even moments after moving on. There were a few exceptions.

After mingling for a solid hour, we were approached by the most austere looking woman I had ever seen in my life. She had to be seventy, with silver hair pulled back into a severe bun, and a navy gown that went from her neckline to her toes, the stark lines showing a sparse figure.

She stood directly in front of us before she spoke. Her tone was icy, her accent crisp and British. "James. And how are you this evening?"

His eyes were cold as he studied the woman, but the moment he spoke, I detected a note of something I'd never heard from him before. It was almost as if he affected a slightly sneering tone, mimicking her accent just enough to goad her. I watched him in fascination. "Aunt Mildred. I am well. And how are you this fine evening?"

Her brow arched. I thought that to her it may have been a way of answering. She never spared me a glance. "Well enough. I have been hearing things about you, though. Disturbing things. Even more disturbing than your usual debaucheries. Please tell me that you haven't invited a penniless flight attendant to live in one of your homes."

I stiffened, but still couldn't look away from James. *How did everyone seem to know that we had moved in together before it had even happened?* I had barely even agreed to the arrangement.

His eyes began to twinkle, but it wasn't a good kind of twinkle. It was as though he had engaged this woman in hostile banter too many times to count, and I thought he just might look forward to offending her. "Aunt Mildred, meet my girlfriend, Bianca. Bianca, this is my charming Aunt Mildred."

The awful woman just slanted me a malevolent stare, giving me a sneer.

"Now, now, Auntie," James began in that goading tone, "you had better play nice with my dearest Bianca. I have not invited her to live in one of my homes. I have welcomed her into *all* of them. And though I know it would break your heart if anything were to ever happen to me, you will be beholden to this angel to cover your living expenses when I pass away, as she will be my sole inheritor."

I shot him a look. I didn't care for him putting me in the middle of what was obviously a family squabble. I let my eyes tell him as much. He just smiled at me, stroking a finger down my cheek.

Mildred harrumphed. "I know you like to have your fun at my expense, you rotten boy, but this is going too far. Really, what a ridiculous thing to say. You'll give the poor chit delusions of grandeur."

He stopped smiling, giving her a very serious look. "It is no joke, Mildred. Meet my future. Her name is Bianca. Come to terms with it. My advice would be to get on her good side." With that, he led me away.

CHAPTER THIRTY-ONE

He was tense as he led me away. "Please don't involve me in that family stuff, James. It makes me horribly uncomfortable."

His mouth tightened. "Just handle it with the practicality that you've handled the press, Love. My family is fucked up to the Nth degree, and you are now a part of it. Trust me, it's best to face them all head on."

"Facing them is different than goading that awful woman with lies about heirs or inheritors."

He pursed his lips, studying me. I could tell that he was debating with himself what he should say to me. "It wasn't a lie, Bianca. You will be inheriting everything, should I pass. I've already begun the process."

I swayed a little on my feet, feeling suddenly quite light-headed. "Please don't, James. Don't say that, and if you're so crazy that it's actually the truth, don't do it. It is the last thing I want. Your family will despise me."

"I'm sorry to say that they will despise you regardless. They are a spiteful nest of vipers, and if something should happen to both of us, all of the family wealth will be going to my mother's favorite charities. I know you will tell me that I am too hasty, that it's all too sudden, but this is how I do things, Bianca. When I'm certain of something, I am decisive about it." His eyes were steady on mine as he spoke, and we stared at each for a long moment while I tried to process what he was saying.

"You won't sway me from this," he continued, "I'm quite set on this course. It only needs to bother you as much as you let it. Go back to pretending that you don't know, if you need to."

I gave him a long, level stare. "You're impossible," I told him.

He had the nerve to grin.

His gaze shot to a spot behind me, and in an instant that grin was gone, replaced by a very careful, very blank mask. It worried me. I didn't want to see what had bothered him enough to close him off so quickly.

I turned, a feeling close to dread in my stomach, and sure enough, it was justified. Jules was less than ten feet away, clearly making her way to us through the crush.

James moved in close to me, tilting his head closer to my ear. "I'm sorry. I didn't know she would be here."

"I'm not avoiding her," I told him, my eyes never leaving the ravishingly beautiful woman.

She was stunning in a cream silk gown. Her shoulders were perfect and delicate in the classic sleeveless gown, her skin a perfect dusky shade against the pale silk. My own shoulders were broad and bony and pale. Her cleavage was perfect, showing just enough to be tasteful and sexy. My own cleavage felt vulgar in comparison. Fair or not, I hated her.

"That's for the best, in general, I suppose," James said quietly into my ear. "I can see from here, though, that she is determined to start trouble for us. Please, my love, don't let her get to you."

I took deep breaths, not answering. The last time I had seen the woman, I had been devastated by the things she had implied about her relationship with James. If I could trust James, and I was beginning to, this woman had to be close to crazy, planting stories to the press about their fictional romantic love affair. I was bound and determined not to let her ruffle my feathers. She wasn't worth it, even if she was one of the most beautiful women I'd ever seen. I despised her for that, for being so close to the female counterpart to James's impossible beauty.

Jules gave us what appeared to be a truly genuine smile as she drew close. "James! Bianca! How lovely to see you both." She air kissed both of our cheeks.

Our responses and postures were nearly identical as she leaned close to us both. Stiff and distrustful. James held me to him with a hard arm around my waist, his hand snaking to grip my hip firmly. One side of the front of his body pressed into my back.

I thought resentfully that Jules even smelled divine as she pulled back with a smile on her blood red lips.

"Give it a rest, Jules. I know about the stories you've been planting. Just what did you hope to accomplish with any of it? And bringing *her* here? What are you doing? Why waste so much energy? Just for pure spite? Or are really so addicted to staying in the headlines?" James spoke in a cold, disdainful voice that somehow managed to be bored. Jules's smile barely slipped, but I sensed how his disdain crushed her as I looked into her gray eyes.

She's in love with him, I thought. I shouldn't have been surprised, all things considered. And of course, the largest consideration was the man himself. *Who wouldn't be in love with him?*

I hadn't noticed the second woman until James mentioned her, though it was hard to believe that anyone could overlook the stunning woman. Perhaps it was her size. She was very petite, maybe five feet tall, with curly black hair that hung loose to her waist.

Her face was devastatingly beautiful. Even Jules was no match for this woman. She had the face of an angel, her eyes a clear blue that stood out on her dusky skin. That dusky skin was nearly the same shade as the woman who stood so close to her side. In fact, their skin tones matched perfectly enough to make me think they could be sisters. Either that, or they'd used the same spray tanner. If so, it was worth every penny.

She wore a crimson dress that matched her pouty bow-shaped lips. It was a classic style that matched Jules's gown almost perfectly, down to the silky material, one of them red, one of them white, as though they had planned it. An angel and a devil. They were holding hands, and I knew this woman was trouble for me. Just knew it.

It was probably the way her focus never wavered from James. *As though he had trained her never to look away from him...*

"Bianca, dear, this is Jolene. Jolene, Bianca. I know you were dying to meet her. What do you think?" Jules addressed Jolene.

Jolene shrugged a lovely shoulder, her gaze never leaving James.

"Hello, Mr. Cavendish," she said softly. Her voice was almost breathy and bled over-the-top sexy vibes across the scant feet separating them.

I looked at James, almost scared to see his reaction to the stunning woman.

He gave her a stiff nod, his eyes cold and unreadable. "Jolene."

Jules ignored all of the awkwardness, beaming at me as though we were longtime friends. "You and Jolene have a lot in common, Bianca. I bet you can guess at some of it..."

The hand on my hip had turned into an absolute death-grip. "Well, we've had about enough of the immature games for tonight.

Please excuse us, ladies. Ah, perfect. I think I see your brother, Jules." I got a fleeting glance of the near-panicked expression on Jules's face as James tugged me away. She was searching the crowd, looking none too happy.

I didn't have time to ask James any questions about the odd exchange, and the conclusions I'd drawn, before he was introducing me to a stunning man who I knew at a glance had to be Jules's brother. They could have been twins, though he was much taller and broader. "Bianca, this is my good friend, Parker. Parker, this is my Bianca."

The man smiled warmly, much as his sister did, though I thought his smile might actually be genuine. "So good to meet you, Bianca. James has instructed me not to scare you off, but I would like to thank you for finally getting him to settle down. My wife and I would love to have you both over for dinner. At your convenience, of course. You should see James with our two-year-old. You'll get baby fever at a glance, I guarantee it."

I was still stiff and upset from the exchange with Jules and Jolene, and this only made me tense up even more. I simply had no idea how to respond to such a statement. Didn't even know where to begin.

James just sighed. "That's not a great way of *not* scaring her off, Parker. Of course, it doesn't help that we just ran into your deranged sister. She's being crazier than ever, by the way. She's here with Jolene."

Parker began to scan the crowd at that. "That little brat. What the hell is she doing, anyways? What does she hope to accomplish? She's only making it so you'll never want to speak to her again. I'll have a word with her. Which way did she go?"

James pointed in the direction we had come from, and Parker was off in a flash. James grinned at me. "He'll lecture her all night."

I couldn't reply as yet another woman approached us, her

smile friendly and warm. She was maybe five seven, with curly white-blond hair clipped up in an elegant style. She was classically beautiful, with even features and soft pink lips. The color of her soft pink gown suited her perfectly. It was one shouldered and mermaid style, with fluffy layers of taffeta making it move playfully as she walked. I didn't think many women could have pulled the style off. She had a very slim figure, and moved with absolute confidence in her own skin. I thought that Jackie would love to dress that figure.

She walked directly into James's arms for a long embrace. I watched the exchange with the cool mask I had adopted for the evening, taking a careful step away from them. I wondered what the odds were that James somehow hadn't slept with this lovely woman. I was guessing not good. I was happy to be wrong.

She pulled back finally to smile at us both, looking back and forth between us. She smiled, her gaze finally just settling on me. "You must be Bianca. I'm so happy to meet you. I'm Parker's wife, Sophia."

I smiled back, but I knew it was stiff. I had become too guarded to even try to adopt a real smile. "Pleased to meet you, Sophia."

"Jules is at it again. Parker has gone off to try to talk some sense into her. She and Jolene came here together."

Sophia grimaced. "That little fool." She looked at me, reaching out to touch my arm reassuringly. "Jules puts on a good show, but she is basically a society princess who's spoiled to the point that she's never had to deal with the notion that she can't have everything she wants. She's being particularly dense about the fact that she can't have James. It drives Parker and I crazy that, to this day, their daddy gives her everything she wants. She's never had to work a day in her life, and she has way too much time on her hands to cause trouble."

Sophia looked at James. "Parker is seriously considering

telling their daddy about some of the things she's done. She's got her parents half sold on some of her delusions about you two. As though she's been holding a torch all these years, as opposed to the truth, which is that she's always done whatever the hell she wants, with whoever she wants, male or female. Hell, she made a pass at *me* when Parker and I became engaged. The fact is, she's thinks she's in love with you, but that's only because she's too selfish to know what love actually is. And you've always been clear about how *you* felt." She took a breath after that little speech. I just blinked at her. Not many people were so open at a first meeting.

"Anyways," she continued, "don't be surprised if you see Jules and Parker's parents and it's a touch awkward. They have no notion of what's *actually* going on."

James sighed heavily. "I can't say I'm looking forward to it. Perhaps I should have a word with them myself. The things she's been telling the gossip mags is unacceptable."

Sophia blanched. "Yes, you're absolutely right, but I think Parker should be the one to speak to them about all of it. I'll make sure he does that sooner rather than later."

James nodded, but he did not look happy about it.

Sophia seemed to spot someone in the crush behind us. She kissed me on the cheek. "Please, you have to come have dinner at our house sometime. I promise the talk will be about more pleasant things." I nodded rather stiffly before she strode away.

James watched her go, waving at whoever she was joining. I guessed it was Parker, though I didn't turn to look. He studied me for a long time, looking solemn and a touch worried. "Are you okay, Love?"

I just studied him, my chest feeling tight and achy. "Jolene was your submissive," I said, my voice very soft.

CHAPTER THIRTY-TWO

His mouth tightened and his jaw clenched, but he didn't look even a little surprised that I had guessed. "Yes, she was. Past-tense. Please, let's not talk about it here. I'll tell you anything you want to know, but later."

I thought of him doing all of the things that he did to me to that perfect creature, and I felt sick. *How could I compete with someone so beautiful? And how could he want me for long, when he had a woman like that, still so obviously infatuated with him?* The thought was daunting and demoralizing.

He gripped my nape firmly. My gaze had gone a little glassy with my thoughts, but I looked back at him squarely. His face was composed, but there was trouble in his eyes.

"Please don't think like that," he said, his voice quiet but pained.

I arched a brow at him. "You're reading my mind now?" I asked him. I was only half-joking. The man had an uncanny ability to read me.

He sighed. "In a way. I could tell by looking at you that you were having doubts about us. About me. I can't change my past,

Bianca. All I can do is be honest with you, and I've done my best."

I tried to make him understand. "I understand that. But understanding and feeling okay with it aren't always the same. Your past, all of the other women...intimidate me. There's no way I can compete with all of that."

His eyes got a little wild at my words. His voice held a hint of cold anger when he spoke. "I've never asked you to. You have no competition for me, Bianca." *Someone should tell his ex-lovers that,* I thought, but even as I had the thought, I knew it was petty.

He studied me, visibly calming himself in that mercurial way of his. "Let's go dance," he murmured, leading me in the direction of the ballroom.

"I really don't know how," I said to him, voice pitched low so I wouldn't be overheard.

"It doesn't matter. I want to show you something. Come."

He led me purposefully into the ballroom, and onto the dance floor without further ado. He pulled me into a dance as though it were the most natural thing in the world. And it turned out to be just that. He led, and I followed. He held me close in his arms, barely a breath between us, and moved us as though we'd practiced a thousand times.

He murmured into my ear as he led us through the steps that turned out to be easy and natural. "You may not like my experience. But it has its uses. It made me see very early on that you and I are different. This thing we have is different. Take this dance, for example. It comes so natural, the leading and the following, because you and I are so perfectly matched. And I knew it would. I had no doubts, and I was correct. That's how it's always been with you, Bianca. You are not experienced. And perhaps that's why you can't see how perfect we are together. Not how I see it, anyways. That's why you need to learn to trust me. I'm sure of this, sure of us. I will endeavor to convince you as well, my love."

I let him lead me through the dance, and it felt like a dream. He took control and it was magic. A heavy violin added a thread of melancholy to the dance, but it added emotion as well. I looked at him as we moved, but I could have closed my eyes, it came so naturally. There were times when I could let him take control, and it was perfect. I had thought that effect could only work in the bedroom, but apparently he dominated the dance floor as well.

"Oh, James," I sighed, not knowing what to do with him. He was a force of nature. "This is all so fast. You overwhelm every part of me."

I hadn't meant to ruin the moment, but I felt him stiffen instantly at my words.

"That sounds ominous," he said, his voice very low and carrying an almost imperceptible hitch. I wondered sadly if I had put the vulnerability in his eyes. If I was the reason for his oh-so-careful demeanor. But then I mentally chastised myself. I was giving myself too much credit. Perversely, the thought made me feel both sad and reassured.

He led me from the floor as the music died briefly. He ignored the music as it started up again, a slow, sensuous chord strong in the instrumental song. I just knew that I had darkened his mood.

"I need to use the restroom, James," I told him quietly. Mostly I needed a moment to myself. I had only spoken the truth. I was utterly overwhelmed by him. Still, it hurt me to displease him, as I knew my constant reluctance did, and I needed a moment alone to compose myself. A wave of sadness rocked me. I was supposed to be the innocent one here, but I simply couldn't trust James in the way he seemed to trust me. The very idea was impossible to me. I didn't even trust my own feelings. Every emotion he made me feel was met with my reluctance, and my skepticism, and my doubt. I felt like half of a person, the part that could trust other people somehow missing from my soul.

"Of course. This way," he said, his voice just as quiet as mine had been, leading my by a hand gripped just above my elbow.

I felt an urge to reassure him, or even to apologize, for what, I wasn't quite sure. In the end, I was silent.

He led me to the restrooms, pointing down the hallway as we parted. "I'll be waiting in the antechamber to the dining hall." He walked away.

Even the restroom was daunting, huge with cream and white marble along the floor, and thick columns that seemed out of place in a bathroom.

The stalls were made of glass that frosted over from transparent to opaque as you clicked the lock into place. I'd seen the trick before in a few hotspot Vegas clubs, but I was still vaguely impressed with the effect.

I just stood there for the longest time, door closed, taking deep, painful breaths. I tried to place what was affecting me so. I felt myself falling, once again, so deeply under James's intoxicating spell, but some part of me just couldn't trust him.

But was it him? Or was it me? Was I so superficial that, just because he was so impossibly beautiful, I didn't believe he could ever really fall for me the way I'd so easily fallen for him?

He had an angel's face, but his eyes were so hypnotically tarnished, a mirror of my own pain in their depths. I had never been superficial, and I knew that his looks hadn't been what made me fall for him. It was the soul underneath all of that beautiful packaging. I had seen that he was more, so why wouldn't I let myself trust that? Why had that seductively beautiful submissive, so much closer to his physical equal than myself, shaken my faith in him with just a brief encounter? Was I insecure, or just realistic? I berated myself, again and again, for being foolish. If he had wanted to be with Jolene, he wouldn't be with me...

Finally, when I felt I had given myself a good enough pep

talk, I let myself out of the stall. I nodded politely to the bathroom attendant as I washed my hands.

I was checking my makeup carefully in the mirror when two figures breezed through the door. I stiffened when I saw who they were.

Jules practically beamed when she spotted me. Jolene's look was even more confusing. It was feral and almost...smoldering.

They moved to flank me, moving together as though they had planned it. I towered over both of them, but they still managed to make me feel overwhelmed.

"Bianca," Jules murmured, running a hand over my hair affectionately.

I stiffened until I felt a little brittle. Her smile grew wider, and perversely, warmer. "How are you, love? Is James sweeping you off of your feet? He's very good at that, you know. No one so beautiful was ever so charming as our James. Wouldn't you agree, Jolene?"

Jolene was studying me in the mirror, barely blinking as her stunning eyes drank me in. "He's irresistible and completely relentless when he wants a new woman. In the beginning, he pursued me with such passion and fire that I still dream about it sometimes. I've never felt as beautiful or desirable as I did when I was with our James. It was the most exhilarating year of my life."

My breath caught, my heart pounding in my chest nearly loud enough to drown out the last of her words. *A year*? My head began to spin.

"Tell her everything, Jolene," Jules prompted the other woman. It was an order, really.

"I was under contract with Mr. Cavendish for a year and two months. I belonged to him for that time, exclusively unless he said otherwise, to do with as he wished, completely at his disposal. I was in my own personal heaven."

Under contract? I tried to take it all in. I had known a little about the contract she spoke of, though he had never tried to do the same to me. Perhaps because he had been afraid to scare me off, perhaps not. But a year and two months? He had claimed never to have had a girlfriend before, but this sounded far more serious than having a girlfriend...

"How long ago was this?" I asked Jolene, keeping my face very carefully blank, my tone very empty.

She ran her tongue over her teeth, and the gesture struck me hard, as though she had learned it from being so familiar with James. *She must know him so much better than I do*, I thought. "Three years ago."

I was somewhat mollified. I arched a brow at our reflections. "A bit long ago for you to still be so hung up on him, don't you think?" I asked her. I didn't mind at all if I came off as a bitch with these two women. The last time I had encountered Jules, her words had crushed me, and I had fled like a wounded animal. I wanted her to know, this time, that I was not such an easy mark.

Jolene's eyes were earnest, as though she felt not even a hint of my malice. "Three years ago was the end of our written contract, but far from the end of *us*. He still calls me often, between whatever fresh conquests he's obsessed with. Just six weeks ago he flew me out to Vegas on his private jet to spend a night with him."

CHAPTER THIRTY-THREE

That one hit its mark squarely, and I felt myself trembling. I did some absent math in my disconnected brain. He had admitted to being with a woman only one day before he had met me. The dates added up for her claim. *At least he hadn't called her while we were on a break...*

I turned my eyes to Jules, studying her and trying very hard to remind myself that this woman was just trying to cause trouble. And still, it was working... "And what is *your* purpose in all of this, Jules? Are you going to map out your own relationship with James for me?"

She gave me that warm smile. The most sincere fake smile I'd ever seen. "I'm not his submissive, if that's what you're asking. He's always seen me too much as his equal to ever treat me that way."

She doesn't get it, I thought, a little shocked. It wasn't about equality. If anything, James had always made me feel that I had most of the power in the relationship, outside of the bedroom. After all of the trouble this woman had caused us, to realize that she wasn't even his type, and that she didn't understand him at all, was stunning.

"I'm his social equal," she continued, "and we have always been perfectly matched. I'm self-confident enough to allow him his kinky little side affairs."

All I could think as she spoke was how pathetic she was. "You realize that he has a completely different opinion about your relationship, don't you? He said it's been at least a year since you've had sex. He claims that you're just a friend."

Her face tightened nearly imperceptibly, but I saw the tension around her mouth. It was written on her young face like an old bitterness. "He's sowing his wild oats. I'm an understanding woman. He needs that in a partner. It's something only someone from our social class could really comprehend."

I had nearly forgotten about Jolene until she pressed her large, soft breasts against my arm. My gaze swung to hers in the mirror. Hers were smoldering at me.

"We don't need to be your enemies, Bianca," she said, her voice nearly breathless. "If you're going to last for any length of time at all with our James, you should know that he only stays interested in women who like other women."

I blinked at her, trying hard to find another meaning to her words. "Excuse me?" I asked her.

I couldn't mistake how she rubbed against me. "There's nothing he loves more than dominating two women at once. Hasn't he mentioned that to you yet? I loved it when he brought other women into the playground with us. And, of course, as his favorite, he brings me back in to play with his new subs."

A wave of nausea hit me, and my fists clenched. I did not want these women to know how they'd affected me, but it was already a struggle, and I knew they weren't finished.

Jolene lowered the sleeveless top of her dress, exposing the perfectly proportioned, overly generous globes of her breasts. I noticed the large silver hoops pierced into her dark red nipples immediately.

Her sinfully full lips curved into a sensuous smile. "He only gives these to his favorites. Didn't you know?

Jules shocked me by pressing hard against me from behind and grabbing my wrists in a hard grip. It didn't even occur to me to struggle at first. A physical threat from these women was the last thing I had expected.

Even as Jules moved, Jolene was reaching her arms up around my neck and pressing her soft figure against me. Her petite, small-framed body was much stronger than I could have imagined as she pulled my head down to hers.

"Just a taste, Bianca," she whispered, just before she crushed her soft mouth to mine. I registered that it felt beyond strange to be kissed by such a soft, moist mouth as she moved her lips against mine. I was frozen in shock at the unexpected assault until she thrust her little tongue into my mouth. I began to struggle against the two women holding me in earnest, then. I bit Jolene's tongue hard enough to make her pull back with a curse.

She looked absolutely shocked at my rejection as she stepped away from me, her hand to her mouth. Jules released me at almost the same moment, moving in front of me to join a red-faced Jolene. Jolene's eyes made a surprisingly quick transformation from shocked to hard and mean as I watched the sensually lovely woman.

She pointed a finger at me. "You're making a mistake, you know. You can't hope to hold his interest unless you're willing to be more open-minded. He's completely insatiable. He needs variety, and if you can't provide it, he'll be done with you in a week." As she spoke, Jules was adjusting Jolene's top back over her breasts. Her touch on the other woman spoke of familiarity.

I glared at both of them. "That's not happening. If James wants other women, he's free to have them. I'll leave him so fast his head will spin. And if you two like women so much, you can have each other. Why even bother with James?"

Jolene's expression didn't change at all. "You won't be able to let him go so easily. And he's impossible to forget. Mark my words, you'll change your mind about wanting me. I'll be waiting." As she spoke, the two women linked their fingers together, a clear sign of their solidarity.

Jules gave me a very 'cat that ate the canary' smile as they sauntered out of the bathroom. They walked out slowly, as though they hadn't assaulted me just moments before.

I just stood there, staring at the closed door for long moments, completely stunned by the whole deranged exchange. In spite of my resolve not to let Jules cause us problems, the things I had been told had shaken my faith in James, and in our ability to have any kind of a stable relationship. I turned from the closed door to look in the mirror. The sight that met my eyes made me angry. My mouth was smeared with Jolene's crimson lipstick, and my eyes were wide and scared. I dragged the back of my hand across my mouth, wiping away the offending color.

I had forgotten about the bathroom attendant completely. I only recalled her presence as she kindly offered me a towel. I thanked her gratefully, wiping at the red on my lips, trying to erase every trace. It clung to my mouth stubbornly. I hated the color.

The bathroom door burst open and a furious James tore inside as though he'd hit it at a dead sprint. He took me in with wild eyes, searching the bathroom as he moved towards me.

A drop-dead gorgeous woman hurried in the door behind him. She had streaky blond hair worn down her back in whimsical mermaid waves. She wore a soft gray sheath gown that managed to be both elegant and sexy. It covered her from neck to ankle but did nothing to disguise her spectacular, supermodel figure.

I couldn't spare her much of a glance as James reached me swiftly, cupping a hand at the back of my head, his other hand tilting my chin up to study me.

"What happened?" he asked.

My hand grabbed his where it held my chin, and his eyes flew to the back of my hand. It was covered in crimson lipstick smears.

His eyes moved from my hand to my mouth and back again. "What happened?" he repeated, his tone harsh.

"Can't you guess? Your Exes got their hands on me. The short one doesn't understand the word no very well," I told him. My voice came out more coldly than I meant for it to.

His hand tightened to a nearly painful grip on my chin. His voice got very quiet, but I heard the panic in it. "They assaulted you?"

"Jules held my wrists while Jolene took her top off and forced me to kiss her. Yeah, I guess you could say they assaulted me. They seem to have some sort of routine down for pressuring your women into trying threesomes." I made my face and voice as expressionless as I could manage. I wanted to see his response and I watched him carefully for it.

He cringed, an awful kind of rawness overtaking his face. He pulled me into his chest. "I'm sorry. I should have done a better job of protecting you. I swear I'll take the necessary steps to make sure nothing like that ever happens again. I just never dreamed they would do something like confront you in a bathroom. And I never imagined they would put their hands on you."

I should have realized that he'd blame himself for it all. I still felt angry and bitter about the entire thing, but even in spite of that, I felt myself wanting to soften towards him.

"Bianca, this is Lana. She's an old friend of mine." James made the introduction while still holding my face buried in his chest. "She happened in on you being harassed in the bathroom and was kind enough to come get me."

I turned to meet the woman, not missing the clear affection I heard in his voice as he said the woman's name.

The woman was even more stunning than I had realized, as I caught my second glance at her, this time closer up. She gave me a friendly, if very careful, smile. She had the face of a fairytale princess, with eyes so bright a blue they were violet. I wondered if they could have been her real eye color. I had never met anyone with purple eyes before.

Her wavy blond hair had every shade of blonde streaked through it as it flowed down her back and around her shoulders like a whimsical cape. Her face was stunning, her features perfectly symmetrical, her eyes big and thickly lashed, her nose tiny and pert, her soft, pouty mouth damn near as pretty as James's.

She stood at eye level with me, which meant she was somewhere between five nine and six feet tall, though I couldn't say for sure without a good look at the size of her heels. As I studied her, I realized that somehow I recognized this exquisite woman, though I hadn't a clue how. She was not the type of woman anyone could forget meeting.

She saw my brow furrow as I studied her. She seemed to read my thoughts, and grimaced. "You recognize me," she said with a sigh. Her voice was soft and musical. She shot James an arch look. "James, you're in the ladies restroom, as you seem to have forgotten. Go wait outside. I'll help your Bianca freshen up so you two can make your escape. I'll even make your excuses for you, but you need to get out of this bathroom before you create a scene. Anyone could come in here at any moment."

James kissed the top of my head before heading to the door. He cast me a worried glance but spoke to Lana. "Don't be long," he warned.

She held out a chair in front of a vanity for me. "Sit down, hon," she said. I complied, responding automatically to the kindness in her voice. She couldn't have been more than twenty-six, but she had an almost maternal countenance, in spite of her bombshell looks.

I studied her in the mirror, but still couldn't place her. "What do I know you from?" I asked her finally. She had a huge, if fashionable, handbag, splayed out on the counter, and was digging through it determinedly.

She cast me a wry smile. "I had a dismally short stint in modeling a few years ago. I wasn't suited for it at all, but people occasionally recognize me from some high profile covers I did. I only ever even got the covers because my mother was a supermodel from the eighties."

As she spoke I conjured up a memory of her in a tiny yellow bikini, straddling a surfboard for a very famous cover of Sports Illustrated. My jaw dropped. "You were a supermodel yourself. You don't model anymore?"

She shrugged, her smile turning very self-deprecating. "It's a fact that I'm much better at working for the family business than I ever was at smiling for the camera."

I studied the fascinating woman, happy for a distraction from the night's drama. "What's the family business?"

She flashed a charming dimple at me. "Don't hold it against me, but my family is also in the hotel business. The Middletons are infamous competitors of the Cavendish family. Imagine everyone's shock when James and I met and became fast friends, over eight years ago."

I wondered if friends could possibly be all that they were. How could two such outrageously good looking people of the opposite sex be strictly friends? Especially if one of them was James...

She seemed to read my mind again. Her eyes widened on mine in the mirror and she vehemently shook her head. "We have been *strictly* friends. We went out to dinner a few times when we first met. I think James was toying with the idea of trying to seduce me, but it never came to that. He's a man that knows how to read women, and he knew I was unreceptive. And I must tell you, I'm quite relieved at the change I've seen in him since he's met you. I had thought, for the longest time, that James was as broken as me, if for different reasons."

"Broken?" I asked, completely drawn in by her candid manner.

She grimaced, but her fairytale lavender eyes quickly smoothed back into a smile. "I'm not usually such an open book, but I can't seem to help it with you. It makes sense, I suppose. You and I just have to be friends. I adore James, and I adore you on principal just for being the woman to finally make him fall in love."

CHAPTER THIRTY-FOUR

I didn't correct her words, though they made me wince as though she'd hit upon a very tender subject. Instead, I turned the focus back on her. "Why did you say *you* were broken?"

She smiled. It was the saddest smile, unarguably heartbreaking. She just had that effect. What she felt showed on her lovely face, and it was impossible not to feel at least a little of it with her.

"Since I can remember, I've been in love with a man who can never love me back. In fact, he's in love with someone else, though it took me a long time to see that. My heart's never been able to move on, so, much to my parents horror, I seem to be immune to the opposite sex. Even to a man as beautiful as James. I tried to be attracted to him, at first, but it's no use. I think that it was after that when I knew not to bother anymore. I'm the type of woman who will only ever fall in love once. Unfortunately, that one time happened to be with a man who could only ever see me as a sister."

"That's impossible," I told her. "You could have any man you wanted."

She just shook her head, finally pulling a brush out of her

monstrosity of a designer bag. She began to carefully pull the brush through my mussed-up hair. "Lovely hair," she murmured to me almost absently. "You and I could pass for sisters, really," she added. I thought it was a hugely flattering compliment. "How many women have naturally blond hair nowadays? You're the only other one I know. But, no, I certainly cannot have any man I want. And I only ever wanted one. Akira Kalua. I shamelessly threw myself at him and the best I got was a pity fuck, pardon my crass language, but that's the best term for it."

"Akira Kalua," I repeated back, surprised at the name. It sounded vaguely familiar, though I couldn't place why. I thought the name sounded very Hawaiian. I had several Hawaiian friends, and there was a large population of them working for my airline.

She smiled almost wistfully, as though just hearing the name brought back bittersweet memories. "I'm an island girl at heart, if you can believe it, though I was banished from paradise a long time ago. God, I hate New York."

I was more than a little surprised at that admission. I had just assumed, with her family wealth and incredible looks, that she would fit right into the big apple. "You're from Hawaii?" I guessed.

She nodded, smoothing my hair with a comforting hand before digging back into her bag. "Born and raised. My dad fell in love with Hawaii when my mother was pregnant with me. Maui, to be specific. By the time they were ready to live in a different house, I wasn't ready to go with them. They had to leave without me, and my adopted Hawaiian family wound up having me more than my actual parents did."

"Tell me about Akira," I prompted. She just smiled, shaking her head. She brought a makeup wipe to my face, wiping off the errant mascara that had bled under my eyes. I wanted badly to hear her story now that she had given me a few juicy tidbits. From the beauty of her face and the sadness in her eyes, I just knew it was a tragic love story that would be captivating.

"Another time, perhaps. You need to join James before he causes a scene. We have to hang out sometime soon, though. James told me you live in Vegas. I spend a lot of time there, managing the family property. It's only five minutes from the Cavendish property, in fact. I'll get your number from James. Have lunch with me?"

I nodded. I had met her minutes ago, but I felt like we were already friends. It was more than a little unusual for me. "Will you tell me about Akira then?" I asked, strangely curious about this lovely woman's love life.

She gave me an exasperated look, digging into her handbag again. She handed me a tube of clear lip gloss. "Just use your finger. I swear it's never touched my lips. It'll make your lips look less bruised. And yes, I'll tell you about Akira when we meet for lunch, if you really want to know. I never talk about him, so maybe it'll be therapeutic to get it off of my chest. But *you* have to tell me about you and James."

I liked Lana, so I agreed as I dabbed on a bit of lip gloss with my finger, handing the tube back to her.

She smiled at me. "Good as new. James will want to get out of here ASAP. He's in a rare state. He was expected to say a few words, but I'm familiar with the charity, so let him know I'll step in for him. I'll call you sometime this week."

When I stood she enveloped me in a tight hug. I hugged her back, more than a little surprised by the affectionate gesture.

"God, I love that you're as tall as me. I don't feel like a giant around you. We have got to hang out," she said with a smile as she pulled back.

James was practically pacing impatiently as we stepped out of the bathroom. He grabbed my arm in a death-grip as soon as I was within reach.

"Go on. I'll make your excuses. Oh, and James, send me

Bianca's number. We're going out to lunch, hopefully sometime this week," Lana told him.

He gave her a grateful, if tense, smile. "Thanks, Lana. I owe you." He began to lead me away, not pausing as he spoke. "The car is being brought 'round. We can make a quick escape. I need to get out of here."

Becoming almost twitchy with impatience, James led us out of the ball and into a waiting town car in a dizzying blur of activity. We exited into a tiny back alley where I saw no sign of photographers.

I sensed James withdrawing as the car began to move. When I gazed out the window I felt him studying me but when I turned back to look at him, he was gazing out of his own window, stone-faced.

I had endless questions that I needed answers to. I wanted to know what Jolene had lied about and what had been the truth. I hoped to god not all of it had been true. I wanted and needed, to know, but I was almost scared to hear his side of it, scared that our relationship wouldn't survive the answers. And it didn't help that I had no idea where to even begin.

We were nearly back to his building before I broke the silence. The feet that stretched between us on the seat felt like miles.

"You said you'd never been in a serious relationship before, but Jolene claims that you were with her for a year and two months, and that you continued to see her often, up until six weeks ago. Was she lying?"

He was silent for an unnervingly long time, his face unmoving as he stared out the window. "We're almost to my building. We'll talk about this inside."

I didn't like that answer. I knew that the only answer I would have liked would have been a quick and unhesitant, 'yes, she was lying.'

The driver took us to the underground garage elevator and we disembarked from the car silently. James took my arm in a proprietary manner as we walked to the elevator, but didn't even touch me once we were alone. It made a little ball of terrible black dread tie a knot in my belly.

He was deeply upset, and it had to do with what had happened in the bathroom. Was he upset about the questions I would ask? Was he troubled about how I would respond to his answers? Or was it something worse? I was starting to worry that it was something even more terrible, like he was about to break up with me altogether. Had the whole relationship idea finally sank in for him, and now he was realizing that it wasn't what he wanted? Had seeing the lovely Jolene made him realize his mistake? A part of me had been expecting him to do something like that all the while.

"Can we talk in our bedroom?" James asked, finally breaking the silence as we neared the top floor of the building.

I studied him. He wouldn't even look at me. I thought I might become physically ill. "We don't have to move this quickly, James. We shouldn't even be talking about moving in together yet, let alone actually doing it." *I've lost all of my pride*, I realized. I was trying to reassure him that we could take a step back instead ending it altogether. Anything to keep him from saying what I feared he was thinking.

He sent me an almost stricken look, but quickly looked away, making me think I'd imagined it. "We'll talk in our room," he said. I wasn't reassured.

The elevator reached his floor, and he led me up to his room without a word. I saw from a clock we passed that it was just past eleven o'clock. I was shocked that it wasn't any later than that. A lot had happened in the last few hours. I thought of Lana Middleton. She had been a welcome distraction. "Do you know anything about Lana and Akira?" I asked James.

He still didn't look at me. "Akira?" he asked. So he didn't know, either.

"Never mind."

He was walking first up the stairs to the floor of his bedroom. "Lana is the worst workaholic I know. She makes me look like a slacker with my seven day work weeks. Everyone who knows her loves her, but even the socializing she does is for work." His tone was impersonal as he mapped Lana out.

"She asked me to go to lunch," I pointed out.

"That means she really likes you. I'm glad. She's a very good friend, and she's very discreet and nonjudgmental, so you won't have to guard your words with her."

I blinked, wondering if he meant that I could discuss *us* with her. "Does she know about your...preferences?" I asked finally.

"Not exactly. She knows that I have atypical sexual proclivities, and she knows that I used to sleep around too much, but I doubt she's heard many more details than that. But I think she would be a good person for you to talk to, if you need that. As I said, she can be trusted with secrets, and she won't...berate you for your own preferences. That's just not her way."

He had basically given me the go ahead to tell Lana about our BDSM activities. I was grateful that I could, though I still didn't know if I would. I hadn't even discussed it with Stephan, and I rarely kept even the most minor of details from him. I decided that it might be easier to tell a woman like Lana than it would be Stephan. He was so protective of me that I wasn't sure how he would react to the things I let James do to me.

Our brief distraction technique came to an abrupt end as we reached his bedroom. He hovered in the doorway, ushering me inside. I glanced back at him. He was acting so unlike himself that it raised every hair on my body.

He just watched me for long minutes, as though trying to get answers just by looking. His face was shuttered, but his hands shook a little as he loosened his silken navy bow-tie.

"Take off your clothes, Bianca." When he finally spoke, his voice was dangerously soft.

I shot him a defiant look, my chin lifting. "We can't put this off, James. We need to talk."

He nodded. "Yes. Take off your clothes and get on the bed. We'll talk then."

I watched him closely, trying to decide if it was a strange joke.

His nostrils flared. "Now," he said. There was a fine tremor in the hand that pointed to the bed. Finally I complied, driven by his strange mood and the desire to know exactly what it meant.

CHAPTER THIRTY-FIVE

I stepped out of my shoes as I approached the bed, shrugging out of my floaty gown with a few easy movements. My tiny lace thong was a distant memory between one step and the next.

I sat on the very edge of the bed, facing him. I was naked, but I didn't feel as self-conscious as I usually did. I had too many other things to be anxious about.

"Lie down in the center of the bed," James ordered softly, still framed in the doorway. He was still fully dressed in that devastating navy tux, only his tie mussed, though it still hung undone around his neck.

I obeyed, but it didn't come as naturally as it normally did. Sheer force of will made me shift my body onto the spot where he'd ordered it.

"Spread your legs and raise your hands over your head," he continued.

I shot him a wild look. He was getting waaay off track. "James," I began.

"Do it," he said with a new trace of steel in his voice. I closed my eyes, nearly shuddering as I obeyed him. I wanted answers, but I couldn't lie to myself. I wanted this just as much.

He only moved after I'd complied, striding towards the bed and using the restraints hidden at each corner of the bed to secure me swiftly. As he stared at my restrained body, some of the tension seemed to drain out of him, right before my eyes.

He loomed over me from the side of the bed for a long time before he finally spoke. "Now you can't run away if you get upset. Ask me whatever you need to. I'll answer all of your questions, and you know I'll be honest, but you don't get to run away if you don't like the answers."

I was looking directly at him, but I could see my chest rising and falling with rapid breaths out of the corner of my eye. If his tactic had been to distract me from the questions that troubled me, he'd succeeded beautifully. Now that I was naked and bound, nothing seemed as important as what he could do to me, not even those answers.

I mentally shook myself, making my mind move back to the discussion at hand with great effort.

"Was Jolene lying, James?" I finally asked, dreading the answer.

He ran a restless hand through his dark golden hair, mussing up its artful evening styling. He began to pace, shrugging out of his tuxedo jacket and tossing it onto a chair. I was ready to scream by the time he answered.

"She wasn't lying. She was my contracted submissive for about that long. But we didn't see each other 'often' after that. We met up maybe six times a year, if that, and generally when I was between subs. I know this doesn't make me look any better, but it was only ever physical between Jolene and I. I know she thinks she's in love with me, so it was badly done of me to keep in touch, but it was a strictly sexual relationship. It's an awful thing to say, but I don't even like her."

I flinched every time he mentioned things like 'physical' and 'sexual', horribly vivid images of the two beautiful people entwined naked together flashing through my mind. I turned my head away and shut my eyes for a moment, trying to compose myself. I knew it was silly to be so jealous, but knowing and feeling were two very different things. "Was she the woman you were with the night before I met you?"

He cursed, a long and fluid rant, but I didn't look at him.

"Yes," he answered after a long pause. "I always used a condom with Jolene, though, if that's what's worrying you."

I counted to ten in my head, the word 'condom' striking at some vulnerable part of me. It wasn't the condom, but rather the act that went with it, and the horrible woman he had done those things with, painting a vivid and painful picture in my mind of the two of them together.

My next question embarrassed me for some ludicrous reason, and my cheeks blushed pink even as I began to speak. "Jolene said a few things about joining you and your other subs..."

I felt him sit down near my hip. His hot hand gripped my wrist. The hold was light, but I thought I could still feel his intensity through the contact. "She joined me and two of my subs in the playground, maybe a handful of times. None of this matters, Bianca. I know it troubles you, but it really is insignificant. How I feel about you is what's important."

"She said that there's nothing you love more than dominating two women at once," I said quietly, wanting to pull my wrist away from the hot contact of his hand.

I heard him suck in a breath, but kept my eyes stubbornly closed. "That's a lie. I've done that with a few subs, but only the subs I knew favored that sort of thing, but that's never been about *my* preferences. I suspect that Jolene herself may prefer that."

"Jolene said you didn't stay with women unless they would do that for you."

His palm made contact with my thigh. It wasn't a slap,

exactly, but it wasn't a soft touch either. "This is ridiculous. I wouldn't ask that of you. I would be distraught if you even suggested it. You aren't just my sub, Bianca. This is much more than just a physical relationship. I feel utterly possessive of you. If someone touched you the way I touch you, male or female, I would lose my mind."

He took a shaky breath before he continued. "I want to share my life with you, to be monogamous with you, and my past is in the past. I wish there was some way I could prove it to you, once and for all. I do have a sordid past, but I've never lied to any of the women I've been with, and I've never promised to anyone the things I promise to you."

My breathing was growing more even, the strange red haze over my vision getting better with every word he spoke. He was charming me out of my doubts, and no part of me wanted him to stop. *I have it bad*, I realized then. It was worse than I had even realized, and I'd known I was already crazy in love with this incomparable man. "Thank you for answering my questions," I told him softly.

He was so quiet for a long moment that I couldn't even hear him breathe. "You're not upset?" he asked finally.

"A little, but I'll get over it. I get insanely jealous when I think about you with other women, and I was sick with worry that you would want me to do things with Jolene that I just can't do, but I'm not unreasonable." I looked at him as I spoke. His face was stricken.

He crawled on top of me still fully clothed. He moved until we were nose to nose, that awful look still on his face. "I would never ask you to do anything like that. Moreover, I wouldn't allow it. You promised me exclusivity, and I intend for you to hold up your end of that as staunchly as I'll hold up mine. Will you still move in with me, still stay with me? Even though I've done a dismal job of protecting you?"

I agreed that I would, even though my doubt was still a thick knot in my stomach, but as I was learning, again and again, he was impossible to resist.

"You can't exactly protect me in the women's restroom, James. That's just silly. And you certainly couldn't predict that they would do that to me. I couldn't believe it even when it was happening. Jolene showed me her piercings. I really didn't ever want to see that."

James got up at my words, moving swiftly into his bathroom. He returned quick moments later with a toothbrush. He was very gentle as he brushed my teeth. It was an awkward angle with me on my back and helpless. "Tell me where they touched you. I want to scrub them off of you."

I thought he was beyond strange, and it went without saying that this was some kind of OCD on his part, but I enabled his strange need to wash them away, telling him every single thing they had done, and every part of me that had been touched.

His face was dark as he worked, scrubbing hard at my wrists. He worked for a long time on my kiss swollen lips. They were swollen more from the way I had scrubbed them myself than from the kisses, but it didn't seem to matter to James. When he was finally done scrubbing, he moisturized me thoroughly, spreading something that felt like vaseline directly onto my lips.

"It would have saved time if you had just let me loose to shower," I told him, trying to make him smile, anything to ease the tense set of his shoulders, and the dark look in his eyes.

"I couldn't bring myself to untie you. I have this nagging fear that you'll run away from me again, and I'll have to suffer through another desolate month. That was the longest month of my life. I'd do anything to never let it happen again."

I felt a strange wrenching in my chest at the thought of him alone and suffering because of me. I hadn't withdrawn to hurt him. I had been scared, scared of the way he made me feel, and the way I couldn't seem to help but do his will.

"Make love to me, James." My voice held a clear plea as I addressed him.

I didn't have to ask him twice. He was on top of me in a flash, kissing my mouth as though he wanted to devour me. He was still fully clothed, and the silk of his shirt rubbed against my chest teasingly. He propped the lower half of his body just out of reach. I circled my hips, trying to reach him, but my legs held me securely against the soft bed. I arched my back, rubbing my chest harder against his. He thrust his tongue deep into my mouth, and I sucked on it, drawing on it like I would his cock. He groaned.

He'd propped himself up on his elbows, setting them deep into my underarms so he could cup my face as he kissed me. I thought this was the closest James could get to sweet lovemaking. But even his sweetest moment was still too fucking hot to bear.

I whimpered against his mouth. It was a plea. My body was throbbing for him, and nothing would feel like enough until he was buried deep inside me. He didn't seem to agree, and just continued like that for long, torturous minutes, only the top halves of our bodies touching as he worshipped at my mouth.

Eventually he began to move down my body with sweet, torturous kisses along every inch of me. His pretty mouth was incredibly and deliberately soft as he rained kisses across my ribs and into my navel. He'd avoided my quivering breasts altogether, seeming to focus on absolutely every other inch of my torso. I realized that he was torturing me systematically when he moved back up my body and began to kiss along my shoulder tops and up one of my bound arms.

He moved off of me as he focused on one fettered wrist. I watched him, his face so sensual, no coldness present tonight. He licked along the spot where the black rope met the inside of my wrist, and I writhed. He rose to his knees to massage my hand for long, agonizing minutes. It felt exquisite, but I wanted to scream.

He moved back down my arm, across my shoulders, and gave the opposite arm, wrist, and hand the same treatment. I felt on the edge of orgasm just from that and the sight of him crawling around me on the giant bed, his full erection clearly outlined even in his navy silk trousers.

I sucked in a breath as he nuzzled into my underarm, licking me there as though it were a rare treat. He licked and kissed just the undersides of my breasts as he moved to my other side to repeat the motion. I squirmed. "Hold still," he murmured, a warning note in his voice.

He continued to torment me for the longest time, kissing and licking and nuzzling into my skin, while skipping all of the obvious spots. I discovered as he did this that he had enough skill to draw exquisite pleasure from even the most innocent parts of my body. He had me panting just by paying special attention to the dimples in my knees. "James," I gasped, "you should be illegal. There can't be anyone alive as good at this as you."

He gave me a heated look from under his pretty lashes for that one. "If there is, you'll never know it," he said, rather darkly, I thought.

That exchange seemed to light a fire in him and he began to pleasure me in earnest. He licked his way up to my breasts, drawing on a nipple until I was ready to come just from that nearly painful pressure. He gave equal attention to it's twin before moving down the center of my torso, past my naval, and into my core. I screamed as he finally buried his face there. This was no idle caress, and he used his fingers and tongue to make me come within seconds. He never slowed as I spun back down from my nirvana, bringing me back to orgasm like my nerves were simple keys on a piano.

He was in a relentless sort of mood, and he brought me again and again, until I lost count, though with the mood he was in, I doubted that *he* forgot the number.

I felt boneless and light-headed when he finally impaled me. He rammed into me with one clean thrust, and my eyes shot open. They had only been closed because he was too absorbed with his face between my legs to notice the slight.

Our eyes locked, and I realized in a corner of my very distracted mind that he was still fully clothed. Even his tie still remained hanging around his neck, thought he had loosened it. I glanced down at our joined bodies and saw that he had only undone his slacks and pulled them down slightly, just enough to give him access. Something about all of those dark, formal clothes against my naked, bound body was one of the most erotic things I'd ever seen.

His forehead nearly touched mine as he held himself over me, working in and out of me with smooth motions. It was downright gentle, for him. He was making slow, sweet love to me, in his way.

Scant drops of sweat dripped from his temples to mine. I thought it was unbelievably sensual. Only Mr. Beautiful could make sweat into something so sexy. I wanted to lick it all off of his body. I told him so.

He grinned, though there was an edge to it as he continued to thrust in and out of me with agonizing slowness. "Not tonight. You were thinking about taking other lovers while I made love to you. Now I have something to prove. Perhaps if I fuck you unconscious, you won't be able to wonder if there's someone better out there for you."

I gave him an exasperated look. As much as I could, considering he was slowly fucking me out of my mind. "You're impossible, James. You took that all wrong. I was only thinking about you, and how lucky I am to have you."

His face went a little slack. It made my heartstrings pull. With a shout he began to thrust in earnest, and from the look on his face, he was completely losing himself. I loved it. I drank in the sight of his composure completely deserting him as he pounded into me, his beautiful eyes made into slits with the strain. He shouted my name, rather desperately, as his orgasm took him. My own caught me moments later as he continued to arch deeply inside of me.

He let his heavy weight sag onto me for several minutes in our aftermath. I nuzzled my face into the hair around his ear, smelling his wonderful spicy scent, mixed with his sweat and just a hint of cologne.

"You're wonderful," I whispered against his hair.

He stiffened, burying his face into my neck, nuzzling there. "I want to deserve you, my love," he whispered back. I could hear the desperation in his quiet voice.

"Do you even know how crazy that is?" I asked in the same quiet voice, as though we could be overheard. "I'm nobody, and you're the most extraordinary man I've ever met. I don't deserve you."

He made a little sound of protest in his throat. "You're my angel, Bianca. You've exorcized my demons. I don't have nightmares when I'm with you. I don't have to work seventy hour work weeks to keep my mind distracted. My life has become more than work and emotionless affairs. You make me a better man."

"You're so good to me," I told him.

He reached up to untie my wrists, kissing me softly all over my face as he did so.

He had me untied and cradled into his chest in swift moments. I cuddled into the soft silken fabric of his shirt, too tired to even try to get him naked.

I was just on the edge of sleep when I felt him shift. "Love, I promised Stephan you would call and text him before you went to bed. He wanted to make sure your night went alright. Don't drift off. I'm going to find your phone."

I quickly found I had to sit up to stay awake as James

disappeared into his closet. He re-emerged in short order, stripped down to his boxer-briefs, and carrying my phone. He maneuvered himself behind me on the bed, pulling me between his legs as I checked my phone. I had several texts from Stephan, asking how I was, and I texted him back that everything was fine and I would see him in the morning.

I checked my phone log next. I had missed three more calls from the strange 702 number, and my brows drew together as I saw that the caller had left a voicemail this time. That was new. I found myself clicking the play button and holding my phone to my ear before I thought better of it. I should have waited until morning, but something about the strange caller and number was nagging at me. If it was my father, I'd just as soon know right away, instead of worrying about it all night.

The voicemail was just silence at first, with the slightest hint of background noise, soft soothing music playing, just like in the phone calls. But eventually a harried female voice began to speak haltingly. There was a familiar paranoid fear in her voice, though I didn't recognize the voice itself at all.

"Bianca Karlsson. This is, um, this is Sharon." A long pause. "Sharon Karlsson." My entire body went still as a corpse and the hair on the back of my neck prickled with a warning. "I'm...married to your father. I, well, I guess that I'm your stepmother. I really need to speak to you. Your father always forbade me from trying to contact you. He would never say why, but, well, um, he's disappeared. He's been gone for over a month with no word, and I'm pretty sure he's gone for good this time. So I would really appreciate it if you would meet with me. Please call me back as soon as you can."

CHAPTER THIRTY-SIX

My hand dropped into my lap still holding the phone.

"What is it?" James asked, apparently not overhearing the strange message. I didn't answer, my mind busy worrying over the bizarre development of my father having a wife.

James took the phone out of my hand, and I watched him retrace my steps and hold the phone up to his own ear to listen to *my* message.

Nosy, rich bastard, I thought, almost fondly.

His brow furrowed as he listened to the strange message. He reached over to put my phone on the bedside table, then came close to cuddle me against him.

"I don't like this. If you decide to meet with her, it should be in public, and make sure you have at least two bodyguards with you. Promise me, Love."

I nodded absently, nowhere near keeping up with his train of thought, my mind still obsessing over the strange knowledge that my father had remarried. *When? Why?* Did he treat this strange woman better than he had my poor abused mother? The woman was alive, so clearly he did.

In spite of my body's exhaustion, my mind became too busy for sleep after that. James cleaned us both, even wiping away my makeup before turning out the lights and spooning in behind me. His presence was soothing, but I still worried over the surprising news for a long time before finally drifting into a restless sleep.

I was in that house again. I lay in my hard, tiny bed. I was hugging my knees to my chest, rocking and rocking, and trying to ignore the harsh shouts just a few thin walls away. If I stayed in my room, it would all go away. They would forget I was even here and in the morning my Dad would sleep all day and leave us in peace so I could tend to my Mother.

But that wasn't meant to be. Not this time. The yelling grew louder, my mothers turning into terrified screams.

When I couldn't stand the horrible noises a moment longer, I crept quietly through the house to investigate. In spite of my overwhelming fear, my need to at least attempt to aid my mother almost always thrust me into the violent thick of things.

I looked down at my thin bare feet, wishing I knew where some clean socks were. I was so cold, an achy kind of cold, down to my very soul.

My parents were speaking in Swedish, and I pieced together some hysterical words as I got closer to the kitchen where they fought. "No, no, no. Please, Sven, put that away."

My father's voice was an angry roar. "You've ruined my life. You and that brat. I've lost everything because of you. My fortune, my inheritance, and now, my luck. You've taken everything from me, just by living. Tell me why I shouldn't take everything from you, you silly cunt?"

"When you're sober, you'll regret it. We have a child together, Sven. Please, just go to sleep. If you sleep on it, you'll feel better."

"Don't you dare tell me what to do! Fuck sleep. Fuck you. And fuck that little brat. Look at her, hovering in the door, frozen like a little mouse." His cold eyes went to me.

I was frozen in place, as he'd said. He changed his tone when he spoke to me, and it turned into a mockery of a gentle tone. "Why don't you join us, sotnos? Come be with your pretty Mama."

I moved to my mother, having learned a very long time ago not to disobey him when he was in this mood.

He sneered at the two of us when I stood beside her. He towered over us. My mother didn't look at me, didn't reach for me. I knew she didn't want to draw more attention to me. She tried to protect me, as I did her. "Look at my pretty girls. The daughter is even prettier than the mother. What use, then, is the mother? Tell me why you're useful, Mama?" he asked her.

I didn't hear her answer. My gaze was focused solely now on the object he was holding at his side. It was a gun. My gut clenched in dread. The gun was a new and terrifying addition to this violent scene.

My gaze flew back to my father's face as a laugh left his throat. It was a cackle of a laugh, dry and angry.

I began to back away, shaking my head back and forth in denial.

"Wrong answer, cunt," he said.

He waved the the pistol in front of her. "You can't take your eyes off of this. Do you want it? Would you like me to give this to you? Take it, if you want it. You think I can't touch you with a gun in your hand?"

My mother watched him, her eyes almost blank with terror. She must know, as I did, from the mocking tone of his voice, that he was testing her. She would pay dearly if she took the gun from him, even if he had told her to.

He laughed. "I insist. Take the gun."

Unexpectedly, and horrifyingly, she did. She pointed it at him with hands that shook. "Get out," she said, her voice tremulous and awful with her terror. "You can't do these things, especially in front of our daughter. Get out, and don't come back." She was sobbing, but she managed to pull the hammer back.

He laughed again. With no fear and no effort, he grabbed her hand. His hand covered one of hers, ripping the other one away. He turned the gun, slowly and inexorably pointing it away from himself and pushing it into her mouth.

I had backed myself against the wall as I watched their exchange, but when I saw his clear intent, I suddenly rushed forward, sobbing, "Mama."

I stopped as though I'd run into a wall when my father pulled the trigger, covering us and the entire room in obscene amounts of glowing crimson blood and gore.

My horrified eyes met my father's. His showed no expression at all.

I awoke to total darkness, a harsh scream caught in my throat. I had no notion of where I was and I began to scramble off of the huge, soft bed, fumbling around in the pitch blackness for a wall, a lamp, a light switch, anything. I needed to wash the blood off. I was feeling along the wall and sobbing like a child when light suddenly flooded the room.

I finally got an inkling of where I was as James rushed to me, cradling me into his chest. "What's wrong, Bianca? What can

I do?"

I gasped in several breaths before I could speak. "Shower. I need a shower. I need to wash the blood off."

He didn't ask anymore questions, getting us both into the shower in a flash. He turned the water directly onto me, and the cold water that hit me for just moments before it began to warm helped bring me a few steps further away from the dream.

Slowly, my broken sobs turned into gasping breaths as I became clean in the water, my mind moving further and further out of the nightmare realm.

"Can you talk about it?" James asked. His voice was so vulnerable with his concern for me that I couldn't resist him.

"It's the same old dream about my mother's death. I was in that room, not three feet from her, when it happened." I felt the floodgates open, and I told him everything, every gory detail, of both the dream and the horrific event. He didn't speak at all, just made sympathetic noises and gave me reassuring touches while I spoke. I was surprised to feel much better when I'd gotten it all out. It had actually helped to tell him about it.

He helped me out of the shower and dried us both off. We lay in a naked snuggle on the bed with only a sheet covering us. He was on his back and had pulled me almost on top of him.

I rubbed my cheek over my name on his chest as he stroked my wet hair back, arranging it over his arm.

"You've done all you can. You told the police everything you saw. It's not your burden anymore, Bianca."

"Yes, I know. I haven't had that nightmare since that other time, over a month ago. I think it was learning about *her*, his wife, that got my mind back into that dark place again. I need to tell her what he did, to warn her. I don't know the woman, but she deserves that much. Lord, I don't want to speak to her. I don't want anything to do with her."

"You could always just send her an email, or hell, a letter.

You don't have to do anything you don't want to."

I mulled that over. It seemed so cowardly to be afraid of a simple phone call. "I'll call her tomorrow," I decided.

His arms tightened on me, his hold becoming almost painful. It was comforting to my twisted senses. "I need to stay in New York this week. Will you come back to be with me on your first day off?"

I thought about it. It didn't take me long. "Yes. Do you mind if I invite Stephan? You have plenty of room, after all."

I had felt all of the anxious tension leave his body when I agreed to come. "*We* have plenty of room," he chastised. "And yes, of course. Invite Javier, too, if you like. Or anyone you want, for that matter. I'll have to work quite a bit anyways. I've been putting some important meetings off that need tending to. And god only knows what a mess my New York management has made of things on the Manhattan property. I would feel better if you had someone to hang out with while I'm working. I wouldn't want you to get bored, though you do have a studio set up for painting downstairs. I never had time to show you. We never seem to have enough time. How many days can you take off this week?"

"I can fly into New York Monday morning, and take a flight back on Thursday. I can take a week off from working overtime."

I began to wonder if Stephan could work his own overtime with Javier, instead of me. My boyfriend was filthy rich. It seemed silly not to at least keep my days off.

My stance had changed so drastically from just a week ago that I felt almost dizzy with it. Instead of intending to continue my life exactly as I pleased, I found myself wanting to compromise to please James, and of course, to see more of him.

He gave me a soft kiss for my concession. "I would love that. Thank you."

I sighed, plunging in deeper. "It seems ridiculous to work overtime anymore, everything considered. My straight time can more than cover my mortgage and food, and you bought me enough clothing to last a lifetime. I'm going to see if Stephan will work his extra shifts with Javier. I'd be willing to bet he won't mind the idea."

"Thank you," he said with quiet sincerity. "I'll make sure to make it worth your while."

I burrowed against him, feeling good. Good about him. Good about us. "You already have."

"You make me so happy, Bianca. I never knew life could be this good. I've been alone for so long, since my parents died, really. But I don't feel alone with you. I feel like I have a family and a home again. You're my home. All of the dark shadows seem to disappear when we're together."

I placed a kiss on my name over his heart, feeling myself drifting off. I didn't even know what time it was, but I wasn't worried. I knew James wouldn't let me oversleep. More and more, I just trusted him.

CHAPTER THIRTY-SEVEN

I couldn't stop yawning as I got ready for work the next morning. James woke up with me, in spite of the ungodly hour. He was alert but quiet as we both got dressed. He wore an elegant pale gray suit. It was so pale it almost looked white at first glance.

He paired it with a brilliant turquoise dress shirt with a stark white collar. A skinny tie as white as the collar hung to his pale gray belt. The pant legs were very narrow and fitted, and he'd chosen faded gray lace-up dress shoes. The full effect was devastating. Only James could have pulled it off.

He approached me from behind as I shrugged into my uniform dress shirt. He held up a tiny silver object in front of my face. It took me a moment to place it as a small lock. "May I lock on your collar now?"

I stiffened, but tilted my head forward to give him access. "Yes," I said.

For better or worse, I had made my decision.

He locked it on quickly, placing a soft kiss to my nape. "Turn around," he told me. I did, and he was holding the key on a chain around his own neck. He tucked it under his shirt as I watched. "There will be security at your house. Please cooperate with them. They're there to keep you safe."

I just nodded. I knew better than anyone that I wasn't safe, and I was grateful for the extra protection.

He rode in the town car with me to the crew hotel. He gripped me tightly to his side and buried his face in my hair. "This is harder than I thought it would be, letting you go like this," he murmured into my hair.

I rubbed a hand over the spot over his heart where he'd etched my name. I knew that the action comforted us both. "It's only for a few days."

"Call or text me when you land, and again when you're safely in your house. I'll worry if you don't."

I nodded, the motion rubbing his face against the back of my hair.

"I can't kiss you goodbye, Love. If I start, I know I'll never stop."

I nodded again. I understood the odd sentiment. Instead, when the car stopped in front of my crew hotel, I held his elegant hand to my lips, kissing the palm and then moving my lips over the faint thin scars on his wrist, placing a soft kiss there as well, and then moving my lips back into his palm, allowing myself just a moment to nuzzle against it.

He made a soft little sound in his throat that made it so hard to get out of the car. He caught my hand as I was about to move away and copied the motion on my own wrist and palm. It was sheer agony to walk away from him. I didn't look back. I knew that would only make it worse.

Only Stephan and Javier were in the lobby when I walked in, Stephan in his uniform, Javier dressed business casual in a lavender dress shirt and beige slacks.

I *was* five minutes early, I saw as I checked my watch. Stephan grinned when he saw me, striding over to hug me tightly.

"I missed you, Buttercup."

I hugged him back, just as tightly. "We have so much to talk about, but I needed to ask you and Javier something."

Javier approached us rather cautiously, as though afraid to interrupt our reunion. "What's up?" Stephan asked.

"How would you like to stay in the swankest pad in New York for our days off this week? Most likely we'd fly in Monday morning and stay until early Thursday."

Stephan's grin grew even wider. "I can't think of anything I'd love more. I take it this means you and James are working things out?"

I nodded, smiling and looking up into his eyes. I let him see all of my happiness but none of my troubles. It was what he deserved.

Javier cleared his throat. "Um, so, did you mean just for Stephan, or..."

I gave him a friendly smile. "I meant for the two of you to come, if you want to. James has an obscene amount of room, considering that it's in Manhattan."

Stephan cleared his throat, shooting Javier a positively wicked glance. I could have sworn Javier blushed just a tad even through his lovely pale mocha skin. "Javier and I only need one room regardless."

I blinked. That was moving incredibly fast, for Stephan. I took it as a good sign. He seemed to be more comfortable by the minute about being in an open relationship with a man.

"I had one more thing I wanted to talk to both of you about. I've decided to stop working so much overtime and just stick with my regular shifts, for the most part. I hope you don't mind losing your overtime partner."

Stephan didn't look in the least perturbed. "About damn time, Bee. I figured you would be catching on to that soon enough. I already asked Javier if he wanted to be my new overtime buddy.

He's doing some trades to share our days off, so it should work out perfectly." As Stephan spoke he stroked a hand over Javier's jet black hair.

Javier closed his eyes, as though savoring the light touch. I didn't know if it was just the only thing I knew with my limited experience with relationships, but it looked to me like Javier was clearly Stephan's submissive. The way he closed his eyes, his hands in his pockets to keep from touching back, just reminded me so much of an act of submission. Stephan's hand moved down to rub at a spot on Javier's thin, straight shoulders. Javier let out a pleased little moan. I thought they were beautiful together.

"The crew bus is here. Let's load up," Stephan said, releasing Javier.

We filed out, handing our luggage to the driver, who loaded it into the baggage compartments mounted along the bottom of the mini-shuttle. "Five more coming," Stephan told the driver, climbing inside.

Stephan and Javier took the backseat, and I sat on the row just in front of them. "Bianca, be our lookout," Stephan said rather cryptically. I turned to look at them. I was as shocked as I'd ever been by what I saw.

Stephan had a flushed Javier pinned down on the bench seat beneath them. He was straddling the smaller man and giving him a very intense, very heated look. He held the other man's wrists pinned tautly above his head. As I watched he bent down and kissed him. It was not a casual kiss but a rough one, and I knew dominance when I saw it. My shocked gaze flew out the window as I suddenly realized that I was the lookout, and that I actually needed to do the job considering the things going on in the backseat.

I heard Stephan murmuring something to Javier, and I could hear that whatever it was was muffled against some part of the other man's skin. "Bianca, do you suppose you could manage ten minutes without me on the flight?" Stephan addressed me. "I know it's going to be hectic, but I would really appreciate it."

"Of course," I answered without hesitation.

"See. I told you she would. Three hours, tops, and I'll take you again. I'm not *that* much of a tease," Stephan said in a low voice to Javier. It made me blush down to my toes, but I stayed alertly watching out the window.

"You *are* a tease," Javier muttered, sounding sullen. "Three hours is forever."

I spotted the pilots in the lobby. "Pilots incoming," I said, sounding a little panicked even to my own ears.

Stephan sat up, releasing Javier. I glanced back at Stephan. He grinned at me shamelessly. I couldn't help it. I grinned back. Javier looked more perturbed but still happy. His blush was like a happy glow around him. His words hadn't shown me that, but his face did. He gave me a shy smile. "Sorry," he muttered to me.

I smiled back. "Don't be sorry. I've never seen Stephan like this. I think you guys are beautiful together."

That made him truly glow. Javier had it bad. It took one to know one, and I knew that lovesick look because a certain Mr. Beautiful had the same effect on me. I was relieved to see it. I wanted Javier to feel that kind of love for Stephan. He wouldn't want to hurt someone he loved that much.

"Quit making him blush, Bianca. That's my job," Stephan said, ruffling Javier's hair affectionately. Sure enough, Javier blushed harder.

I turned around, shaking my head with a strange smile on my face. I had never seen this side of Stephan, didn't know he had it in him.

The Saturday morning flight into Vegas was hectic, as it always was. Stephan took his ten minutes with the meeting with Javier in the bathroom that I had expected. Both men emerged looking flushed and happy. We all grinned at each other like fools before Stephan and I got back to work and Javier returned to his seat.

Stephan and I clutched hands as we landed, grinning at each other. We didn't say much, just enjoying the moment.

I texted James as we taxied in.

Bianca: Just landed in Vegas. How r u?
James: Fine. Keeping busy with work, but still missing you like crazy.

I hesitated, then just said to hell with it.

Bianca: I miss you too.
James: Call me when you get to your house.

I put my phone away after that, since I'd be contacting him again soon enough.

The drive home was a jovial affair, with Stephan and Javier smiling about just about everything. My expression matched theirs. I couldn't seem to help myself.

I was met at my front door by the security guard, Paterson. A woman I'd never met before was standing beside him, looking grim. She was short and stocky, and I knew at a glance that she was a tough woman. She had dark hair held back in a short, no-nonsense braid. Her face was round and pale, but her eyes were hard and assessing. She didn't wear a scrap of makeup, I doubted she ever did, and her mouth was set in a grim line.

Her body could have been bulky or just big-boned. It was impossible to say with the baggy, short-sleeved mens button-up shirt she was wearing over wide-legged slacks. She was like the agents, in her own way. Just looking at her made you think of law enforcement.

Paterson gave me a polite nod as I approached my front door. I could feel Stephan hovering behind me. I didn't have to ask to know that he wouldn't leave until he knew I was settled into my house, safe and secure. He had done so ever since the attack.

"Ms. Karlsson, this is Blake. She's new to the team, but I've known her for years. She's the best. She'll be your personal bodyguard detail for public excursions. It's been very clearly brought to my attention that I had overlooked your security in public restrooms."

I flushed, recalling the incident in the restroom. Of course James would take extra measures after that. I should have seen it coming. I nodded to Blake. "Nice to meet you, Blake," I said. I wouldn't protest the extra security. I certainly couldn't argue that I needed it.

She nodded back solemnly. "A pleasure, Ms. Karlsson."

I wondered if I could get her to call me by my first name. I had sort of given up on trying that with the security after Clark. He'd stubbornly refused in spite of my prompting.

"Please, allow us to secure the house before you proceed inside," she said solemnly.

I nodded, unlocking the door and going inside to punch in the security code. Both Paterson and Blake sucked in a breath when I stepped into the house first. I saw how I had erred, and apologized. The least I could do for my bodyguards was make it easy for them to do their job. "I'll get you guys some copies of my keys and give you my security codes to make it easier."

Paterson cleared his throat, but it was Stephan that spoke. "I already did, Bee. I got copies for them, and for James."

I imagined that they were all holding their breath, waiting for me to throw some kind of tantrum, but I wasn't unreasonable. Stephan might have been a tad premature, but it was only a convenience at this point. "Thank you," I said. I thought I heard all three of them let out relieved breaths. *What has the security team been told about me*? I wondered.

Paterson and Blake asked me to stay near the front entrance while Blake hovered near me and Paterson did a rather long search of the house. I was too distracted by the new additions to my living room to care much. A Mac with a large screen had taken residence in the spot where my old computer had been. I just stared at it for awhile, blinking, my tired mind blank. "What happened to my old computer?" I asked out loud.

Stephan answered. "It's gone. That one has everything you need. I wiped the other one and put everything on this one for you. James asked me to do it so he wouldn't have to hire a stranger to go through your computer." His voice held a sheepish apology.

I sighed, becoming more and more resigned to James's constant need to buy me things. "That was nice of you. Thank you."

"You aren't mad?"

"It seems silly to get mad about getting a new computer, doesn't it? I'm growing accustomed to this sort of thing." I looked at Stephan as I spoke.

He grinned at me. "It was no trouble at all. James bought me one, too."

I thought of all the things I needed to tell him. There just hadn't been any time. "I have so much to tell you. Will you come over tonight?" Javier had already gone to Stephan's house and was waiting for him. The two men seemed inseparable. "Can we get a little while to talk, just the two of us? Then we could have dinner with Javier, unless you two want to be alone." It felt awkward to have to request his exclusive company, but I told myself to get used to it.

He gave me a chastising look. "Of course. I'll come over right after a nap. Just text me when you wake up. And yes, we'll all have dinner. At my place. I'll cook. I've missed you, Bee. I know I need to get used to it, but just a few days without you is tough. You never have to ask when you want to spend time with me. You give me the time and the place and I'll be there. Always."

I moved to him, and he opened his arms. I walked right into them, barely aware that we weren't alone. His words had touched an emotional chord in me. "Go get some sleep. As you can see, I'm in good hands. I'll text you when I wake up."

He kissed the top of my head. "Good night," he murmured. I walked him to the door.

Blake was studying me when I turned back into the room. She quickly schooled her face into a carefully blank expression.

"All clear," Paterson said as he strode back into the room. He addressed me, "If you have any problems, any problems at all, one of us will be right across the street, in a black SUV, at all times."

"I have a spare room. I don't mind if you guys want to sleep in there. There's only a twin bed, but it's better than sleeping in a car."

Paterson and Blake shared a look, but not before I saw the surprise in both of their eyes.

"Thank you for the kind offer, Ms. Karlsson," Blake said.

"I'll discuss it with Mr. Cavendish," Paterson said.

Of course control freak Cavendish would have the rule that he had to approve all decisions.

Paterson cleared his throat. "Mr. Cavendish has also asked me to tell you to please answer your phone." Paterson's voice was carefully polite, but I'd have been willing to bet that James hadn't been when he made the request. My phone was buried somewhere in my flight bag and I dreaded seeing how many calls I had missed since I'd left the plane.

"Excuse me, please. I need to go take a nap," I told the two security guards awkwardly. I wasn't used to having staff, and my first instinct was to treat them as guests in my home.

They both nodded rather deferentially, as though it had been taught to them amidst all of the other training they must have been through. "As I said, we'll be just outside. And my number is in your phone, under 'Security.'"

I thanked them both politely before I went into my room, shutting my door gratefully behind me. I meant to call James, my mind was on him even as I got half undressed and fell facedown on top of my covers.

CHAPTER THIRTY-EIGHT

A barrage of strange noises woke me up. It took me long disoriented minutes to sort them all out.

The most persistent noise came from my bedside table, in the form of an Ipad I hadn't even known existed. I recognized the thin object, but I certainly didn't know what one was doing in my bedroom, or how I hadn't noticed it before I went to sleep. I had passed out rather quickly, I remembered. It was letting out a loud chiming noise, over and over again.

I decided that wasn't my biggest problem as someone knocked, rather frantically, at my bedroom door. I felt fear curl in my stomach until I realized that any real threat would hardly be knocking at an unlocked door.

"Yes?" I called, my voice still full of sleep.

The door burst open and Blake stood framed in it. She had apparently taken my yes as an invitation to enter. Her eyes darted around my room, looking for threats. When she deducted that there was none, her eyes shifted to me. She quickly looked away uncomfortably.

I realized that I was basically naked, wearing only a pair of panties and one errant stocking. I had managed to pull a corner of the covers over most of my torso in my sleep, thank god, but it was obvious that I was nearly naked underneath.

A muffled sound from my flight bag drew my attention briefly, and a I realized that my phone had been going off constantly, just like the the mysterious Ipad.

"What's going on?" I asked Blake. I figured she had to have a better idea than I did.

"Mr. Cavendish has been unable to get ahold of you. He was...concerned. He said you were supposed to contact him when you got to your home, and you did not." Her voice held a world of condemnation, as though forgetting to make a phone call were the worst sort of offense.

I studied her. She wore only a tight navy T-shirt and athletic shorts, her shoulder holster and gun clearly visible. I realized that instead of being stocky, as I'd originally thought, her figure was solidly covered in stark muscles. I couldn't remember ever seeing a woman quite so ripped up with muscle. She could have been a female body builder.

"I just sort of passed out. I guess I was more tired than I realized."

She sighed heavily. "Well, please call Mr. Cavendish now. He's more than a little upset."

Before I could respond, a shirtless and disheveled Stephan appeared behind Blake, looking distraught. "Are you okay, Bee? James just woke me up. He's frantic, says you were supposed to call him hours ago and he hasn't been able to get ahold of you. He's got me feeling guilty for falling asleep before making you call him." As he spoke, Stephan brushed past Blake to my bed. He climbed in with me wearing only his boxers, stroking a hand over my hair. I thought Blake's eyes were going to bulge out of her head.

"That is highly inappropriate, Mr. Davis. I would ask that

you please remove yourself from Ms. Karlsson's bed."

I gave her a baffled look. Stephan's was downright unfriendly. "Stephan is my adopted brother," I explained to Blake, even though we didn't owe her an explanation. Still, I didn't see the need for her to get the wrong idea. And he really was my adopted brother, if not technically than at least emotionally.

She looked relieved. "That is a relief. Still, I will have to report this to Mr. Cavendish. Just so you know."

I shrugged. Stephan leaned over and kissed me on the forehead. "I'm going back to bed, Buttercup. Call James before he gets on a plane."

Stephan left, but Blake still hovered in the doorway.

I began to get annoyed, as much with James as with my stern bodyguard. "I got it. I'll call James as soon as you give me some privacy." I felt rude even as the words left my mouth, but she just nodded and left.

I opened the pumpkin orange case of the chiming Ipad, sitting up as I did so. I was startled to see myself topless for an endless moment before an image of James, dressed in the suit I had said goodbye to him in that morning, and with a huge window with a killer view of New York in the background, took over most of the screen. He looked wild, his hair disheveled as though he'd run his hand through it impatiently. The curl of his pretty mouth gave me a good idea of his dark mood.

"Why didn't you call me when you said you would? And why are you topless?" he asked. His tone was harsh, and I saw not an ounce of softness in his angry face.

"I fell asleep before I realized it. I didn't mean to. I had no idea I was so tired."

"You said you would call. Are you toying with me? Is that what this is? Do you like to drive me wild?"

I let my annoyance show clearly on my face. "That's ridiculous. It's exactly what I said, and you're overreacting.

Obviously I was fine. You have this whole place patrolled day and night. What did you think had happened?"

His jaw clenched hard enough that it looked like it hurt. "I don't know. And not knowing is worse than just about anything. You might have been mad at me again, or freaked out that you'd agreed to live with me. Perhaps you were leaving me again. And in the back of my mind, I was even worried that your father had somehow gotten ahold of you again." He didn't bother to hide his vulnerability during his little tirade, and I felt myself involuntarily softening towards him. It was a talent of his.

I sighed. "Oh, James. I'm sorry I didn't call when I said I would, but I wasn't being deliberately hurtful. I was just more exhausted than I realized by the time Paterson had finished searching my house. I barely got undressed before I passed out."

His face went a little slack and I saw his gaze shift down to my naked breasts. They'd been uncovered when I'd sat up in bed. He swallowed. I felt a surge of unadulterated lust shoot through my body. "I see that. I'm sorry I overreacted. You're more precious than my own life to me, Bianca, and knowing that you're safe and sound is my first priority."

I felt my face, hell, my whole body, soften. He said the sweetest things to me, the most romantic things. I tried to remind myself that he'd never once told me that he loved me, but still I felt that raw emotion for him like a drug to my system.

"I miss you," I told him softly.

His lids got very heavy. "I can't wait for Monday. Is your bottom half as naked as your top half?"

I couldn't help it, I blushed. "Are you in your office? On a Saturday?"

His pretty mouth twisted into a wry smile. "Yes, though I'm quite alone. The hotel industry is a seven day a week business. Don't change the subject. Shift the camera down for me. I want to see what you're wearing."

I blushed harder, but I did as he said. It was just more natural to obey him than to fight him when he spoke like that. I showed him my lower half, my lap covered in a thin blanket, my one stockinged leg clearly exposed. I couldn't see his face anymore with the way the screen was angled. "Take off the cover."

I removed it, showing him the tiny scrap of nude-colored underwear I wore. I heard his guttural moan of approval and let my legs fall open.

"Use the magnetic cover to prop the Ipad up on your bedside table. Point it at the bed."

I did, seeing him clearly again. He had rearranged himself as well, pushing his chair far enough back from the desk so that I could see his lap.

He was still fully dressed but I could see his stark erection tenting his pale gray slacks obscenely. As I watched him he opened up his pants, using both hands to pull his naked cock free. It sprang out and up with a little bounce that made me gasp.

He shifted, pulling his slacks down far enough to give it total freedom. He unbuttoned the last three buttons on his shirt, pulling it open wide. He threw his long thin white tie over his shoulder and out of his way. I had an unobstructed view of his hands as he stroked himself. "Take off your panties and lie back on the bed."

I obeyed, my face turning pink all the while.

"Prop yourself up on the pillows and open your legs wide. Wider. Open yourself for me. Perfect, yes, just like that. Push two fingers inside of you. Deeper. Yes. Reach a hand up to cup your breast. Knead around it, but don't touch the nipple." As he spoke and I acquiesced to his demands, he stroked himself with hard, almost brutal thoroughness. "You're so beautiful, Bianca. Every inch of you is perfection. I can see the moisture between your legs. It's the hottest fucking thing I've ever seen in my life. Stroke yourself harder and faster. Imitate me fucking you."

"It's not the same," I gasped, stroking myself faster and faster. It wasn't at all the same as him touching me, a sad imitation in fact, but I was still getting close to orgasm, more from his voice and the sight of his beautiful hands on that perfect cock than from what I was clumsily doing to myself.

He gave me a pained smile. "I know it's not. Not even close. We shouldn't be separated like this. Not ever. But we'll work with what we've been given. Now move that hand on your lovely tit down to your clit. Yes, perfect. Rub very soft, small circles on it with your finger. Tell me when you're close, my love. I could come on a dime, and I want us to go at the same moment. Mmm, there, shove those fingers in as hard and fast as you can manage. If we get separated like this often, we'll have to get you a vibrator for your house. Or a dildo that's a perfect replica of my dick."

His voice and his words brought me closer and closer to the edge as I watched him work himself so roughly with his hands. The sight of him touching himself was incredibly erotic to me. "I'm close," I gasped to him.

He bit his lip as he wrenched at himself. His neck arched but his eyes never left me as he came into his hand with a rough little groan. The sight of him coming in spurts that hit nothing but air brought me with him, and I gave a little whimper as my orgasm took me. It felt good, but nowhere near as intense as where James usually brought me. I sat up and watched in fascination as he cleaned up the mess he had made, giving me a self-deprecating smile all the while.

"Was it good for you, Love?" he asked, his eyes tender in spite of that smile.

I wanted to cry for some strange reason. I didn't want to analyze the urge at all, but I couldn't help but worry about how much I was coming to depend on James. I felt an addictive need to be near him. "It was good. I loved watching you touch yourself, but it all just made me want you with me even more."

His face changed so drastically that I blinked. There was a calculation there now, and a resolve that made me tense. "We don't ever have to be apart. You could work from home, and have a career with your paintings. I won't rush you, but it's something I'd like you to start thinking about."

I tensed up even more, and he held up a conciliatory hand. "I'll drop it, love. Paterson tells me that you offered to let Blake sleep in your spare room. Are you really okay with that? For security purposes it would be ideal, but I want you to be comfortable in your own home."

I shrugged, and his eyes moved down to my breasts. He began to tuck himself back into his slacks, making a visible effort to tear his eyes back up to my face. I wasn't totally comfortable with it, but I thought that with all of the other bizarre things I would need to grow accustomed to, it was a very little thing in the scheme of it all.

He gave me an almost grateful smile. It looked a little off on his too perfect face. "Thank you. That will help me to sleep better when you have to be away from me." I shifted as he spoke, sitting cross-legged and pulling a corner of my bedspread over my lap. His smile changed to a smirk. "Take the blanket off your lap. I love the one stocking, by the way. You really passed out, huh?"

We chatted for a long time, both of us in a lighter mood by the time he finally had to get back to work. I wondered how my heart could be both light with happiness and heavy with love at the same time.

CHAPTER THIRTY-NINE

I was heading from my bedroom to the kitchen, clad only in a robe, when I heard a commotion at my front door. I moved to see what it was before I could think better of it. I blinked at the unexpected sight that greeted me.

A strange, middle-aged woman stood just in the front doorway, Paterson behind her, Blake in front. She had hair dyed a garish red, with overdone makeup that couldn't disguise the drawn look of her too thin face. She looked how I thought a retired showgirl might look, with a thin body and too large breasts that seemed to hurt her posture.

Her spine stiffened when she caught sight of me. Her eyes were neither friendly nor hostile, but held a desperate sort of appeal that I couldn't understand showing to a complete stranger.

She addressed me right away. "I'm not here to hurt you, as these people seem to think." She held up a plain white envelope. "I just wanted to give you this. There are some things you need to know. I would have told you before, but your father wouldn't let me contact you. Now that he's disappeared, I saw no reason to delay. Please, just read this. I can see why you wouldn't want to talk to me, but this isn't about me." Her speech was a little desperate, and I recognized the nervous fear that seemed to sit on her shoulders, a fear that she had to live with every second of her life, living with my father. I remembered it well.

"Sharon Karlsson," I said, my mouth stiff around the words. The name felt so wrong to me.

She nodded, her arm shaking badly as she held the envelope towards me. I moved forward to take it.

Blake moved to block me. "She hasn't let us search her, Ms. Karlsson."

I studied Sharon. She wore a thin shift of a dress, flowers faded from many washes. I didn't see how she could hide anything in the dress, but I wasn't the expert. "Will you hand me the envelope then?" I asked Blake, trying to be practical.

Blake took the envelope from Sharon, and the red-headed woman began backing immediately out the door. I remembered that I had something to tell her but she was retreating swiftly. I had to shoulder past my bodyguards to catch a last view of her getting into an old clunker of a sedan that was parked on the curb.

"Wait, Sharon," I called out. She cast me a panicky look, but didn't pause. I moved closer. "I need to tell you something important," I shouted, but she was already peeling away from my house like a madwoman.

"Please, Ms. Karlsson. Step back inside. It could be some kind of a trap," Paterson said, scanning the street with focused thoroughness.

I cooperated, walking back inside with a sigh. Now I would have to call her. I had so just wanted to get it over with. I had an almost overpoweringly strong aversion to speaking to that woman. I held my hand out to Blake as I passed her. "May I have that letter?"

She looked hesitant but handed it to me.

Paterson cleared his throat. "May I inspect it first, Ms.

Karlsson?"

I already had the thing open, and I could see that it contained nothing more than a thin scrap of paper. I showed him.

He grimaced, holding out his hand. "I'm asking to read it first."

I shook my head. I would cooperate with them for the sake of my safety, but I had no intention of sharing my personal business with them. "No. I'm sorry, but this is private." I went into my bedroom without another word.

I could hear Paterson's voice through the door. "I'm going to have to tell Mr. Cavendish about this, Ms. Karlsson."

"You do that," I said, opening the letter. It was short and to the point.

> *Bianca,*
>
> *I understand why you don't want anything to do with me, but I have a son. He is your half-brother, your father's son. He's only one year younger than you. His name is Sven Karlsson, and he lives in Manhattan. His phone number is at the bottom of the page. I think he would like to hear from you. We have no other family, and he has been estranged from me and his father for several years.*
>
> *Sincerely,*
> *Sharon Karlsson*

My vision went a little fuzzy after the first few sentences. *I have a brother?* Only a year younger than myself? The ramifications took long minutes to sink in as I sat perched on the edge of my bed.

I had been fourteen when my father had murdered my

mother. He had been seeing this other woman the entire time, had a child with her. Is that why he had killed my mother? Had the shooting been even more calculated than I'd realized?

I thought of my mother, my beautiful mother. That Sharon woman never could have held a candle to her, with her garish looks and lack of class, and she was obviously much older than my mother would be, if she were alive. My mother had been the very epitome of class, holding a quietly reserved grace in every line of her elegant body.

It seemed impossible that anyone would have killed such a woman, let alone for someone like Sharon. I found myself hating that woman with a passion usually only reserved for my father. But my half-brother... I had not a clue what to think about the idea of that.

My phone distracted me out of my reverie, though it had been ringing for awhile, I realized. I saw that it was James and answered it.

"What's going on, Bianca? Paterson tells me you wouldn't let him check a mysterious letter." His voice was more worried than angry but I still felt myself bristling.

"It's *my* letter, James. And what harm could there be in a letter?"

"Who was that woman?"

I sighed. Of course he'd gotten a detailed report of everything. "My father's wife, Sharon Karlsson."

He cursed. "What did she want?"

I studied the short letter. "Nothing much. She was in full panic mode, so she didn't say much. I didn't get a chance to tell her anything, either, so now I have to call her. The sooner the better, so I need to let you go."

"Wait. What did the letter say?"

I pursed my lips, debating what to tell him. Why not everything? His investigators probably knew more than I did, at this point. "She just wanted to tell me that I have a half-brother. She and my father have a son."

He was silent for a long moment. "Okay. Thank you for telling me. I'll let you go so you can make that phone call. Will you call me before bed?" I agreed to call him, and we hung up.

I went back to my missed calls, calling back the number that I knew was hers. It rang five times and went to voicemail. I was a breath away from just leaving her a message when I realized how that might endanger her. I couldn't say anything about my father or she might have to answer to him for it. I finally decided that any message from me would be bad, if my father had access, which he very well could have. I tried calling her again, with the same result. I realized with resignation that I would have to keep calling her until I got the woman herself.

I had taken such a long nap that I found myself having dinner at Stephan's house just thirty minutes later, dressed in an overlarge T-shirt and cheer shorts. Stephan gave me an arch look when he saw my attire. "Bet you wouldn't be caught dead wearing that when James was around."

I gave him a half smile as I moved into his house. "James isn't around, now, is he?"

Stephan, Javier, and I had a very pleasant dinner, laughing and talking while we all ate too much of Stephan's chicken cacciatore. It was as fabulous as it always was, one of his best recipes by far.

After dinner Javier slipped away without an awkward moment to give us some privacy to chat. "I need to make some phone calls," he murmured and slipped away. Stephan gave him a very affectionate smile.

We caught up on everything, nearly talking over each other to get it all out. He was shocked about my mysterious half-brother. I was shocked when he glanced at the doorway where Javier had exited then leaned forward to say in a whisper, "I'm totally in love with him, Bianca. I'm in deep. I can't seem to help it, with Javier. Falling for him is just too easy, when I don't hold myself back."

His eyes were so earnest and vulnerable that I wanted to cry. I hoped with all my heart that it worked out for them. He sighed and smiled, happy to enjoy the moment, instead of analyzing it all to death like I seemed to. "What about you? Do you think you love James?"

I looked down at my hands. They were suddenly fisted in my lap. I nodded. "Hopelessly. I don't know about the rest of it, but I know I love him. Hell, I don't even know if he loves me back. I'm not even sure he's capable of it, or if I'm capable of letting him, you know?"

His soft eyes just about undid me. "Oh, he loves you alright. I think he's loved you from the start. That man would do anything for you. I know it in my heart."

I thought about what a beautiful thing Stephan's heart was, to always see the good around the mess that it was buried in.

I wanted to ask him something, but even thinking about it made me blush. But Stephan and I had established a pattern of openness so long ago, that it was as ingrained in me as my love for him, so it wasn't long before I got up the nerve. "You and Javier seem to have a sort of, um, dominant submissive vibe going on. Is that how it is between you?"

I studied his face, but saw no hesitance or embarrassment there. He just smiled happily. "We aren't into the BDSM stuff, if that's what you mean, but I'm his top. We don't switch, not ever. It doesn't appeal to either of us."

He had explained the top/bottom thing to me a long time ago. He only ever topped. I had known that. I just hadn't connected his preference to a dominant/submissive relationship so clearly, though it obviously was just that.

Stephan cleared his throat. "You and James are into the

BDSM stuff, aren't you? He's your dominant."

I nodded, meeting his eyes squarely, though I couldn't bring myself to smile, like he had. "I know it's not...normal, but I've found that it's just the way I'm hardwired. And he mostly only acts that way in the bedroom. He really doesn't boss me around outside of it, though he does manipulate the hell out of my life."

He stroked my hair. "You don't have to explain your preferences to me. I want whatever makes you happy, and I see that James does that, when you let him. You weren't even slightly interested in men before you met him, so he obviously gives you something you need. I'm glad you found someone who seems to compliment you so well."

I nodded, sighing in relief. I had been half-afraid that he would be mad at James if I told him about our strange sexual preferences, and it was good to know that he wouldn't judge us. I knew better, and as always, Stephan deserved only my blind faith.

We finished out the night watching a few episodes of New Girl, the three of us laughing and eating ice cream. Stephan walked me home around ten o'clock. My security was waiting for me, of course.

I called James, and we spoke for nearly an hour before we reluctantly said goodnight. It hadn't even been a day since we'd parted, with just one more to go, but as I tried to fall asleep that night, it felt like forever.

CHAPTER FORTY

Work the next day was beyond busy, but still managed to feel like it took ages. We were actually running early on our hour layover in DC. I called James but he didn't answer. He had told me he had some important meetings that day, so I wasn't surprised. Just disappointed.

Stephan was speaking excitedly to Javier on his phone in the galley just before we boarded. He beamed at me as he hung up the phone. "The JFK flight is delayed two hours. If we keep running on time we can actually take the redeye flight tonight. Javier is going to meet us at the airport with my overnight bag. James has things for you at his place, right?"

I nodded, feeling suddenly light and happy. If everything worked out just perfectly, I would get to see James a good eight hours earlier than I could have hoped for. My day was looking up.

When we finally arrived back in Vegas we deplaned with efficient and single-minded purpose, still hoping to catch the flight to New York. "Javier says it's at D39, the gate next door. He's waiting there now. He's all checked in, and we're listed. We just need to get there in the next twenty minutes."

And we did, rushing off the plane at the first possible moment, barely saying goodbye to the rest of the crew. Stephan left his paperwork with Jake, who would drop it off for him.

Javier grinned when he saw us running up to the podium.

We got on the plane, if only barely. It departed not ten minutes after we got on board. I only had time to leave James a brief text telling him that we were on our way, and what time we would arrive.

Stephan and Javier fell soundly asleep in the back row of the plane, but I got up to help the main cabin crew with drinks since I was in uniform, the flight was nearly full, and the people were downright cranky with the delay. As though a sleep wand had been waved over the passengers, they all seemed to fall asleep right after they got their drinks. I was prying empty cups out of the hands of sleeping passengers when I caught the flight attendant I'd been helping studying me with a strange intensity.

I'd never met her before, but she'd seemed friendly enough when she realized that I was going to help her with their service, no strings attached.

She was a very small, very nondescript woman in her early twenties. She was hispanic and had long black hair and eyes so dark they looked black.

We were back in the galley, just the two of us, when she seemed to get up the nerve to ask the question that was obviously on her mind.

"You're that flight attendant who's dating James Cavendish, aren't you?" she asked. Her tone wasn't hostile, merely curious. In fact it was a little too curious for a complete stranger, something in her voice suggesting that she knew something about him, or even about me. I shouldn't have been so surprised by it, but it was the first time I had experienced that sort of strange interaction with a co-worker.

I sighed. "Yes, I'm dating him," I finally said.

She didn't smile, just gave me that fascinated stare. It was unnerving. "It must not be serious. I'm right, aren't I? You wouldn't still be working here if he were serious about you."

I felt myself getting instantly defensive about my job. "I like my job. What's wrong with working here?"

She gave me a stare that was way too direct for a stranger talking about my personal life. "Come on. He must make more money than this just brushing his teeth in the morning. I'm just saying that if he wanted to live with you or marry you or whatever, it would be beyond pointless for you to be spending all of your time making peanuts while he makes billions. If he was serious, he would let you quit."

I felt myself flush, but tried to maintain my composure. "For your information, we are living together, and I haven't quit because I *like* my job. So what if he makes more money than me? I still have to work. I'm not going to sit around all day and wait for him." I realized even as I made the argument that that would never be the case, whether I had this job or not.

I didn't need to worry about waiting around for him all the time because I just wouldn't do it. And he knew me well enough to know not to expect it from me, either. *What would I do if I could do anything I wanted?* I wondered, kind of stunned that I was even letting myself think that way.

I remembered that I was in the middle of a conversation with an obnoxious woman who seemed to think she knew something about my life. "And why on earth do you assume that you know anything at all about either of us?"

She had the nerve to give me a conspiratorial smile as she reached into her flight bag. She handed me a rolled up magazine. "I've been keeping up with *all* of the drama," she said, as though it were an accomplishment.

I cringed as I saw the cover of the gossip mag she'd handed me. It was a picture of me wearing a transparent white slip and standing in my driveway, looking stunned and confused. You could just make out the outline of my nipples in the thin slip. At least it wasn't obvious that I hadn't been wearing panties.

James was behind me in the shot, obviously striding towards me, but giving the man taking the shots a positively murderous look. He looked absolutely gorgeous wearing only his boxers, even his hair perfectly disheveled. My own hair looked like it had just been through a wind-tunnel.

When I was done working through my own feelings about the horrible pictures getting out, my mind went to James. He must know about it by now. He probably had people who brought it to his attention. If I was this upset, I knew he would be livid.

"He's so hot. Do you have any idea how hot he is?" the strange flight attendant was asking me. I really needed to remember her name.

I gave her a very direct stare with lots of eye contact. "As a matter of fact, I know exactly how hot he is. Trust me when I say that *you* don't have any idea just how hot he is."

She made a motion as though she were swooning. "That is awesome," she said with a sigh, and I realized for the first time that, though she didn't have any manners at all, she meant no harm. In fact, she didn't seem to have a malicious bone in her body as she stared at James on the cover of the magazine. "Good for you, girl. He's a total dreamboat."

I threw her a bone, feeling tired but suddenly a little delirious about the fact that I might see James in just a few short hours, depending on if he was at work by the time we got there. "There's a chance he might be picking me up from the airport. If he is, it will probably be right by the crew van pickup, so you might get a glance at him."

She grinned at me as though I had just done her a huge favor. "That's so awesome. He can't possibly be that beautiful in person, though, so I'll brace myself for disappointment."

I had to smile back. "Actually, he's even more gorgeous. Sometimes I call him Mr. Beautiful."

She giggled. "You're very pretty and all, but he can have any woman on the planet. No offense, but how did you manage to land him?"

I gave her my little shrug, strangely no longer offended by her candor. "I really have no idea."

Our strange little talk was interrupted as the two other members of the main cabin crew came through the curtain. They were less pushy, but both of them gave me strange, probing looks, and I figured they'd heard or seen something about me.

I asked them politely if they needed any more help. When they declined, I ducked back into the cabin and found my seat beside Stephan. I lay my head back and tried my best to get a short nap in.

I awoke with a start as the plane touched down. I was so conditioned to stay awake on red-eyes that I was surprised I'd been able to sleep that long on a plane.

I sent James a text as we taxied in.

Bianca: We just landed.

He responded immediately.

James: There's a car waiting at the curb for you.

That didn't seem to need a response, so I put my phone away, deplaning as quickly as possibly. We were in the last row of the aircraft, though, and it was a frustratingly slow process.

We wound up walking with the crew through the airport. Stephan grabbed my small flight bag from me without a word, as was his wont.

The strange girl, who was named Marie, as I discovered when she reintroduced herself, made her way to my side as we walked. She chatted on and on about celebrity gossip.

She seemed to think that because I was in the tabloids, I would also like reading them, and be caught up on the latest drama. She seemed crestfallen when I disabused her of the notion. I really had no idea who she was talking about.

She had me half-distracted with her endless chatter as we stepped out of the sliding door and began to make our way to the pickup spot at the curb. But I wasn't so distracted that I didn't instantly see the tall figure step out of the limo parked just behind the crew van. Even if he hadn't gotten out of the car, there was no way I could have missed Clark's imposing figure waiting on the sidewalk for us. But James stepping out of the car with the warmest smile on his face made me instantly forget that there were even other people in the world, let alone that one was babbling at me.

Without even thinking about it, my steps quickened until I was nearly running to him.

He wasn't indifferent to my enthusiasm. He began to walk briskly towards me, obviously determined to meet me at least halfway.

When we got within arm's reach of each other he grabbed me to him in a bone-jarring embrace, his hold painful but oh so comforting to me. I had thrown my arms around his neck at the same moment he'd grabbed and I held on tightly as he lifted me, moving back towards his car, one hand cupping the back of my head firmly. I felt like I was five years old, my feet dangling inches from the ground. I nearly laughed.

"James, put me down," I sputtered.

He just gripped me tighter, moving purposefully towards the car. "I can't be in public like this, Bianca. I feel too raw. God, I missed you. It felt like Christmas when I heard you were getting in ahead of schedule."

I gripped his silky hair in my fists. "I missed you, too. It's scary just how much. I don't know how it happened so fast, but you feel like home to me, James."

A hoarse, pained sound escaped his throat. "Yes," he said, his voice rough with emotion. "This is home."

CHAPTER FORTY-ONE

James had me in the car and securely ensconced on his lap when Stephan and Javier finally joined us, both of them grinning widely. They had obviously found our over-enthusiastic reunion amusing.

"I have to warn you guys; that crew is going to tell the world about that little scene. That small sassy one, Marie, was even making noises about giving an interview to the press," Stephan said, his voice more amused than worried.

I rolled my eyes. That little gossip-monger probably would, too. I tried to remember if I had told her anything I wouldn't want shared, but mentally shrugged the whole thing off. There was nothing I could do about any of it now, and it was much more pleasant to bask in the presence of Mr. Beautiful than to worry about what-ifs.

James greeted the other men politely before he began to nuzzle into my hair. I felt him breathing me in, and my eyes closed in pleasure.

His arms were wrapped around me snugly, but suddenly they tightened to the point of pain and I felt him tense.

"I need to tell you something," he whispered, his mouth at

my ear. From the tension in his body and voice, I immediately knew that something was terribly wrong.

I stiffened, turning to study his face. His strange change of mood was troubling, to say the least. And his eyes were haunted, just the sight of them making my chest tighten in dread.

"What is it?"

"Sharon Karlsson was found dead in her home last night. She was murdered." His voice was quiet, but the car went deathly silent at his news.

I just froze, staring at him as I processed his words. I had been trying to call her, to tell her about my father, but I had failed to get ahold of her.

Could I have prevented this? Was I to blame?

It wasn't even a question to me who had killed her. It was just too big of a coincidence, and I had stared too fully into the murdering eyes of my father not to know that he was fully capable of killing again. It was only a wonder that he hadn't killed again before this. Though, for all I knew, he had.

"How?" I finally asked.

He ran a hand over my hair, a gesture that I thought was to comfort himself as much as me. "She was shot in the head."

I thought of the way my mother had died, a mock suicide where she'd 'eaten the gun.' "Like my mother?" I asked, my voice very small.

His eyes were impossibly tender, and infinitely worried, on my own. "Yes, like that."

"I tried to tell her. I've been trying to call her since I found out she existed, but I feel responsible. He's a killer, and he stayed free because I lied for him. I don't know why, but I never imagined he'd kill again. I've known for all these years, and somehow it just never occurred to me. Why do you suppose that is? I should have thought of it." My voice was pitched low, but it seemed to crack through the stunned silence of the car.

Everyone began to speak at once.

"You are *not* responsible for this," James said, his voice firm and harsh and full of pain.

"You couldn't have known, Buttercup," Stephan said, his voice passionately sincere.

"Please don't do that to yourself," Javier implored quietly.

I ignored the reassurances, feeling the weight of her death like a heavy burden on my soul. And shamefully, even stronger than that guilt was the fear. My father had killed at least two women now, something he'd threatened to do to me more times than I could count. Even with the numb state my brain seemed to be in with the disturbing news of Sharon's death, what I felt the most was a chilling terror that ran so deep I couldn't remember a time that it hadn't been a part of me.

I shared a long look with James. In his eyes I saw a wrenching helplessness that mirrored my own.

SERIES BY R.K. LILLEY

THE WILD SIDE SERIES

THE WILD SIDE

IRIS

DAIR

THE OTHER MAN - COMING SOON

TYRANT - COMING SOON

THE UP IN THE AIR SERIES

IN FLIGHT

MILE HIGH

GROUNDED

MR. BEAUTIFUL - COMING OCTOBER 15TH, 2014

LANA (AN UP IN THE AIR COMPANION NOVELLA)

AUTHORITY - COMING SOON

THE TRISTAN & DANIKA SERIES

BAD THINGS

ROCK BOTTOM

LOVELY TRIGGER

THE HERETIC DAUGHTERS SERIES

BREATHING FIRE

CROSSING FIRE - COMING SOON

TEXT LILLEY + YOUR EMAIL ADDRESS TO 1-678-249-3375 TO JOIN MY EMAIL NEWSLETTER.